"Arrangements like ours are not meant to last, Alice."

"They're not," she agreed.

"I have to do my duty." His mouth, which had always been so warm and smiling, was unhappy and determined, the expression in his eyes unreadable.

Her heart was beating harder than a horse at full gallop. "Maybe you should have thought about your duty six months ago." When he had wooed her and swept her off her feet and made her his mistress within weeks of their meeting.

"Maybe I should have," he said.

His quiet admission stripped her raw.

"For what it is worth, I really am sorry, Alice." He took a step toward her, reached out a hand as if he meant to touch her.

Alice recoiled. It was a hand that had caressed her lips and stroked against her naked skin, a hand that had touched her in the most intimate of places. It was all she could do to stop herself from striking it away with every ounce of strength in her body.

"You should go now," she said with feigned calmness.

* * *

Mistress to the Marquis
Harlequin® Historical #1146—July 2013

Author Note

You met Alice and Razeby in *Dicing with the Dangerous Lord*—the story that belongs to their best friends, and in which Alice becomes Razeby's mistress.

During the Regency era it was considered completely acceptable for a gentleman and nobleman such as Razeby to keep a demirep woman such as Alice as his mistress. Marriage between them, however, would have been viewed very differently. But there were cases in which mistresses went on to marry their noblemen protectors. Margaret Farmer, a commoner and daughter of an Irish spendthrift, married Lord Mountjoy and became the Countess of Blessington. Sophia Dubochet, courtesan and sister of the infamous Harriette Wilson, married Lord Berwick.

So with those exceptions in mind, here in *Mistress to the Marquis* is Alice and Razeby's own story of a love strong enough to defy the strictest social class rules of their time. I truly hope you enjoy reading it.

Mistress to the Marquis

MARGARET MCPHEE

HARLEQUIN® HISTORICAL

Recycling programs
for this product may
not exist in your area.

ISBN-13: 978-0-373-29746-7

MISTRESS TO THE MARQUIS

Printed in U.S.A.

Also available in *Undone!* ebooks:

How to Tempt a Viscount

**Did you know that these novels are also
available as ebooks? Visit www.Harlequin.com.**

For my wee Wee Sister, Joanne—
an extra spicy story especially for you!

MARGARET McPHEE

loves to use her imagination—an essential requirement for a trained scientist. However, when she realized that her imagination was inspired more by the historical romances she loves to read rather than by her experiments, she decided to put the ideas down on paper. She has since left her scientific life behind, retaining only the romance—her husband, whom she met in a laboratory. In summer, Margaret enjoys cycling along the coastline overlooking the Firth of Clyde in Scotland, where she lives. In winter, tea, cakes and a good book suffice.

Chapter One

London, England—April 1811

'Razeby, you surprise me! I wasn't expecting you until later.' *Much, much later.* Miss Alice Sweetly's fingers were flustered as she shoved the sheet of paper she had been writing upon into the drawer and rammed it shut, but her sudden anxiety had nothing to do with not being ready for her protector. Within seconds she was on her feet and hurrying towards the Marquis of Razeby to distract his interest from the desk. 'You've caught me unawares.'

'Forgive me, Alice. I did not mean to startle you when you were so absorbed.' Razeby said in his rich, aristocratic voice.

'Hardly absorbed. I was just writing a letter to a friend.' In her nervousness her natural soft Irish lilt grew stronger than ever and she felt her face burn with traitorous colour at the lie.

'Lucky friend.' Razeby smiled with his usual good nature.

She tensed in case he meant to quiz her on the fictitious letter and friend. But, true to form, Razeby trusted her and did no such thing. He did not even glance over at the little bureau.

'Finish your letter. I will fetch myself a brandy while I wait.'

'I'll do no such thing.' Embarrassment rippled through her, making her face grow hotter just at the thought of sitting back down at the desk with him watching. With a glance down at her shabby moth-nibbled woollen shawl and the morning dress beneath it, with its old-fashioned style, the pretty muslin faded and worn, she changed the subject. 'Look at the state of me! I'm only wearing this old thing to keep my fine clothes good.' It was a habit she found hard to break, having grown up with nothing. 'And I've a lovely silk ready to wear tonight. I best get up the stairs and change into something decent.' She made to pass him.

But Razeby swept an arm around her waist, stilling her panic and pulling her against him. 'Relax, Alice. You look beautiful just as you are. As ever.' His eyes, deep brown and true, met hers as he stroked an escaped strand of hair away from her cheek. 'And have I not told you, it is not the clothes that are important, but the woman beneath?'

'Flatterer,' she accused, but she smiled and his tall, masculine body in such proximity sent waves of attraction and excitement crashing through her.

'It is the truth as well you know it.' Razeby could charm the birds down from the trees. He was still smiling as he pulled her closer. 'But if you have a wish for a new wardrobe, then you shall have one.'

'I've no wish for a new wardrobe. I've enough dresses up those stairs to clothe half the women in London!'

'I like buying you things—it makes you happy.' He gathered her right hand in his left. 'And I want you to be happy, Alice.'

Alice tried to curl her fingers to hide the black ink-stains that marred her fingers, but Razeby did not let her. He slid his thumb to rub against the marks on her skin.

'Mmm…' His eyes lingered over the inkstains before moving teasingly to hers. 'I do believe a new pen is a requirement.'

'No.' She laughed, but her face flamed anew at the mention of writing and of the precious silver pen that was so dear to her. 'I don't want another pen. I like the one I've got just fine.'

'I am very glad of that,' Razeby murmured huskily and pressed her inkstained fingers to the warmth of his lips.

'You know I'm happy. Very happy…' She paused before adding softly, 'And not because of the things you buy for me.' It was the truth.

He smiled a strange, almost poignant, smile, stroked his fingers against her cheek and stared into her eyes.

And it did not matter that she had been his mistress for six months, sleeping with him nearly every one of those nights. When he looked at her with that look in his eyes she felt that same flare of desire that had sparked between them the very first moment they met in the Green Room of the Theatre Royal in Covent Garden. Indeed, familiarity had not diminished the passion, or all that had grown alongside, between them, only sharpened and heated it. Her stomach turned cartwheels, her skin tingled all over and her thighs seemed to burn. He glanced away, over towards the window, a pensive, sombre expression upon his face. 'Alice…'

But whatever he meant to say was lost as she gently took hold of his face, turned it to hers and kissed away the worry that she saw there.

Razeby retaliated in kind, his mouth passionate and warm and irresistible as the night he had first kissed her in the moonlight outside the theatre stage door.

Breaking the kiss, she watched him as she smiled, a mischievous smile this time, and let her hand stroke lightly over the hard bulge in his breeches. He swallowed and she felt the shiver that rippled through his body, felt the way it strained to meet her and heard the slight catch of the breath in his throat.

He caught her hand in his own and moved it away from temptation, his eyes darkening to that familiar smoulder that made the fire of desire twist and curl and dance all the more, low in her belly. 'Alice, you are a wicked woman,' he breathed in a velvet voice that tickled against her ear and sent a shiver tingling across her skin.

'Very wicked, indeed, Razeby.' Her top teeth caught at her bottom lip. 'So wicked that you might need to put me across your knee and spank me.'

'I would be remiss in my duty to you if I did not do so.' She could hear the low stroke of desire beneath his words.

'And the one thing about you, Razeby, is that you're never remiss in your duty.' Again she thought she saw the shift of a shadow in his eyes so she teased her skirts higher to flash him a glimpse of a stockinged ankle, wanting to make him forget whatever was troubling him. And it worked.

'Be careful, Miss Alice Sweetly,' he cautioned.

'I prefer to be reckless, James Brundell, Marquis of Razeby. But isn't that the truth of why you like me?' She arched an eyebrow and playfully unfastened the buttons at the top of her bodice, allowing the dress to gape and reveal the bulge of her breasts over the transparent linen of her shift.

Razeby's eyes darkened. His focus narrowed and sharpened upon her. He swallowed, then wetted his lips. 'Alice, you are a temptation I cannot resist.'

'I hope so.' She laughed, and one by one she plucked the pins from her hair, until the neatly coiled length of fair hair loosened and tumbled long and wanton over her shoulders.

Razeby discarded the neatly fitted dark tailcoat on the sofa behind him. His fingers moved to the buttons of his pale waistcoat, unfastening it and shrugging it off. Around his neck his white cravat was still neatly tied in a fashionable knot. She reached and tugged an end of it, pulling it free and draping it over the back of the sofa. Through the fine white lawn of his shirt she could see a hint of his flesh and the dark peppering of hair that covered it. Her eyes swept lower to the tight buckskin of his breeches that did little to disguise the extent of his arousal or the long muscular thighs beneath. And lower still to the glossy black riding boots that were coated with dust from his having ridden from his own town house in Leicester Square to the one he kept for her here in Hart Street.

She knew the body beneath those clothes, intimately, every inch of honey-coloured skin, every hard taut muscle. She knew the sweep of his tight buttocks and the breadth of his chest, the feel of his skin beneath her fingertips and the way his heart beat fast and hard after he had loved her. She knew the scent of him, the feel of him, the taste of him and the way he made her heart blossom with such warm tenderness. It just made her want him all the more.

She turned round and, sticking out her bottom, wiggled it to taunt him.

'You are playing dangerously, Alice.'

'Are you close to yielding?' she asked over her shoulder.

He stepped towards her.

She skirted around the other side of the sofa so that they faced one another as opponents across that barricade.

'When I catch you, Alice...'

'*If* you catch me...' She smiled and arched an eyebrow. 'What are you going to do to me?' she asked, as excited by the game she had instigated as he was.

'I am going to pull up your skirts.'

'Yes...' she breathed.

'And bend you over my knee.'

'And then...?' She felt breathless at the thought.

He stepped closer to the sofa, lowering his voice to little more than a husky whisper as he did so. 'You know there is only one way this can end, Alice.'

'Really? How might that be, my lord?'

He lunged over the sofa for her.

Alice dodged clear, making a run for the door of the drawing room. 'You'll have to be faster than that, Razeby!'

She made it to the first landing of the staircase before he caught her, his arm fastening around her waist and pulling her to him.

She gave a yelp and a giggle.

'Minx,' he whispered in her ear as he kissed the side of her neck, where the blood pulsed strong and wild.

He scooped her up as if she weighed nothing at all. Her breathing was loud and ragged while Razeby's was barely changed at all. For all her squeals he threw her over his shoulder like some marauder from olden times abducting his woman and strode up the rest of the stairs.

'Razeby!' she protested and gave a wriggle, but all she got in return was a slap on the bottom before he kicked open the door to their bedchamber and threw her down upon the bed.

'Now, woman of mine,' he said. 'We have a score to settle—a matter of some spanking, I believe.'

'Oh, you think so?' She laughed and, rolling on to her stomach, began to quickly crawl across the bed to evade him.

'I will not let you escape me,' he said in a strict voice as his fingers fastened around her ankle and hauled her back across the bed towards him, catching her skirts on the bedcovers and hitching them up her legs in the process. She was still lying on her stomach, her stockings revealed. He pushed her skirts higher to expose her naked thighs and bottom in full.

'Now there is a sight to behold,' he murmured and she caught her breath as his fingers traced down the curve of her hip.

The mattress dipped as he sat down upon it and she gasped as she felt herself hauled to lie across his thighs, her skirts twisted high around her hips, her buttocks bared for whatever he chose to inflict upon them.

'Mercy, my lord Razeby, I beg of you,' she pleaded,

but she was smiling and the words were breathless with anticipation.

'I swear, my love, that when it comes to you I have no mercy…or resistance.' His hand stroked against the fullness of her buttocks, then he spanked her bare bottom, several small light slaps that were little more than cupped caresses.

She laughed again, as did he, as he turned her in his arms, cradling her to him and kissing her mouth. She wound her arms around his neck, kissing him with all the passion that was burning within her. He rolled her flat on to the mattress and she pulled him down on top of her, stroking his face, threading her fingers through his hair.

'Alice,' he whispered, and caressed her cheek. His eyes were a dark liquid brown, so filled with both tenderness and desire as they stared into hers.

'Razeby,' she said softly.

Their eyes held as he plucked a single deep intimate kiss from her lips.

He rose, long enough to divest himself of his shirt over his head and unfasten his breeches and drawers. Her fingers were still working upon the buttons of her bodice when he returned.

'Allow me to assist,' he offered, and then in a move that would have done justice to any Viking warrior in the midst of some rape and pillage Razeby took hold of the neckline and tore the length of the bodice open.

'Such impatience, my lord,' she chided.

'It is the state you push me to, wench.'

'You'll be tying me to the bed next.'

He glanced up at the lengths of black silken cord that

dangled from the headboard of the bed. 'Let us save that game for later.'

'If you insist, Lord Razeby.'

'I do, Miss Sweetly.'

She smiled at that and felt the place between her thighs grow hotter at the thought.

He gave a growl as he pushed the flimsy torn linen and sprig muslin aside, exposing her nakedness to the hunger of his gaze.

'Do you know what you do to me?' She could hear the strain in his voice, see it in his face. He touched her lightly, trailing his fingers across her breasts, making their tips harden and grow unbearably sensitive.

'I could hazard a guess,' she murmured as he lowered his face, all the while keeping his gaze locked with hers, and flicked his tongue to taste her.

The gasp escaped her, loud and needful, and in response his torture grew only more exquisite.

She groaned her need of him, arching her back to thrust her breasts all the more into his mouth so that he suckled her in earnest. Her fingers threaded through the dark feathers of his hair, clutching him to her, wanting him never to stop, wanting this, and more, so much more. He laved her, worked each rosy nipple in full until it was bullet hard and so sensitive that she was in danger of finding the fullness of her pleasure before he had even touched between her legs. She tried to hold back, tried to resist, but, seeing how close she was teetering to the edge, he smiled.

'No mercy, Alice,' he said in his low, sexy velvet voice and then did something so clever with his tongue that rendered all resistance futile. She let go and exploded in a bliss that was blinding and overwhelming, making her body ripple and shimmer as the pleasure, absolute and all consuming, filled her from head to toe and she was gasping aloud with the wonder of it.

She was still pulsing inside as his face came up to hers. 'Razeby,' she whispered.

'Naughty girl,' he said and he was smiling.

She let her hands glide over the pale honey-coloured contours of his shoulders, over the muscles at the top of his arms. He was strong and lean from all the fencing and horse riding and pugilism, his body so different from hers, so much bigger, so masculine.

'It's all your fault,' she said.

'Guilty as charged,' he admitted, and his eyes smouldered all the darker. He kissed all the way up the column of her neck, kissed the line of her jaw, kissed her chin.

Already she could feel the desire stoke again within her. Her woman's place between her legs ached for him.

She scraped her teeth against the naked skin of his shoulder, licked him there, sucked him there while one hand slipped lower to caress the long hard length of him.

She felt the involuntary contraction of his muscles, heard the sharp intake of his breath as she stroked him.

'Alice…'

She smiled and bit his shoulder.

Razeby took her mouth with masterful possession, plunging his tongue into its depths as she wrapped her legs around him and welcomed him home.

They moved in a dance as old as time itself. A man and his woman, mating, bonding, sharing all that was possible to share on this journey that could have only one destination for them both. Striving together until she was gasping and crying out his name as he spilled his seed within her and she pulsed around him and shattered into a myriad of stardust and magic that transcended all else.

And afterwards, as ever, he held her safe in his strong arms, curving his body around hers as if he would protect her from all the world. She could feel the stir of his warm breath against her hair and the possessiveness of his hand around her breast, the warmth of his hard masculine body preventing the cooling of her own lover's rosy glow. His lips brushed against the top of her head and her heart gave a little dance of utter happiness and joy. She snuggled in closer and basked in the aftermath of their lovemaking.

But when she opened her eyes to look into his she glimpsed again something of that same pensive undercurrent that she had seen in the drawing room. She stroked her fingers against the faint blue stubble of his cheek. 'What's wrong, Razeby?' He was not his usual self. He had not been entirely himself for the last weeks. 'You've something on your mind.' Please God, don't let it be what she had been writing upon the desk. If he asked about that, she was not sure what she was going to tell him.

He looked into her eyes, studied them, and just for a moment she thought he was going to tell her. Then it was gone, replaced by that smile of his that made her melt inside.

'Nothing that cannot wait a little longer.' He caught her fingers from his cheek and pressed them to his lips.

But she was not so easily reassured. A little whisper of unease stroked down her spine. 'Razeby,' she began, but he rolled her on to her back and followed to cover her, staring down into her face all the while.

'Please not yet,' he said, and it sounded almost like a prayer; then he silenced any further protestations with a kiss. The kiss led to another, and another, until the passion that consumed them made all else fade away.

Chapter Two

Razeby stood by the window of his study in his town house in Leicester Square, observing all of normality go on in the street outside. A carriage rolled by, the Earl of Misbourne's crest painted upon its door. A coal cart rattled slowly out of the nearby mews, its load lessened following its delivery. Two gentlemen upon horseback had pulled over by the gardens to greet each other. Servants hurried along the pavements on errands for their masters. A nursemaid was taking a baby for a walk in a child's pushchair. He turned away from the window at that last sight.

The brandy decanter was sitting on his desk. The heavyweight crystal engraved with the Razeby coat of arms and motto—The Name of Razeby Shall Prevail—was a taunting irony. Regardless of the earliness of the hour he lifted the decanter, filled one of the matching engraved glasses, and took a sip.

The heat of the brandy hit the back of his throat, the smooth warmth tracing all the way down to his stomach. He took a deep breath and set the glass down upon the letter that lay open upon his desk. A bead of the rich tawny liquid trickled down from the glass's rim, slipping slowly, inexorably, down the stem to the base, where it finally crept upon the paper beneath to blur the inky words his cousin Atholl had written there— Atholl, who had defied all advice to buy a commission in the cavalry and taken himself off to fight against Napoleon. Yet another reminder. Everywhere Razeby looked there were reminders.

There was not a sound within the house. Only the slow steady tick of the tall clock in the corner, marking how quickly time was slipping away. He had left it so late, almost too late. He could leave it no longer.

He thought of Alice, his Alice, with her beautiful dark blue eyes and her passion and her warmth of heart and spirit, of how much she had been looking forward to the fireworks tonight. He thought of Alice and all that had been between them these past months, and felt an ache in his chest. His eyes strayed to the long, slim brown-velvet box that lay beside his pen holder. Just a momentary pause, as he steeled himself to the task. Then he slipped the box into the pocket of his tailcoat.

Razeby downed the remaining brandy in one go, but it did not settle the sourness or dread in his stomach.

The night sky was a canopy of clear midnight-blue velvet sewn with a smattering of diamonds that twinkled and glittered. The moon was a thin crescent hanging high in their midst. Although the winter had passed, the spring night air was cold, turning Alice and Razeby's breaths to smoke as they climbed from the little boat and walked hand in hand across the grass to Vauxhall Gardens.

Alice wrapped the cloak around her more tightly and felt Razeby's arm pull her closer.

'You are cold.'

'Only a little.' She smiled up at him. And he stared down into at her face with a curiously tender expression, as if he were branding her image upon his memory never to be forgotten. 'Why so serious? Hmm?' she asked, still smiling, and cupped his beard-scraped cheek.

He moved his lips to kiss the palm of her hand. 'It has been an unpleasant day.'

'Then we'd better make sure we enjoy tonight.'

'Every last precious minute.' The words were so softly murmured she had to strain to catch them. Then he seemed to shake off his megrims, and, taking her hand in his, led her to watch a host of entertainers: jugglers and knife throwers, dancers and musicians. A hurdy-gurdy man with a little monkey upon his shoulder, its tiny furry body all dressed up smartly in a fine coat and matching hat, was drawing quite the crowd. They could smell the food from the banqueting tables beyond, but the night seemed too chill for the wafer-thin cold ham and champagne that was being served to the guests.

'I'm glad we ate at home,' she said.

'Me, too.' Razeby pulled a bottle of champagne from his pocket. 'No glasses. I am afraid we will have to slum it. Even if it is the best bottle from your cellar.'

'*Your* cellar,' she said and laughed, as he timed the popping of the cork to merge with the explosion of the fireworks in the sky.

The froth exploded over the top of the bottle, cascading down the bottle's neck as Razeby offered it to her.

Alice took a swig from the bottle and spluttered at the furious fizz of bubbles.

Razeby's swig gave not the slightest hint of choking.

Then she leaned back against his chest as his arms wrapped around her waist, and together they looked up and watched the magnificent explosion of coloured lights and flashes fill the sky. All around them the crowd was 'oohing' and 'aahing' with amazement and appreciation at the spectacle. She could smell the sulphurous stench of the fireworks and catch the drift of the scent of smoke from the braziers not so very far away.

Razeby leaned down to kiss her and he tasted of the green grass and of strawberries and champagne, and of Razeby and all that was wonderful in life. They watched the fireworks and they drank the champagne and they kissed, not caring who saw them, because it was dark and because this was the slightly *risqué* Vauxhall Pleasure Gardens, and because it would have been too much to keep their lips from one another. As the fireworks began to wane Razeby took her hand, not even waiting until they had finished in full, and led her back towards the boats so that they would not have to wait in the crush that would follow.

Within their bedchamber at Hart Street the glow of the firelight burnished the dark blonde of her hair a red-gold. He reached out and caught a vibrant strand that had loosened from her pins, running it between his fingers before tucking it behind her ear. His thumb stroked against the softness of her cheek. She closed her eyes and angled her face into his hand for the breath of a moment before stepping away beyond his reach.

He shrugged off the midnight-blue tailcoat he was wearing, throwing it to land on a nearby armchair. But as he did so the slim brown-velvet box fell from the pocket to land upon the rug beneath their feet.

Alice smiled when she saw it. 'You bought me another gift. What did I tell you the other day?' she demanded.

He picked up the box, kept his eyes on it and could not rise to her teasing.

'Honestly, Razeby, you shouldn't have.'

He gave a small tight smile and passed the brown-velvet box to her.

'I'm mystified as to what it can be.' She stared at the jeweller's box, stroked her fingers once against its velvet, hesitating for a moment before finally opening the lid. The radiance of the diamond bracelet, lying within on its cream-velvet cushion, caught the firelight to glitter and sparkle and illuminate the room around them.

She gave a soft gasp. 'Oh, Razeby! It's beautiful!' She pressed a kiss to his cheek. 'It must have cost you a fortune.'

'You are worth every penny, and more.'

'I love it.' Her hands came to caress his face, her eyes scanning his. 'Thank you.'

His heart squeezed tight.

Slowly she touched her lips to his.

'Alice,' he murmured and, pulling her into his arms, he kissed her.

He kissed her and he could not stop. He kissed her and lost himself in her, as ever he did. She made him forget everything else, all of his responsibility that weighed upon his shoulders, all of the darkness that was coming. Her eyes were filled with a passion and need that matched his own.

'Make love to me, Razeby.'

He could not deny her. He could not deny himself, or all that he felt for her.

He undressed her in silence, their eyes clinging together all the while, and laid her down gently on the bed. He never took his eyes from hers even while he stripped off his waistcoat and shirt and cravat. Nor while he unfastened the fall of his breeches and freed himself from his drawers.

He took her tenderly, with reverence, with meaning, all of which seemed to make the force between them only stronger and rawer. Claiming her as his own, gifting her all he could, so neither of them would ever forget. And she rose to meet him. He opened himself to her entirely, gave all, held nothing back. And in Alice's reply he felt her do the same, this woman for whom he would pluck both the sun and moon from the sky and give them to her if he could.

Their bodies had been made to be together. To merge. To be as one. She was his complement, and he hers. Together they found another place distinct from the world. But the lovemaking between them tonight took them further than he had ever known. It was poignant, special, a bonding between them like no other. As if she touched an even deeper part of him he had not known existed. They clung together, strove together, looking into one another's eyes as their bodies reached a new nirvana, and together stepped over the edge to tumble into a shared climax the force of which made them capture each other's merging cries. And afterwards, he could feel her heart and his beat in time, as they lay entwined together watching the flicker of the firelight dance upon each other's naked skin.

Her fingers gently caressed the muscle at the top of his arm.

'Alice…' he said, and there was a terrible pressing tightness in his chest.

'Did you get the tickets for tomorrow night's show?'

'I have the tickets.'

'Well, that's a relief.' She smiled but Razeby could not reciprocate. 'We'll have a grand time. Ellen says the horses are amazing. That a body wouldn't believe they could be trained to do such tricks.'

He closed his eyes, took a breath, forced himself to say the words aloud before he could not. 'I cannot accompany you to the show tomorrow night.'

'I thought you said you had the tickets.'

'I do, but there is…another occasion…which I am obliged to attend.'

'What occasion?'

The small silence hissed loud.

'A ball at Almack's.'

'Almack's is not usually one of your haunts.' She gave a little laugh. 'All those débutantes and fierce matrons intent on landing eligible husbands for their daughters. Is Devlin finally on the hunt for a bride?'

'I am not going with Devlin, but with Linwood.' Viscount Linwood, who almost six months ago had married Alice's best friend and London's most celebrated actress, Venetia Fox.

And he felt the withdrawal of her body and saw in her face that she realised the truth even before he said the words he did not want to say, 'We need to talk, Alice. There is something I have to tell you.'

Chapter Three

Razeby fixed his drawers and breeches into place before sitting up in the bed. Leaning his spine against the massive carved-oak headboard, he stretched his long still-booted legs out before him over the counterpane.

Alice felt the rush of cold air fill the space where he had been. She shivered at its icy touch as she pulled the sheet to cover her nakedness and sat up next to him, leaning back to rest against the headboard in the same manner.

And even though he moved his hand to cover hers, threading their fingers together, her stomach dipped and a cold draught moved across her heart. She waited, knowing what Razeby was going to say and willing with all her heart and mind and soul that it would turn out to be something different, that later she would laugh over this foolish pound of her heart and tight fear in her throat.

'You best get on and tell me then.' She smiled as if dread were not trickling like ice through her veins.

'I have a duty, Alice, to my title, to my estates and the people upon them. A duty to safeguard them for future generations. And part of that duty is to marry and produce an heir. I was raised for that purpose. I must produce a son who will do the same. I must marry.'

'Of course you must.' She had always known it, they both had. But he would marry at some distant time in the future, not now, not when what they had together was still so fresh and vital. 'But you're young enough yet. Surely you don't need to step upon that path right now?'

'I'll be thirty in six months' time.' He glanced away and raked a hand through his hair.

'What's the significance of thirty? Is there some kind of stipulation that you have to be married and breeding an heir by then?'

A shadow moved in his eyes as he glanced away. 'Something like that,' he said. 'Atholl will be coming home on a stretcher. It could too easily have been a coffin.'

'Your cousin who got shot in battle.'

'As it stands he is my heir, Alice.'

'I thought he was on the mend.'

'He is. Now. He very nearly was not. What happened to Atholl…it has forced me to reconsider things. I have deferred my duty for too long. I can defer it no longer. I have to find a bride for Razeby.'

Their fingers still lay entwined together. Neither of them had moved, both just sat leaning back against the headboard of their bed, as if this was just an ordinary conversation, one of the thousands they had had before, when it was anything other. She sat motionless, feigning relaxation, pretending that she was not shocked and reeling from his words.

'So is this you giving me my *congé?*' She smiled

with the incredulity of it, half-expecting him to deny it, to tell her they could still go on as before. On the ivory of the bedcover she could see where the dust of his riding boots had smudged dark.

But he made no denial. 'I am sorry, Alice.'

She slipped her fingers from his. Looked round at him, but he stared straight ahead, as if seeing into the distance, and did not meet her eyes.

Not five minutes ago they had been making love, their breaths and bodies and hearts merged as one in that ultimate act of intimacy. Now he was sitting there dismissing her. It felt like she had just been punched in the stomach.

She glanced down at the diamond bracelet that glittered as beautiful as a night sky full of stars. 'That's why you bought me the bracelet!' She laughed a mirthless laugh. 'As a pay off.'

The silence hissed.

Her fingers unfastened the latch and slipped it from her wrist. The diamonds sparkled and cast shimmering lights against the shadowed walls as she let it fall on to the pale counterpane.

She could not think straight. Her thoughts swayed and staggered as she struggled to understand. 'You were going to tell me the other day, weren't you? That's why you came round unexpectedly.'

Again he did not deny it.

She gave an ironic laugh and shook her head.

His eyes were dark and serious.

The tide of emotion threatened to engulf her. She turned her face away, barely able to conceal her anger and incredulity, and the splintering unbelievable hurt. How could she have been so blind? Six months of thinking that everything was happy and good and wonderful. And believing that he had felt the same. She could barely take it in that he was telling her it was over.

'You can stay here as long it takes to find other lodgings. There is no rush to leave.'

'How kind of you.'

He ignored the irony. 'I will, of course, make a settlement of money on you.'

'I don't want your money, Razeby.'

'It is part of our contract.'

'Oh, so it is.' She thought of the piece of paper with its fancy black writing, secure and tied neat within its green ribbon. 'How could I have forgotten?'

The silence seemed to pulsate between them. There were so many thoughts running through her head, so many words crowding for release upon her tongue. She closed her mouth firmly to prevent their escape.

Climbing from the bed, she grabbed an old dressing gown from where it hung over the back of a chair, pulling it on and tying the belt around her waist as she walked to stand by the window and stare down on to the lamp-lit street below. In the continuing silence she watched the occasional group walking along the pavements. Theatre goers who had gone elsewhere after a late show. Women who, despite the quality of their dress, were ladies of the night, plying their trade; Alice could pick them out with an expert eye—like could always recognise like. A carriage passed and then a gentleman on a horse.

She heard him move and glanced round to see him get to his feet, all six feet of him, with his tight dark breeches and his naked chest, and that ruggedly handsome face. And, despite what he had just told her, her traitorous body reacted with the usual rush of desire for him.

'Arrangements like ours are not meant to last, Alice.'

'They're not,' she agreed.

'I have to do my duty, Alice.' His mouth, which had always been so warm and smiling, was unhappy and determined, the expression in his eyes unreadable.

Her heart was beating harder than a horse at full gallop. 'Maybe you should have considered your duty six months ago.' When he had pursued her while the play in which she and Venetia had starred together took London by storm. When he had wooed her and swept her off her feet and made her his mistress within weeks of their meeting.

'Maybe I should have,' he said.

His quiet admission stripped her raw.

They stared at one another. He was grim-faced, serious in a way she had never seen him before.

'For what it is worth, I really am sorry, Alice.'

'So you said.'

He swallowed. 'Thank you for everything.' His eyes clung to hers. He took a step towards her, reached a hand as if he meant to touch her.

Alice recoiled, sweeping her eyes over his extended hand with its long manly fingers and its lightly tanned skin. It was a hand that had caressed her lips and stroked against her naked skin, a hand that had touched her in the most intimate of places. It was all she could do to stop herself from striking it away with every ounce of strength in her body.

She raised her gaze to meet his with fierceness.

He swallowed, glanced away, let his hand drop to rest by his side. 'If there is anything more you need—'

'There isn't. You should go now,' she said with feigned calmness before turning away again to the window. Clutching her dressing gown all the tighter around her, she stared down at the gas-lit street, seeing nothing of it, waiting only for him to leave.

But he did not leave.

She heard him come up behind her. He did not touch her, but she could feel the heat of his proximity scorch the length of her spine.

'Alice...' there was a straining pause '...I hope I have not...hurt you.'

She turned to him, held her head up to look him defiantly in the face. 'Hurt me? Don't flatter yourself, Razeby. It was nice while it lasted, but...' She gave a shrug as if she did not care and bit hard at her bottom lip to stop the threat of the betraying tremor.

She saw the bob of his Adam's apple in his throat, the way his dark eyes studied hers.

'That at least is something.' He gave a nod. 'Goodbye, Alice.'

'Goodbye, Razeby.' The words were tight. She forced a smile and turned away to the window again as if she were more interested in the dark view.

He turned and walked away, but she could see the reflection of his leaving in the glass of the window pane and her own face watching, pale and haunting as a ghost.

The bedchamber door closed with a quiet click that seemed louder than an almighty slam.

She stood there and listened to the stride of his booted footsteps along the corridor and down the stairs. Her breath caught in ragged gasps, but she caught her hand to her mouth to silence them. Five minutes later the front door shut. Only then did she let herself sag back to lean against the wall and allow the sob to escape.

For what remained of that night Alice sat in the little blue armchair by the fireplace and stared into the flames. They licked high around the fresh coal she had thrown on to it, devouring the black rocks with a ferocity that matched the force of emotion whirling and tumbling through her. It did not matter how much heat they threw out, it did not warm the chill from her bones. Nor did the dressing gown or the woollen shawl clutched tight around her shoulders. It was the shock, she thought to herself. And the anger. And that feeling that she had drunk ten cups of coffee and that it did not matter if she lay on the bed and closed her eyes; her thoughts were running so wild she would never sleep again.

Don't you dare shed a single tear for him!

But her eyes were swimming and she felt she could have wept a waterfall. She swallowed down the lump in her throat, but no amount of swallowing could shift the boulder from her chest that felt like it was crushing her.

It was just sex. It had always been just sex. And the way she was feeling now, so scraped and raw and bleeding, was down to the shock of it; that was all. Razeby's words had come out of nowhere, catching her with her guard down.

She breathed, calmed herself. Stared into the flames. She had survived worse things than this. She thought of her family back in Ireland, of her coming to London to find a job that she might help them, of the hunger and the desperation. She thought of playing the role of the masked Miss Rouge in Mrs Silver's high-class brothel, her identity hidden from the world. So few people knew. But Razeby did. God only knew why she had told him. She was regretting that now.

Her eyes glanced across at the bed with its sheets still rumpled from their lovemaking. Amidst them she could see the sparkle of the diamond bracelet, so brilliant and beautiful and expensive. She gave a shaky laugh and shook her head at what a fool she had been.

Never let them see how much they hurt you. Her mother's words, drummed into her across a lifetime, played in her head. *The bastards can't take your pride away from you unless you let them. Look life straight in the face, Alice, and always, always keep smiling.*

Alice was not clever. She was not smart. But she was practical and hard-working and determined. And she still had her pride, every damn inch of it.

She turned her face away from the bed and, staring into the low golden flickers amongst the red glowing coals, made her plans.

Chapter Four

Within the hallowed grounds of Almack's ballroom, the chandeliers sparkled beneath the flames of a thousand candles. The walls were painted a soft cream and outlined in antique gold. The ceiling had recently been reworked in an array of white plasterwork. In its centre was a line of three elaborate roses, from each of which hung an enormous crystal chandelier. There was a three-piece matching peering glass set above the fireplace, with candles fitted to the fronts and a series of matching mirrored wall sconces positioned at regular intervals around the room. Small chairs and tables were seeded around the periphery. The musicians played from the balcony above, the music floating sweet and melodic to fill the ballroom and haunt Razeby.

'I was not sure they were going to let you in,' he said to Linwood standing by his side.

'I did have to call in a few favours.'

'I am glad you did,' he admitted.

There was a small silence as the two men let their eyes wander to the other side of the dance floor and the crowd of white-dressed débutantes there that posed and giggled and chattered amongst themselves while their stern-faced turban-wearing chaperones looked on.

'Does Alice know you are here?' Linwood asked.

'It is over between me and Alice.' Razeby felt the weight of Linwood's gaze, but he did not shift his own, just kept his face impassive and remained staring straight ahead so that nothing of his feelings showed.

'I am sorry about that.'

'So am I.'

There was the music and the droning hum of surrounding conversations and the tinkle of women's laughter.

'You could have kept her on at least until you found—'

'No.' Razeby did not let him finish. 'A clean severance is for the best.' He met his friend's eyes.

Linwood raised an eyebrow. 'I was under the impression that you and she dealt very well together.'

'We do.' He glanced away and corrected himself. 'We did.' He swallowed to ease the sudden tightness in his throat. 'But she was my mistress, Linwood. And now it is time to find myself a wife.'

Linwood looked at him with that too-perceptive gaze of his, as if he could see the way that Razeby's stomach clenched at just the mention of her name. He was doing the right thing, the thing that had to be done. The thing he should have been doing six months ago, before Alice Sweetly came into his life and changed his best-laid plan. Six months and he could regret not one day of it. Six months and… He changed the subject, pretending something of his usual lightness of spirit when what he felt was anything but.

'See what you missed out on by not playing the marriage mart?'

Linwood smiled, which was a sight that was a deal more

common since his recent marriage. 'I would rather be tried for murder and catch a wife in the process,' he said, referring to exactly what he had done just a few months ago. 'Scandalous and dangerous—but more than satisfying in its end result.' He smiled again and there was a softening of his expression so that Razeby could tell he was thinking of his wife, the former star of the Covent Garden stage, Venetia Fox. Venetia, who was Alice's best friend.

A vision of Alice swam in his mind. Alice, with her mischief and her heart and her laughter. Alice standing in their bedchamber looking at him with that expression of shock in her eyes as he told her it was over. Something churned in Razeby's stomach. He forced that last image away and turned his gaze to the hordes of white-frocked débutantes across the floor, one of whom by the end of the Season would be his wife, in his bed and carrying his child. He felt numb at the thought, but it had to be this way. He had had his fun and Alice had been more than he had ever anticipated, but now it was time to bite the bullet and do his duty...before it was too late. He turned his mind from all other distractions and summoned a cold determination.

'So which lucky débutante are you going to ask to dance?' asked Linwood.

'The first one I come to,' replied Razeby with a smile that did not touch his eyes and, setting his champagne glass down on the silver salver of a passing footman, he made his way across the room.

The day had been a long one, following a night in which she had not slept, but Alice was not tired.

It had been a mammoth effort and one which had seen her travel round half of London. But it had been worth it.

The large travelling bag lay open at her feet.

'Shall I help you, ma'am?' The maid hovered awkwardly in the doorway as if afraid to enter the bedchamber. The girl's cheeks were flushed with embarrassment, her manner awkward. Alice saw the way her eyes dropped to take in the travelling bag before meeting her face.

All of the servants knew, even though she was sure that Razeby would have told them nothing of it. Alice had two sisters in service in Dublin. She knew that servants always knew these things.

'No, thank you, Mary. I'll see to myself. But if you could have Heston see that a hackney carriage is summoned for me.'

'Yes, ma'am.' The girl bobbed a curtsy and hurried off to update the rest of the staff.

Alice went through the wardrobe, pulling out a minimal selection of clothes, all of which she had brought with her when she had come to this house, and ignoring the expensive silk dresses and accessories that Razeby had paid for.

She made short work of gathering up the rest of her possessions. There were not many. Alice travelled light. She preferred it that way.

It was when she moved to close the wardrobe doors that she stopped, her eyes drawn, as if not of their own volition, to the dress hanging on its own at the very end of the row. She hesitated, bit her lip, knowing that she should shut the door upon it just like all the rest, but unable to do so. Before she could think better of it, she slipped the emerald-silk evening dress from the hanger and folded it into her bag.

Of all the gifts that Razeby had given her, she took only one, opening the lid of the long thin cherrywood box just long enough to check that the engraved silver pen was inside. But she did not look at it. She did not touch it, just snapped the lid shut and stuffed it into the travelling bag with a tortoiseshell comb and the rest of her toiletries before buckling the bag closed. Then she swept the black-velvet cloak over her shoulders and lifted the travelling bag.

One final glance around the bedchamber, at the dressing table and its peering glass, at the wardrobe and the armchairs and the pretty little table with its ivory vase of deep-pink roses that had had their day. The heads were blown, the petals starting to fall. But their perfume was still sweet and lingering in the room. She moved her gaze to the bed, which she and Razeby had shared, let her eyes rest there for only a moment. Then, with her bag in hand, she walked away, down the stairs and out into the waiting hackney carriage.

The driver flicked the reins and the carriage drove off into the sunset. Alice kept her focus on the glorious rosy-streaked sky. She clutched her hands tight around the travelling bag and kept her mouth set firm with determination.

And not once did she look back at the house.

Razeby lost track of the number of women he danced with. They all seemed much the same. He made conversation. He went through the motions. But all the while he could not get last night's scene with Alice out of his head.

She knew more than most how the games between men and women played out. She had been under no illusions. Neither of them had. And yet...

I don't want your money, Razeby.

The words whispered again in his ear. It was that one phrase more than any other that worried him.

Last night had been about a clean, quick break. It was the only way. The best way for them both. Just as he had told Linwood. The theory of it had been easy, the practice anything but. He had handled it badly. More than badly. He wondered if he could have handled it worse.

Alice had been good to him, good for him. She was like no one he had ever known. It explained the gnawing feeling he had felt since telling her. Guilt. He should make sure she was all right, now and for the future. He should up the sum of her severance payment from that which his lawyer had specified in the contract, regardless of what she said.

He delivered Miss Thomson back to her mother. And bowed.

Hurt me? Don't flatter yourself, Razeby. He was not sure he believed her. The thought niggled him. He felt the guilt gnaw harder, even though he had spoken the truth to her. Arrangements like theirs were not meant to last. But he could not stop wondering how she was.

'Leaving so early?' Linwood raised an eyebrow. 'The night is still young, Razeby.'

'Breaking myself in gently, Linwood,' he lied. 'There are only so many débutantes a man can endure in one evening.'

'Do you want to go to White's to recover?'

'Another night,' said Razeby.

* * *

The lights glowed through the blind-shuttered windows. The house in Hart Street looked as welcoming as ever it had done. He wondered if he had made a mistake in coming here. But he needed to reassure himself that she was all right.

'What do you mean she is gone?' It had been the early hours of this morning when he had left her here alone. Not even twenty-four hours had elapsed since that botched confrontation.

He saw the awkwardness of the butler's expression before the man remembered his professional decorum and schooled his face to the usual attentive impassivity.

'Miss Sweetly was out all day, my lord, returning earlier this evening to pack a travelling bag.'

Something twisted in his chest. 'Did she leave a note?'

'There is no note, my lord.' There was something in the way the old man's eyes looked at him that made him feel even more of a bastard. He paused before adding, 'She gave instructions that she would not be returning.'

'And did Miss Sweetly say where she was going? Or leave a forwarding direction?' Razeby knew in his heart what the answer to those questions would be, but he asked them in the hope that he was wrong.

'No, my lord, she did not.'

'But she must have given a direction to John Coachman?'

'Miss Sweetly did not travel by your lordship's coach when she left.'

He understood the significance of that very clearly. She did not want him to find her, and, in truth, he could not blame her.

Razeby dismissed the butler and climbed the stairs

to the bedchamber they had shared. Everything looked just the same as it always did, as if last night had been just some bad dream. The wall sconces on either side of the fireplace were lit, the flames of their candles reflecting soft and subdued in their adjoining looking glasses. The roses he had brought her not a week ago were still in their vase. A small fire burned on the hearth, making the room cosy and warm. The scent of her was in the air, the sense of her entwined in the very fibres of the place.

Her jewel casket still sat upon her dressing table, beneath the lid all of what he had given her lying neat in their own little compartments.

He walked to her wardrobe, opened up the door. There were only a few spaces where garments no longer hung. The myriad of coloured dresses that he had paid for from Madame Boisseron's were still there. Their matching slippers and shoes sat in neat pairs at the bottom of the wardrobe. On an impulse he opened his own matching wardrobe and saw all of his clothes just as he had left them.

He closed the doors over, letting his eyes survey the rest of the room. Nothing was out of place...except... His gaze stilled when it came to the ivory bedcovers, neat and smooth upon the mattress, for laid carefully upon them, in their very centre, was the brown-velvet box opened to reveal the cream-velvet cushion and the diamond bracelet that lay sparkling upon it.

He felt his jaw clamp tight and a cold realisation seep through his blood. Alice had gone. He did not know where. Without her severance payment. Without a single thing he had bought for her. And there could be nothing for the best about that.

* * *

'I came as soon as I got your message.' Alice's best friend and mentor, the woman who had saved her from her life in Mrs Silver's bawdy house and set her up as an actress, Venetia Fox, or Viscountess Linwood as she was now, handed her cloak to Alice's new maid and followed Alice through to the drawing room of her new home in Mercer Street.

'You must have dropped what you were doing and come straight away. I only sent the boy half an hour ago.'

'You are my friend, Alice. What else did you expect I would do?' There was a concern in Venetia's face that made Alice feel guilty.

'I didn't mean to worry you, Venetia. I was just letting you know where I was.'

'I am glad that you did. I really have been worried.' Venetia sat down next to her on the sofa and took her hands in hers. 'What happened?'

Alice smiled as if the words were easy to say. 'He gave me my *congé*. Said it's time he found himself a bride.'

'Oh, Alice, I am so sorry.'

'Don't be. It had to happen one day. I'm an actress. He's a marquis. How else was it going to end?' She shrugged and gave a little laugh. 'Besides, I was tired of him. I fancied a bit of a change, myself.' The joking words tripped easily from her lips.

Venetia did not look convinced. 'Neither of you could have anticipated what happened to Atholl. I suppose it made Razeby see things differently.'

'Atholl was a grand excuse for the both of us.' An excuse for Razeby, more like. She knew now what had been bothering him all those weeks and months leading up to it and she was more fool for being worried over him. 'Our time was on the wane.'

'You left Hart Street very quickly.'

'Striking while the iron's hot.' She smiled. 'I've got myself sorted out. What do you think of the new rooms? I've had my eye on them for a little while.' The smile broadened to become a grin. 'Nice and handy for the theatre. And not too high a rent.'

'They are very nice. But I did not come to see the rooms, Alice,' Venetia said carefully.

'You did warn me not to become his mistress. Do you remember?'

Venetia gave no reply, only held her gaze with eyes that were filled with compassion.

Alice hated to see it. It made her feel angry and even more determined. She did not want anyone's pity, not even Venetia's. 'You told me it was better to earn your own money than put yourself in any man's power.'

'And did you put yourself in his power, Alice?' Venetia asked softly.

'Of course not! I'm not that daft. I knew the score with him. Just as he did with me. With my background, how could I not?' The secret of her scandalous past whispered between them. She smiled again as if it meant nothing. 'I kept my hand in at the theatre, didn't I? Doing the odd appearance. Which is why Kemble's agreed to take me back full time.'

'I am glad of that.' But whether Venetia's gladness was due to Kemble taking her back full time or her attitude over Razeby was not clear. 'But there is more to power than money, Alice.' Venetia looked at her. 'I do understand something of how it has been between you and Razeby. How it was even in the very beginning.'

'You're imagining things, Venetia.' Alice gave a dismissive laugh. 'What was between Razeby and me was a kind of mutually beneficial business arrangement, nothing more. Great sex and a good time, and money, of course, lots of money.'

'It seemed as if there was a lot more than that.'

'I'm a good actress. What can I say? You trained me well.' She smiled again.

'You are,' said Venetia, 'a very good actress.' There was no edge to the words. Alice did not know why they brought a blush to heat her cheeks.

The little clock on the mantel ticked, reassuring and steady.

Alice busied herself in pouring tea into the pretty bone-china cups that came with the fine furniture and everything else in these rented rooms. She added a lump of sugar to each and a few drops of cream before passing one small cup and saucer to Venetia.

'You seem as if you have everything in hand, Alice.'

'I have, indeed.'

'If there is anything I can do to help...'

Alice glanced across the room to the side table, where the folded cream paper lay with its red ribbon tied around it. 'Actually, there is one thing you could do for me, Venetia, as you're here. Kemble's given me the contract for the theatre. I was going to come and see you. But I was waiting for a quiet time.' She fetched the document over and set it down next to the coffee tray.

'You can come round any time, you know that.' But that was not true. They both knew it.

'We move in different worlds now, Venetia. You're

no longer an actress, but a viscountess. If I'm seen visiting, it wouldn't look good for you. Reputation is everything in the *ton*. They're starting to accept you. It's going well. I don't want to ruin it.'

'You will not ruin it. You are the very height of discretion.'

'I try.' She laughed. 'Well, only where you're concerned, if I'm honest.'

'I am glad you are keeping your spirits up.' Venetia smiled.

'Why wouldn't I? Razeby's in the past. Ahead there's only the future. And the future looks good for me.' She smiled again. 'I'm planning to throw myself into the theatre life. Make a real go of it. You have to get on with life, don't you?' Another of her mother's teachings. Very easy to say, not so easy to do. But Alice would do it. She was very determined of that.

'You do,' Venetia agreed. Then she lifted the document Alice had set before her and slipped off the red ribbon that bound it.

A small companionable silence opened up as they sipped their coffee and Venetia read the wording of the theatre contract.

'Is it all in order?'

'It seems to be. You are in a strong position, Alice. Your return to the stage full time will fill the theatre. You could push Kemble to pay you more.'

But Alice shook her head. 'I'm happy with what he's offered me. I just want to get on with it. Get started.'

'If you are sure?'

'I am. Although I must confess to being a little nervous at playing so many leading roles.'

'You will be fine upon that stage, Alice. More than fine. You will be great. I know you will.'

'I hope so.' Alice bit at her lip and her cheeks turned pink at the compliment.

'Kemble has told you the plays that are scheduled?'

'Right up to the summer. There's nothing new, nothing I haven't done before, thank the Lord.'

Venetia met her gaze. 'If something new does come up…any new part to be read, come to me.'

Alice gave a nod. 'I will.'

The two women looked at one another, bound by more than this secret that they shared. By sensitivity and friendship and past histories that were too much alike.

Alice took a deep breath. 'Go ahead, sign it,' she said.

Venetia gave a nod and then, moving the tray aside, she lifted the plain black pen, another one of the house's possessions, from its holder and dipped the tip into the ink well. Very carefully she signed at the end of the contract, *Alice Sweetly,* then sprinkled some fine sand upon the still-wet ink of the signature.

'It is done, Alice,' she said.

They both knew that it was more than the signing of the contract Venetia was referring to. This commitment to going back to the theatre full time was the drawing of a line under all that had gone before with Razeby. It marked the end of that chapter in Alice's life and the beginning of a new one. She was fortunate to have such an option, and more fortunate still to have such a friend as Venetia who had helped her. Alice knew that, so she smiled and held her head up. 'It is,' she agreed. 'Thank you, Venetia.'

'I will come and see you in your first performance.'

'You do that. I'll be looking out for you.' Alice smiled.

They walked towards the front door.

The thought was pounding in Alice's mind, and the words whispering in her ear, and Alice tried not to say them. But once Venetia walked out that door it would be too late and Alice had to be sure.

Just as Venetia was about to leave, Alice placed her hand on her friend's arm and said quietly, 'If Razeby should enquire, which I'm sure he won't, you won't tell him the direction of my new rooms, will you?'

There was the tiniest of hesitations in which Venetia looked into her eyes in a way that made Alice regret speaking the words.

'Rest assured I will tell him nothing, Alice.'

There were no accusations. No denials or admissions. Just a hug of understanding. And a farewell.

Chapter Five

Within the study of Razeby's town house in Leicester Square, Collins answered the question he had just been asked. 'Two maidservants, no menservants. Apart from that, no one.'

'Thank you, Mr Collins.' Razeby slid a neat pile of folded bank notes across the gleam of the mahogany desk top.

The wiry, sharp-eyed man pocketed the money without counting it. It was not first time the Bow Street Runner had undertaken a little work on the side for Razeby. Although it was in all probability the last, thought Razeby with a macabre sense of humour.

'All in a day's work, Lord Razeby.' Collins made no comment as to the information he had just given Razeby, although he could not have been unaware of its significance. The Bow Street Runner was too smart for that. It was why Razeby had used him. 'I will bid you good day, my lord.' Collins gave a small bow and left, closing the study door silently behind him.

Razeby sat where he was, staring at the panels of the door without seeing them. A man had his duty and his fate. And honour. None of which he could escape, no matter how much he willed it. That knowledge was ever present in his mind these days.

A few thousand pounds and his duty to Alice would be discharged, all monies owed paid. The severance between them finalised. And after that maybe then he would be able to stop thinking of her, maybe then he would be able to focus on the task in hand. Finding a bride. Breeding an heir.

His gaze lowered to the desk, to the scrap of paper that Collins had given him. He looked at it again, his eyes lingering on it even though the words written there were already imprinted on his memory. There could be no room in his life for sentimentality or faltering. Only getting the job done. He knew that, but he still folded the paper carefully and stowed it safely in the pocket of his waistcoat before ringing the bell for his valet and moving to ready himself for tonight's dance.

In the days since Venetia's visit Alice had done just as she had said and thrown herself into the theatre. She was working hard in preparation for her opening night at Covent Garden's Theatre Royal. The enormity of the challenge before her left little time for that. She rose early and tumbled into bed late, exhausted. She loved the smell of the theatre, that dusty polished scent unique to the grand stage. The way it gave her a purpose on which to focus.

Every day brought new challenges, refreshing herself as to the plays and the roles, running through lines last heard a year past. She took home scripts at night and returned them the next morning, pretending she had read them, as if she could, but Alice had no need to read a single line. She only had to hear something once to remember it for ever. It was her special gift. And she was truly thankful for it.

All day, every day was spent at the theatre, with Mr Kemble and the other actors and actresses, rehearsing. Everything that she feared she might have forgotten of the art of playacting came back to her as easily as if she had last stepped upon a stage in a leading role only yesterday. Even the feeling of fear but also of excitement, like walking a knife edge. It made her concentrate, made her focus. It took away the luxury of time during which she might dwell upon Razeby.

Alice was about to leave for rehearsals one morning when the maid brought her a letter.

'A footman has just delivered this, ma'am.'

She lifted the letter from the maid's small silver salver, wondering who had written. So far, only Kemble and Venetia knew the address of her new rooms. Kemble she saw in person each day and Venetia knew better than to write. But as soon as she turned the letter over in her hands she knew without opening it, without needing to be able to read a single word of it, the identity of the sender.

'Have him wait, Meg,' she instructed.

The thick red-wax seal impressed upon the back was a crest she recognised too well. One that made her pulse thrum uncomfortably hard and her heart beat too fast with anger and too many other emotions she would rather not name. She swallowed, torn between not wanting to open it and the need to know what lay beneath that seal. Wetting her lips, she swallowed again and cracked the wax. The letter unfolded. Inside was a cheque with Razeby's name signed against a sum she could not read. The letter itself was blank other than signed with his name. That familiar bold black scrawl—Razeby.

It was her severance pay, a common enough negotiation between mistresses and the men in whose keeping they had been. A lump sum to tide them over until they found their next protector. Or to keep them for life. But for Alice there would be no new protector. And she would keep herself, earn her own money. Venetia had been right in that. Too late she realised just what her friend had been warning her against.

She stared at the cheque. She might not know the figure written there, but she knew it was high. Common sense and practicality told her she should accept it. Take it to the bank this very day. You had to be careful with money. Save it. Look after it. The future was never certain and life without money could be very hard indeed. Who better than Alice knew that? But when she looked at the cheque, Razeby's money, and all that it meant, she could not bring herself to do it.

Folding the cheque within the letter just as it had been, she heated a blob of rich red wax and let it drip to cover and melt away Razeby's crest. Within a few moments it had cooled and the letter was sealed once more, the wax disc smooth and even.

She took it out to the footman who waited in the hallway. A footman she recognised from Razeby's town house in Leicester Square. He recognised her, too, although he said nothing. If he knew the contents of the letter, he gave no sign.

'If you would be so kind as to return this to Lord Razeby.'

'Certainly, Miss Sweetly. Is there a message you wish relayed?' he enquired.

'None other than what is within the letter.' She smiled at him.

'Very good, miss.' He bowed and left.

Alice watched him go.

It had taken Razeby less than a week to find her. Just for a minute she wondered if Venetia had told him. But she knew in her heart her friend would never have broken her word. Razeby was a marquis, a man of power and money and contacts, all of which he had clearly used.

But he could keep his money. She would not touch a damn penny of it.

Chapter Six

Razeby had checked every entry in the estate account books. The task kept his mind from wandering to other thoughts he had no wish to think. Thoughts of the future. And even more thoughts of the past…with Alice.

Lifting the pen, he made to enter the figure in the column at the bottom of the open page and found the inkwell dry. He opened the top drawer of his desk to find a fresh bottle of ink and saw, lying there, the cheque he had written to her.

He stilled, his eyes fixed upon it. Four thousand pounds, twice what was specified in their contract, and she had sent it back as if it were some kind of insult. Some men might have construed it as a means of angling for more money, but Razeby knew in his gut that it was not. There was a finality about it, a closure rather than an opening of negotiation, and it made him uncomfortable. Had she asked for three times the sum he would have felt happier. Maybe then he would not be worrying over her.

The memory came again of the expensive dresses still hanging in the wardrobe at Hart Street, all the jewellery still in its casket, the diamond bracelet abandoned upon the bed. And the same uneasiness rippled through him, the gnawing feeling that it was all wrong, the unmistakable essence that there were layers between the two of them that he dare not explore. He quelled the feelings, reassured himself that he had done everything he could. He could no longer be a part of Alice's life, nor she a part of his. What she chose to do was no longer his concern. Lifting out the bottle of ink, he turned his eyes from the cheque and shut the drawer.

He had just blotted the entry and closed the books when the butler announced that Linwood had come to call.

'Were we supposed to be riding this morning?' Razeby asked.

Linwood shook his head. 'Not this morning. I came to ask if you are attending the Lords this afternoon.

'I am.'

'It is the debate on Wellesley-Pole's circular letter.'

'The Irish issue.' Razeby could almost hear the whisper of Alice's Irish accent, so soft against his ear.

'I heard that there are plans to bring up the fact that you are biased on the matter.'

Because of Alice. The words went unspoken between them.

'Do they not know she is no longer my mistress?' he asked.

'I am sure they are well aware, but they will still use the association against you. Feelings are running high on the subject. Better be prepared, Razeby.'

'I will,' he murmured. 'Sit down. You'll take a brandy?'

'A trifle early in the day, Razeby.' It was, but he needed it.

'Coffee, then?'

Linwood gave a nod.

They spoke about horses and other inconsequential things while waiting for the coffee. He waited until they were sipping their coffee, bitter and strong, before he asked what he could no longer stop himself from asking. It was natural, he justified. Any reasonable, fair-minded gentleman would do the same, although the words perhaps would not have clamoured so desperately for release.

'Have you heard anything of Alice?' He did not meet Linwood's eye.

'She opens tonight in Covent Garden's Theatre Royal, playing Lady Macbeth,' said Linwood. 'Kemble has made quite a fanfare. It has sold out. There is not a seat to be had in the house.'

'So I saw in the newspapers.' He paused. 'Has Venetia seen her?'

'I believe so.' Linwood sipped at his coffee. 'They are as much friends as we two.'

The silence was loud between them

Razeby swallowed, wondering how far he dare go without raising his friend's suspicions. 'How is she?'

'I understand that she is well.'

Razeby gave a nod and cleared his throat. There was another awkward pause. 'If you should ever hear otherwise…'

'Do not worry, Razeby,' Linwood said quietly. 'Should that be the case, I would let you know.'

'Thank you, Linwood.' He breathed a little easier.

* * *

There was a rap on the dressing room door. The same dressing room she had shared with Venetia all those months ago, before Venetia had married Linwood and Alice had become Razeby's mistress.

'Five minutes to curtain up, Miss Sweetly.'

'Thank you.'

It was Alice's opening night, her grand return to the Theatre Royal as a full-time actress.

Her palms were clammy with nerves, her stomach turning somersaults at the prospect of walking out on that stage alone before a packed house. It had always been this way. But it had not been as bad when Venetia was here as the leading lady and Alice just sharing the spotlight. And thereafter, during her occasional appearances, there had been Razeby. Just his presence, with his easygoing manner and his smile, with his utter belief in her and the way he could rub that little spot at the back of her head that, no matter what, relaxed her tension and made all of her nerves and worries fade away.

There was no Razeby tonight. She sat alone and looked at her painted face in the peering glass, lit bright with candles. She looked strong and capable and determined, even if she said so herself.

She inhaled slowly and deeply. She could do this. She would do this. Pour all of everything she did not feel over Razeby into the part. It was a simple strategy.

Another deep breath and Alice rose and walked out of the little dressing room, along the corridor and through the wings.

'Miss Sweetly on stage in five, four, three, two...' They counted her down with every step she took.

'One.' She walked out on that stage before a packed Theatre Royal.

Her eyes slipped unbidden to Razeby's box.

It was empty. And she was glad of it.

She shifted her eyes to Linwood's box. And there, beside Linwood, was Venetia. Just as she had promised.

Alice smiled, and when she opened her mouth to speak she was not Alice any more but Lady Macbeth.

The clock ticked on the mantel. The sunlight streamed into the study, catching on the crystal drops of the wall sconces on either side of the fireplace and making them shimmer and sparkle with a rainbow of colours. From somewhere in the house there was the quiet opening and closing of a door.

Razeby noticed nothing of it. He stood, rather than sat, at his desk, his focus trained on the newspaper spread open on his desk before him, more specifically on the article about the woman whose return to the stage had taken Covent Garden by storm. London was in awe, as it regaled the delights of the previous night's play with Alice in the role of the leading lady. His eyes followed down the printed column, reading each and every word.

Since her separation from a certain Lord R., Miss Sweetly's acting talent has blossomed and taken on a new and vibrant dimension. She has a passion and realism that quite transfixed the audience and left them shouting, nay, begging, for more.

He had always known she had such wonderful talent upon the stage and he was truly gladdened by her success. But beneath his happiness for her was also an ache.

A subtle rap of knuckles against his study door and then his butler was there, showing his lawyer in.

'Mr Ernst of Ernst, Spottiswoode and Farmer, my lord.'

Razeby's eyes lingered on the words for only a second longer. Then he closed the newspaper and set it aside.

'You sent for me, Lord Razeby, to undertake an audit of the Razeby estate and monies.'

Razeby did not allow himself to think of Alice, but only of what lay ahead.

He took his seat at his desk. 'Please sit down, Mr Ernst.'

Alice was in the middle of removing her stage make-up after her fifth evening of performing when Sara, her fellow actress and mistress to Viscount Fallingham, popped her head round the door of Alice's dressing room.

'Hawick asked if you'll be coming with us tomorrow. There's a little outing arranged to Hyde Park, a promenade at the fashionable hour. I've already run it past Kemble and he's all for it. There's me and a couple of the other actresses, Hawick, Monteith, Frew, and Fallingham of course, not that he doesn't trust me.' She smirked.

Alice thought of her theatre contract. Being seen with the top gentlemen of the *ton* was all part of the promotion she was required to undertake. And now that the performances had started there was no longer any reason to avoid this side of it.

'You don't need to worry, Alice. Razeby won't be there. I checked for you.'

Alice felt her blood run cold. 'You checked?' she said softly.

'I didn't think you would want to bump into him any time soon.'

It was the truth, but she knew she could not let the comment go unchallenged. 'Why not?'

'Because it's only been a couple of weeks since…' Sara glanced away awkwardly.

'He gave me my *congé*,' Alice finished for her with a smile. 'You can say the words. I'm perfectly fine with it.' She knew whatever she said to Sara would be all round the theatre by this time tomorrow.

'I thought that you and he…the way the two of you were together…that maybe you were loved up on him.'

Alice dreaded that was what they were all thinking. She gave a scornful laugh. 'Don't be daft. It was an arrangement, nothing more.' She still had her pride.

'But the way you looked at one another. If Fallingham looked at me like that…' Sara fanned a hand before her face as if just the thought brought her out in a scorching flush.

'We had a good time.' Alice gave a shrug of her shoulders as if it was nothing so very special. 'But these things aren't meant to last.' A parody of the words Razeby had said to her, standing there in that bedchamber.

'Was it an amicable separation?' Sara's curiosity was getting the better of her. She looked surprised, making Alice wonder just what the gossipmongers had been saying, given that they had so little to go on. Maybe she needed to give them a little grist for their mill.

'Sorry to disappoint the girls, but, yes, it was.'

'We thought you were upset, you've not been seen out anywhere on the town.'

'I've been busy. Give me a chance. I've not even finished my first opening week!'

'I suppose so,' said Sara.

'And I'm not upset in the slightest.' Alice smiled to prove it.

Sara gave a grin and looked like she believed her. 'So you'll come tomorrow?'

'I'm looking forward to it already.'

The door closed behind Sara.

Alice took a deep breath. There could be nothing of avoidance. Avoidance was tantamount to admitting that she cared, that she was hurt, that she could not bear to face him. And none of that was the case, as London would see soon enough.

She was getting on with her life. And if Razeby happened to cross her path, then so be it.

It would make not one jot of difference to her. *He* would make not one jot of difference to her.

Within Hyde Park Miss Pritchard was strolling by Razeby's side, her concentration more on the people in the park who were looking at them than anything else. Behind them, Mrs Pritchard, her younger daughter by her side, was espousing on the merits of good breeding and outlining a detailed Pritchard family lineage in the process.

The Pritchards were wealthy and well connected. A suitable alliance for Razeby. But Razeby did not know if he could suffer Mrs Pritchard's incessant boasting. Or, indeed, Miss Pritchard herself. All he had to do was marry her and bed her. It should be simple enough, especially for a man like him who had bedded no shortage of women in his life. But the prospect left him cold.

He stared into the hazy afternoon distance and tried to not to think about it.

The last time he had been here in Hyde Park was with Alice. She had shunned the use of his curricle and insisted they walk. She did not care about being seen on his arm or not. What she had cared about were simple things—the glory of the sunshine, the freshness of the air, the birdsong and the furls of new green buds on the trees; riches for the eyes, as she called nature or art or anything that she liked to look at. He had been unable to prevent his fingers from curling in hers. And she had smiled and not given a damn about who was watching them.

The memory made his heart swell.

He felt Miss Pritchard's hand upon his arm stiffen. Mrs Pritchard was still talking, but he could hear the increased arrogance and volume of her tone, that sudden slight edge of superiority and distaste.

And then he saw the reason why. Ahead, rounding the corner was a small party of men and women, out taking the air and being seen at this most fashionable of hours in the park. But not just any men and women. The men were some of the highest in the *ton*. Of the women, Razeby only noticed one. A woman who stood out from the others because she was golden and beautiful and she just seemed to glow with life and with happiness. He could hear the playful banter within the little party, the laughter, the teasing, flirtatious air.

Alice, clad in her plain pale-yellow walking dress and contrasting cream spencer and gloves, was walking by Hawick's side, listening to something the duke was saying to her. Perched at a jaunty angle on her head was a small stylish hat he had not seen her wear before.

Beneath it her fair hair, so haphazardly pinned up, had allowed pale golden strands to escape and waft artlessly around her neck. It was fresh and simple. He had watched her so many times twist her hair up and pin it all within a minute, only to have him unpin it and slip his fingers through those long silken skeins and take her into his arms and kiss her.

She looked comfortable, confident and yet with that same slight shyness that had always intrigued him. Her eyes were lowered as she listened to something that Hawick was saying, but she was smiling. The sight of her made Razeby feel things he did not want to feel. Not now that it was over and he had set his mind to doing what must be done. There was the hard thud of his heart. The fast rush of his blood.

And the awful sinking sensation of his predicament.

Miss Pritchard was by his side, her mother and sister walking behind. Razeby realised what he was going to have to do. What any gentleman in his position would have to do. And the prospect of it sent a chill all the way through him.

Alice had been his mistress. The woman walking by his side could be his wife.

Duty. The word seemed to resonate with every beat of his heart.

Du-ty.

Du-ty.

Du-ty.

He had no choice.

He turned his eyes away from Alice. Kept his focus steadfastly elsewhere. Cutting her, as the rules of polite society dictated. As if she were some stranger. As if she were not the woman he had loved every night of the past six months.

But he could see her in his peripheral vision, that blur of yellow and cream and blonde, slight beside the tall loom of Hawick's darkness. And he could hear the rustle of the silk of her skirts, hear the distinctive lilt of her softly spoken words, smell the faint scent of her perfume.

His heart beat faster.

He could sense her, feel her, the awareness as sharp as if his eyes were studying her every detail.

He measured every step that brought them ever closer on this path, knowing that they must pass one another, that it was far too late for retreat. Neither of them could turn away from this.

He knew that Alice's attention was all fixed on Hawick. As if she had not even noticed Razeby. As if she were cutting him every bit as much as he were cutting her. And he should be glad of it. Truly he should. But it was not gladness that he felt as the little group strolled towards him and his party through the sunshine.

Every step brought her nearer.

Five feet… She was so close now that he could hear the soft breathiness of her laughter at Hawick's joke.

Four feet… Everything sharpened. Everything focused. The hushed ripple of grass blades in the breeze. The sweep of her eyelashes, soft as a butterfly's wing.

Three feet… The sound of his breath. *Alice.*

Two feet… The beat of his heart…and of hers. *Alice.*

One foot… Razeby turned his gaze to Alice. And in that very last moment, that second in which all of time seemed to slow and stop, she raised her eyes to meet his.

The jolt hit his stomach and rippled right through his

body. It was as if they were the only two people in the park. As if all of the past six months flashed between them in stark vivid clarity. As if the dark blue depths of her eyes swallowed him up and submersed the whole of him in this moment and this woman and all that was beating through him.

Their gazes locked and held. And he could not look away, not if all of the future depended on it, which in a way it did.

And then the moment was past.

She was past.

Walking on with Hawick and the others. Walking away from him.

His steps never faltered. He kept on walking. As if nothing had just happened.

No one else noticed. Everything else went on just the same. Miss Pritchard's fingers still lay upon his arm. Mrs Pritchard was still selling the family pedigree behind him, her younger daughter chipping in smart little comments here and there.

But Razeby was not the same.

Something had just happened and the force of it shook him more than he wanted to admit. Something had just happened, something which Razeby did not understand.

Alice did not hear what it was that Hawick had been saying to her, all she could hear was the rush of her own blood too loud in her ears and all she could feel was the tremor that vibrated through her body. She deliberately kept her gaze low as if playing coy with Hawick, when in truth, it was to hide the storm of emotion suddenly raging within her.

She had seen Razeby and his party, the rich, beautiful young woman clinging so possessively to his arm, and the women who could only be her mother and sister walking so proudly behind, the minute she had rounded the corner. And she had prepared herself. Knowing that he had no choice but to cut her. Knowing she had no choice but to not give a damn. To cut him right back.

And she had almost done it. Would have done it, despite the pound and throb of her heart, and the raw rush of air that rasped in her lungs, and the tight knot that worked itself ever tighter in her stomach, except for that last moment, when it felt like his voice had whispered her name, calling her. The sound of it stroking right down her spine. Tingling against her skin. And she had answered without pausing to think. Yielded to it instinctively.

And when she looked, those liquid brown eyes had been on hers, not looking away, not cutting her, only holding her as intensely as they ever had done, perhaps even more so. As if all that had gone between them had not ended, but grown only stronger. Her heart was still beating nineteen to the dozen.

By her side Hawick shifted infinitesimally closer.

'So you will come, Miss Sweetly?' he was saying.

She calmed herself, hid the shock of what had just passed between her and Razeby. By the time she raised her eyes to meet Hawick's she had herself under control again.

She smiled at him, although she had not the slightest idea of what he had just invited her to. 'If I'm free,' she said. 'I'll need to check my diary.' Truly the consummate professional. Venetia, her teacher, would have been proud of her.

Hawick smiled, too, with a particular interest in his eyes that made her want to shiver in the warmth of the spring sunshine. She hid the urge, along with all the others.

The party walked on through the park.

Hawick began another story, but Alice was not listening to Hawick or his story. She was thinking of Razeby and why, despite everything, it felt just like it had done when she had seen him for the very first time.

Chapter Seven

Razeby dreamed that night that Alice was with him in the bed, that they were still together and all was as it had been.

'Razeby,' she had whispered in her soft Celtic lilt and stroked her fingers against his cheek. 'Razeby.'

Alice. In the dream he had whispered her name through the darkness. 'Alice,' the word murmured aloud on his lips as he held her to him, so glad she had found him, to save him from the terrible thing that was coming, although in the dream he could not remember the nature of the dawning threat, no matter how hard he tried.

The early morning sunlight danced across his eyes, waking him from sleep, dragging him back from his dream world to reality. His body was primed and hard, his erection throbbing for release, but Alice was not in his arms.

He was alone.

And he knew the terrible dark thing that was coming.

The warm comfort of the dream world fell away, leaving in its place the hard coldness of reality and a sinking feeling in his gut. His arousal deflated.

The sunlight that had crept through the crack in his curtains dimmed behind the greyness of cloud. Razeby threw aside the covers and sat up, swinging his legs round to sit on the edge of the bed, relishing the sting of the cool morning air against the nakedness of his skin. It helped clear his mind of Alice and the bittersweet echo of the dream.

The clock chimed nine just before his valet knocked on the door and entered, followed by a maid bearing a pitcher of hot water and his secretary carrying a diary that Razeby knew was crammed full of appointments. He pushed aside the dream as surely as he had pushed aside what had happened yesterday in Hyde Park. Guilt, lust, desire—whatever it was. He could not name it otherwise. He would not name it otherwise.

Not Miss Pritchard, he thought. But tonight there was dinner at Mrs Padstow's at which twenty young respectable women would be present. And tomorrow afternoon, a débutante picnic organised by Lady Jersey. Then there was Almack's, and Lady Routledge's matchmaking ball. And he would find a wife at one of those.

He raked a hand through his hair and, taking a deep breath, rose to face the day.

Alice came offstage to rapturous applause that night. Three curtain calls and still the audience were whistling and calling for more. Her dressing room was so crammed with flowers there was scarcely room for the rail of costumes and table of face paints with its peering glass. Their perfume filled the air of the little room: roses, lilies, sprays of blooms she did not recognise. All with letters and cards attached. All sealed with red wax which displayed the crests or monograms of their senders so prominently. Her eyes scanned over the seals, searching for one in particular. She could not help herself. He had been too much in her mind since yesterday and Hyde Park. Although heaven only knew why. She caught what she was doing and, with a harsh sigh of annoyance, averted her eyes and got on with wiping the make-up from her face. Then she slipped into the fawn-silk evening dress that was hanging over the dressing screen.

A knock sounded on the dressing-room door. The stage hand's voice shouted through the wood.

'Five minutes to the Green Room, Miss Sweetly. Mr Kemble says to tell you that both the Duke of Hawick and the Duke of Monteith are in again tonight.'

'Right you are, Billy. I'll be right there.' She checked her appearance in the peering glass. The woman that looked back from the glass was pale without the thick grease and colour of the stage make-up. And she thought again of that moment in Hyde Park.

'Don't be such a damned fool, Alice Flannigan, you're imagining things,' she whispered to herself, using the name with which she had been born, rather than that she had taken for the stage. 'You put a smile on your face and get through there, girl. Life goes on— if you're lucky. And he isn't worth it.' She rubbed a little rouge on to her cheeks, added a spot to her lips and tucked an errant strand of hair into place.

Taking a deep breath, she held her head high, fixed a smile on her face and went to sparkle and entice the gentlemen of the Green Room, just as her contract required.

* * *

'Razeby,' Viscount Bullford exclaimed, wandering over to where Razeby stood filling a plate with choice selections at the débutante picnic. 'Thought Aunt Harriet would have lampooned you into coming this afternoon.'

'Bullford.' Razeby gave a nod.

The weather was sunny and dry, although a slight chill still sat about the fine spring day. The trees surrounding this corner of the park lent a level of protection against the breeze, but not enough to stop the gentle flutter of bonnet ribbons and muslin skirts amongst the ladies milling all around.

Bullford lifted a small, perfectly formed pork pie from one of the serving dishes on the nearby table and took a bite. 'Couldn't get out of it myself. Pater had m'arm up my back. Insisted I had to bring m'friends with me. Apparently too many ladies and not enough gentlemen.'

'You managed to persuade the others to come?' Razeby raised an eyebrow in surprise.

'Not an easy task, I can tell you, old man.' Bullford took a deep breath as if the memory of what that had entailed was difficult to bear. 'Will be years till I can clear the favours owed over this one.'

Razeby smiled.

Fallingham, Devlin, Monteith and a few others wandered up, glasses of champagne and large chunks of food in hand.

'How goes the bride search, Razeby?' Devlin asked.

'Well enough.' He felt himself tense just at the question.

'Found one yet?' Fallingham enquired.

'Not yet.' He kept his face impassive, his manner cool.

'Don't seem quite yourself of late, Razeby,' Monteith observed.

He smiled at the irony of Monteith's remark. Would any man be the same were he to stand in Razeby's shoes? 'Can't imagine why,' he said drolly.

'Losing one's freedom, weddings, wives and nurseries,' Devlin supplied and gave a shudder.

The rest of the group chuckled as if that was the reason.

'Not regretting giving up the delightful Miss Sweetly, are you?' Monteith asked as he helped himself to a bottle of champagne from a passing footman and topped up all their glasses.

Nonchalantly uttered words, yet they cut through everything to touch some raw inner part of Razeby. It was all he could do not to suck in his breath at the sensation.

'Not at all,' he said smoothly and held Monteith's gaze, denying the suggestion all the more.

'Do not know why.' Monteith smirked. 'The common consensus is that you have run mad. Dismissing such a little gem when all of London is panting after her.'

It took every bit of willpower to keep his jaw from hardening and the basilisk stare from his eyes, and to prevent the curl of his fingers into a fist.

'You could have kept her on,' said Devlin. 'I would have, had it been me.'

'We all would have,' said Monteith.

'I am not you.' And Alice deserved a damn sight more respect than that.

'Why exactly didn't you keep her on?' asked Fallingham and stopped sipping his champagne to hear the answer.

The rest of the group looked at Razeby expectantly, a speculation in their eyes that had not been there before.

'Do you really have to ask?' he drawled with a deliberate ambiguity that did nothing to answer the question.

'What you need is to get her back in your bed,' said Fallingham.

'What I need is to get myself a wife.' He gritted his teeth.

'The two need not be mutually exclusive,' Monteith commented.

'For me they are,' Razeby said it with nothing of his usual jest or charm. He smiled, but the smile was hard and his eyes cool. He saw the look that was exchanged between his friends. And he did not care.

The awkwardness of the moment was alleviated by Bullford's mother, the formidable Lady Willaston, who appeared amidst their circle. 'Sorry to interrupt your little chat, gentlemen, but, Lord Razeby, Miss Frome is nigh on ready to swoon with hunger from waiting for the plate of food you went to fetch her some considerable time ago.'

'My humble apologies, ma'am.' Razeby gave a nod. 'If you will excuse me, gentlemen…' Picking up the plate from the table next to him, he made his way back to Miss Frome and her friends.

On the day after the débutante picnic Alice's visitors sat in her new little drawing room while she poured tea into the three china cups set on their saucers on the table before her.

Ellen and Tilly were old friends—they worked secretly as Miss Vert and Miss Rose at the blot in Alice's past, London's infamous high class brothel, Mrs Silver's

House of Rainbow Pleasures, in which the courtesans each dressed in a different colour and hid their identities behind feathered Venetian masks.

'You ain't half landed on your feet, Alice,' said Tilly, glancing wide eyed round at the warm yellow decor of the drawing room with its gilt-and-crystal chandelier and peering glasses. 'Razeby must have seen you all right in his severance settlement.'

Alice smiled and passed the teacups to each of her friends in turn. 'Of course he did.'

'What did you manage to wangle from him? A suitably large sum and a nice piece of expensive jewellery, I hope,' Ellen said.

Alice thought of the diamond bracelet and felt that same chill ripple through her. 'I couldn't possibly comment,' she said, still smiling. She could not tell them the truth. Everyone knew the deal in relationships like hers and Razeby's. Everyone knew she would have taken everything she could from him. It was what any mistress would have done to her protector.

'You held him to the letter of the contract between you?' Ellen asked.

'Absolutely.' But Alice had no idea what was written within the legal contract that had defined her and Razeby's arrangement. The document had never been unfolded; it still lay, tied in its green ribbon, in the drawer of the desk in Hart Street. She remembered the day that Razeby had presented her with it and how she had refused to accept it until the red ribbon that was used to secure all such legal documents was changed. Razeby had sent out immediately for a green ribbon and tied it in place himself as she stood and watched.

'Don't let the bastard wriggle out of it.' Ellen grinned.

But Razeby had not tried to wriggle out of anything. Quite the reverse. It made her feel angrier, both at him and herself.

She stretched her smile wider, pushing the feeling away. 'I've a good head on my shoulders when it comes to money.' It was true. She thought of the money that Razeby had given her through the months they had been together, little of it spent on frivolities. A regular sum had been sent to her mother in Ireland, the rest she had saved.

'And a good head when it comes to men.' Tilly grinned. 'You did all right out of Razeby.'

'I did,' she admitted and turned her mind away from why the knowledge made her feel queasy.

'You're a clever girl, Alice.' Tilly poured her tea from her cup into her saucer and sipped it as daintily as any lady.

'Aren't I just?' she exclaimed in a voice that made them all laugh.

'Thank you, Mr Brompton. We will continue our discussions later, when you return.' Razeby dismissed his steward from his study and turned to where Linwood was standing by the fireplace, examining the portrait of Razeby's father that hung on the wall above.

'I would have come back another time when you were not busy,' said Linwood, turning to him. 'I did not realise you had summoned Brompton down from the Razeby estate.'

'One has to get one's affairs in order...' he glanced away '...before one's marriage.' The ticking of the clock punctuated the silence.

'You do not seem yourself, Razeby.'

He did not feel himself. 'Prospect of parson's trap does that to a man.' He attempted a light-hearted response. 'You should know.'

Linwood's dark eyes met his and there was not a trace of humour in them. 'I do not,' he said, admitting the truth outright of what lay between him and Venetia. 'But then you are already aware of that.'

Razeby turned away and poured them both a brandy, handing one to Linwood.

'It is not that. There is something more. There is a change in you,' said Linwood, still holding him under scrutiny.

Razeby gave a laugh and turned his gaze away from those shrewd black eyes. 'You grow both fanciful and poetic in your old age, Linwood. Have you been in Byron's company?'

'No.' Linwood was to the point.

Silence.

Razeby gave a shrug, but made no more denials. 'Maybe it is time for a change. A man must face his fate, sooner or later.' The inescapable fate that they all would face in the end.

'He must indeed. But it does not need to be like this.'

'Believe me, it does,' said Razeby with a grim smile.

'There is a rumour circulating about you and Hart Street.'

'There is always some rumour or other circulating,' he said curtly, not wanting to discuss anything of that.

'And Alice?'

'I have already told you, it is over with Alice.' His voice sounded too harsh and defensive.

Linwood knew better than to probe further.

* * *

Before heading to the Green Room within the Theatre Royal that night, Alice called in at the dressing room that Sara shared with two other actresses.

'Oh, Alice, I'm not ready yet! I just can't get my hair to sit right. All the curls have fallen out because of that damn wig! Look at the state of it!' Sara wailed.

'Just leave it as it is, Sara!' one of the other actresses said. 'Or we're all going to be late for the Green Room and Kemble will have something to say about that.'

'You two go on ahead and keep Kemble happy. I'll help Sara with her hair,' Alice said.

'If you're sure, Alice?' They did not look certain.

'Go! The pair of you!' Alice ordered with a grin.

The two younger women smiled and hurried away, while Alice, elbows akimbo, hands on hips, turned to where Sara sat before a peering glass, her hair lying limp and straight from three hours of compression beneath a hot heavy wig.

'Lucky for you I'm a dab hand with hair that'll not take a curl. Now, missus.' Using just her fingers she scraped Sara's hair back into a ponytail, twisted it round, gave it a flick and secured it in place with just three pins.

'Alice, you're a wonder!'

'I am, indeed,' Alice teased. 'Now, come on, get yourself moving, girl.' She turned to leave.

'Just before we go through…' Sara put a hand on her arm. 'The gaming evening at Dryden's, the one I told you about last week.'

'It is still on, isn't it?'

'Yes.' Sara smiled and gave a nod, but there was a slight look of unease in her eyes. 'It's just…well…I was talking to Fallingham about it last night and it seems that he's invited Razeby.'

Razeby. Just his name made Alice's heart skip a beat.

Sara screwed up her face in an expression of awkward apology. 'Sorry!'

'What's to be sorry about?' Alice gave a smile. 'It doesn't matter to me whether Razeby's there or not. I've already told you, it's fine between us.'

'Really?'

'Really,' Alice reassured her.

'I hope so, or it's going to be an awfully uncomfortable evening.'

'You don't have to worry about that, honestly.' Such confidence. Truly worthy of her best performance upon the stage.

Sara smiled her relief.

'Now come on.' Alice slipped her arm through Sara's. 'Kemble will be wondering where on earth we've got to. Better make sure you dazzle him with that new hairstyle of yours.'

Sara gave a giggle as the two of them hurried from the dressing room towards the Green Room, to dazzle and sparkle, to tease and entice. But beneath all of Alice's air of glamour and charm was the constant knowledge that tomorrow would bring Dryden's and a night spent gaming with Razeby.

Chapter Eight

Dryden's Gambling Palace was busy. It was a luxurious affair that rivalled Watier's, with tables to cater to every taste and every pocket. The top room had a chandelier reputed to have real diamonds amongst its glass. Entry was by invitation only and the stakes could stretch to match the highest in all of London.

The room was spacious, airy, the walls papered in plum-coloured paper embellished with real gold patterning. The floor was tiled in marble imported from Italy, black and gold to match that of the blinds that masked the windows. There were no footmen, only the prettiest girls dressed up in footmen's livery who served free drinks to the men who came here to game.

Along the full length of one wall was a bar that housed any drink a man might desire, whatever the time of day. On the opposite side was an enormous Palladian-style fireplace of black marble. The walls themselves were hung with expensive works of art depicting Rubenesque women and wondrous exotic landscapes. But no clocks. Not a single one.

A champagne fountain flowed in the centre of the

room, the filled glasses from which were being served and replenished all around. There was a faro table in one corner, casino in another, and tables for *vingt-et-un,* hazard and piquet in between. In the furthest corner a whist table catered for the more elderly gentlemen or the few ladies who ever dared enter this hallowed place. Women of the *demi-monde* were a different story.

Alice stood with Sara looking over the men seated round the *vingt-et-un* table. Razeby was not here and Alice felt a curious mix of both relief and disappointment at his absence.

'Do you play tonight, ladies?' drawled Monteith.

'I'm here only as Fallingham's good-luck charm,' said Sara, stepping up close behind the chair at which Fallingham was already seated and resting her hands upon his shoulders in an intimate fashion. Alice watched while the viscount lifted one of her hands to his mouth and kissed it. The display of charm and affection reminded her too much of Razeby, making her feel awkward. The smile felt stiff upon her mouth.

'Somehow, gentlemen, I feel my luck is in tonight whatever chances to happen upon this table,' Fallingham said in a playful tone.

Sara's smiled deepened and Monteith and several of the men smiled in that knowing way.

Alice swallowed her discomfort and glanced away.

'And what about you, Miss Sweetly?' Monteith raised an eyebrow. 'Which one of us lucky gentlemen will be fortunate enough to have you act as our charm this evening?' There was speculation and interest in his eyes, in Frew's, and too many of the other men's. She knew what playing the part of any of their lucky charms in this place would entail and she would be damned if she would do that, no matter that she wanted to prove that Razeby meant nothing to her. Flirtation was one thing, an illusion of sparkling enticement, but an illusion just the same. She could not go so far as to let any of them actually touch her.

'Oh, I'm my own lucky charm,' she said smoothly. 'I play tonight, Your Grace.'

She saw the stir of interest around the table, the way they liked that idea.

Monteith smiled, as if amused by both the double meaning of her words and her challenge. 'Do you need anyone to…refresh your memory as to the rules?' He put it so delicately, but she knew what he was thinking, that she had no idea how to play a serious game of cards.

'No, thank you, Your Grace. I think I can remember them.'

They smiled at her indulgently.

As if she could ever forget. Razeby had taught her the trick behind stacking the odds in your favour of winning in *vingt-et-un*—the way to count and memorise the cards. It was a game that they had liked to play often. A game that they had played not for money, but for the removal of their clothes. Razeby always said that the excellence of her memory made her a natural at it—either that or a desire to have him stripped naked before her.

The last time they had played it had been only three weeks ago and they had ended up making love on the dining-room table on top of the forgotten scattered cards. The memory made her heart skip a beat and brought a slight blush both of anger and embarrassment to her cheeks. She thrust it away and took her seat beside Fallingham.

The *vingt-et-un* dealer, dressed in the smart black-

and-gold livery of the gaming house, sat in the middle of the other side of the table. There were empty chairs on either side of him, one of which would not have been empty had Razeby been here. She felt a slight sense of pique at his absence, part of her wanting him to see this proof of how little he had affected her.

'The house rules apply. Are you ready to begin, gentlemen…and Miss Sweetly?' The dealer smiled politely at her.

There was common agreement.

'Then we shall commence.'

Alice kept her eyes on his hands as he dealt a card to each of them and himself last of all, before dealing a second card in a repeat of the process.

'Not too late, am I, gentlemen?'

The smooth velvet voice stroked all the way down her spine. A voice she knew too well, which the mere memory of could set her skin a-tingle and her heart racing. Alice froze in that moment, her heart skipping a beat before setting off at a thunderous tilt. She forced herself to breathe, to stay calm, to focus. And only then did she raise her eyes to look at Razeby, at the very same minute his eyes met hers.

There was the tiniest of moments—that catch of time, that ripple of tension. And then he bowed smoothly. 'Miss Sweetly.'

'Lord Razeby,' she replied politely, as if all of the previous six months had never been. Round the table every pair of eyes looked not at the cards upon the table but at Alice and Razeby.

She had prepared herself for seeing him this time, she reminded herself. And she *was* a very good actress. She breathed, calmed herself, smiled.

'Miss Sweetly decided to play tonight,' Monteith said, the unnecessary explanation a subtle message to Razeby, as if Alice would not understand.

Her eyes met Razeby's, a silent comment upon Monteith's transparent and wasted subtlety passing between them. She remembered what she had come here to do and she smiled at him, a smile that only he would understand.

He knew her challenge. Accepted it by selecting the chair directly opposite her to take his seat.

'I hope you have deep pockets tonight, Razeby,' she said.

All the men laughed, not appreciating the full depth of her tease.

But Razeby did. 'Perhaps not deep enough,' he said. She could see it in his eyes as they met hers, knew it for certain with his next words. 'Maybe we should lower the minimum stake on account of Miss Sweetly's playing.'

There were murmurs of assent as the men around the table mistook his meaning. They all thought it was because, otherwise, she would be out after the first few hands.

'Afraid, Razeby?' She arched an eyebrow, and held his gaze boldly, all the while letting the small smile still play around her mouth.

'My concern is all for you, Miss Sweetly.'

She smiled at that, a smile of genuine amusement, and only then released his gaze, so that she could place a counter onto the green baize.

Bullford looked at the size of her stake, then leaned to her, a look of concern on his face. 'I say, Miss Sweetly, you have played before?'

'Once or twice. But, I admit, not usually for money,'

she said carelessly, and could not resist flitting a glance at Razeby. His eyes were on hers, deep and intent. He was remembering all the times they had played when it had not been for money.

Bullford lowered his voice a little. 'Razeby is considered something of a shark when it comes to *vingt-et-un*. Perhaps he did not tell you.'

She smiled at Bullford in a wickedly flirtatious way, knowing that Razeby was watching, then leaned in closer to him as if they were two conspirators. 'I thank you for the warning, my lord.' Then to Razeby, 'I hear you have something of a reputation when it comes to *vingt-et-un*.'

'I make no such claim.' His voice was soft, his manner subdued, his eyes sharply watchful.

'If you do not wish to play, Razeby...' The same words with which she had teased him on a hundred nights before.

'I do want to play, Miss Sweetly.' His eyes darkened ever so slightly as he gave the same reply he always had done.

Like two players in a script full of secret meanings to which only Razeby and Alice held the key.

She felt the tension tighten between them.

His eyes flicked to the dealer. 'Deal me in.'

Two cards came his way.

His eyes held Alice's. 'I hope you know what you are doing, Miss Sweetly.'

'Oh, I know all right, Lord Razeby,' she said softly. 'You needn't worry about that.'

'In that case...let us play.' He smiled.

And she returned the smile. A real smile. It was impossible not to. Despite everything.

* * *

After fifteen rounds, only four of them remained in the game—Monteith, Devlin, Razeby and herself. Monteith and Devlin were almost out of counters. The pile of counters in front of Alice was only marginally larger than that in front of Razeby. Men had wandered over from the other tables to watch the play so that a small crowd now surrounded them.

The sixteenth hand was dealt.

For all her laughter and sparkle and feigned joviality, all evening Alice had been watching the cards very carefully, memorising who held what, the cards that had gone from the pack and therefore, by default, those that remained. It was an easy enough task when she could hold the whereabouts of three packs in her head at any given time.

Razeby was rolling a counter within his hand. 'Fifty pounds.' He threw a pile of ten counters into the centre of the table.

She swallowed at the enormity of the bet.

Monteith glanced down at his three remaining counters and shook his head. 'Too high. Out.'

All eyes moved to Alice. She stayed calm, relaxed, still. Leaned back in her chair and met Razeby's warm brown eyes.

His gaze seemed to stroke against hers as he waited with everyone else for what she would do.

She smiled. 'Fifty pounds.' She matched the stake with ten counters of her own.

Monteith gave a chuckle. 'You do not frighten her, Razeby.'

She did not let herself think of the sums of money with which they were playing. Enough to last a poor man a lifetime. If her mother knew just how much money was on that table being gambled away...! Alice pushed the thought away, focused her mind. Money or clothes, in the end the game was just the same, if she kept her nerve.

Razeby did not so much as raise an eyebrow. He stayed cool, impassive. Just the hint of a smile upon his face.

Devlin met the stake. But when they turned over their cards Devlin lost his counters and was forced to bow out of the game, leaving only Alice, Razeby and the dealer to play the seventeenth hand.

The dealer dealt each of them their two cards.

It was Alice who was to set the stake this time. She met Razeby's gaze. Their eyes held, each knowing the other's strengths and weaknesses in this game. A test of nerve, a test of so much more.

Never let them see how much they've hurt you.

She smiled, hearing the words from so long ago in her head. Hurt just made you stronger. She did not let her gaze drop from his, held it as boldly as she had done that first night in the Green Room before he had been hers, and she, his. Held it and did not let it go.

'All in, two hundred pounds,' she said, and pushed all of her counters forwards.

The gasp rippled round the table.

'Good Lord,' she heard Fallingham mutter.

Beside her, Bullford produced a handkerchief and mopped at his brow.

The whole room was tense, poised for the next step. They stared at Razeby to see what he would do.

His eyes met hers again.

The attraction, the affinity that had always been be-

tween them was still there, stronger than ever. Powerful. Dangerous. Beguiling.

'As you will, Miss Sweetly,' he murmured, and
pushed all of his counters in to match hers.

Not a single voice spoke, not a glass sounded. Even
the serving maids stopped where they were and stared
to see what would happen.

The dealer's voice broke the silence. 'Lord Razeby...'

Razeby looked his cards. 'Stick.' He smiled at her.

'Miss Sweetly?' the dealer prompted.

She lifted her own, glanced down at them. 'Twist.'

The dealer dealt her a third card.

'Twist again.'

A fourth card came her way.

'And again if you'd be so kind, sir.'

There was a murmur of voices all around.

The dealer looked at Razeby. 'Please show, Lord
Razeby.'

There was a craning of necks to see as Razeby laid
his cards down on the table.

'Queen of hearts, king of hearts. Twenty,' the dealer's voice intoned.

There was an irony in both cards. She wondered if
Razeby realised it, too. That deep dark look in his eyes
was so full of meanings that she could not tell.

'Please show, Miss Sweetly.'

Everyone looked at Alice as she laid the five cards
down on the green baize: ace of hearts, two of hearts,
three of spades, five of diamonds, queen of diamonds.

'Five-card trick,' said the dealer.

The buzz of excited voices spread throughout the
room around them, followed by a silence as the dealer
turned over his own cards. A ten and a seven. He

added another from the pile—the six of clubs. 'Bust.' He cleared the cards with one smooth movement of his hand. 'Miss Sweetly wins.'

'Congratulations, Miss Sweetly.' Razeby was magnanimous in defeat, his dark gaze lingering on hers.

'Thank you, Lord Razeby,' she said with an innocence that belied the look in her eye.

'Alice, I cannot believe your luck tonight!' Sara exclaimed and hugged her, and the gentlemen clamoured excitedly all around.

'I say, Miss Sweetly!' Bullford was beaming by her side.

'Congratulations, Miss Sweetly.' Devlin was shaking her hand.

'Well done!' Frew took her hand next. 'You have a lucky streak to rival Razeby's.'

She smiled. Both Alice and Razeby knew that when it came to winning *vingt-et-un,* there was a great deal more to it than luck.

'I think you have played this more than a few times, Miss Sweetly.' Hawick was by her shoulder.

'Maybe,' she conceded. Her eyes flickered to Razeby's, resting there only for the briefest of moments. 'But never before in public.'

'We must have a game together some time,' said Hawick.

She saw the tiny telltale narrowing of Razeby's eyes, the slight flicker of tension in his jaw at Hawick's words, and she smiled a mischievous smile.

'Indeed, we must, Your Grace,' she said, and wandered away from the table with Hawick.

Chapter Nine

The early morning was bright, the air in Hyde Park fresh and filled with spring and all the promise that came with it. Razeby could smell the scent of leather and of horse, mixed with the freshness of earth and dew-laden grass, and feel the warmth of the early morning sun on his face.

'You seem in better temperament this morning, Razeby.'

Razeby smiled. 'It is a fine morning and I am out riding with my friend.'

Linwood kept his gaze forward facing. 'I heard that Alice was at Dryden's last night.'

'News travels fast.'

'It *is* London, Razeby.'

Razeby gave a laugh.

'Indeed, the news is that she was in your party and that she fleeced all of the table.'

'She did,' Razeby admitted.

'With a skill that matched your own.'

Alice's skill far exceeded his own. She had been a most ardent pupil. Razeby remembered how too many of those long dark winter nights had started between him and Alice, of him sharing his secrets, of her sharing hers....

'Strange, that,' commented Linwood.

'Is it?' said Razeby, all innocence.

'Who would have known she was so skilled at *vingt-et-un?*'

'Who indeed?' Razeby answered, revealing nothing of it.

'There is nothing of…awkwardness…between the two of you?'

'Nothing.' Awkwardness was not what lay between them. There was as much desire, tension and excitement as ever there had been. She had been flirting with him, flirting with the others. Light-hearted, teasing, mischievous. Just as she had done before. But there was a difference this time. There were other layers there that had not been present then and a subtle sense that she had removed herself from his reach—that he might look, but not touch. He could not get her out of his head.

'It was an enjoyable evening.' He told that part of the truth. Enjoyable, and exciting, in a way nothing had been since the last time he had glimpsed her in Hyde Park. He could still feel the thrill of it running through his blood. The thrill of her. Right up until Hawick and that naughty little jibe about playing cards with him. Razeby did not like the thought of that one little bit. That had not been enjoyable. That had been something else altogether.

'I am glad that the separation seems to have been an amicable one.'

But what things seemed and what they were in truth were not always the same thing. Razeby gave no reply.

He did not fully understand what was between him and Alice. But he knew that it was anything but amicable. It was raw and powerful and hungry. There were complexities to it that he did not understand, depths that were downright dangerous.

'It makes no difference whether it is amicable or not.' He needed to stay away from her and keep his mind focused on the marriage mart. But last night and this morning the marriage mart had never been further from his mind.

'In that case, you will not have an interest in which of your events Miss Sweetly is booked to be present.'

'I did not say that,' said Razeby quietly and looked over at him.

Linwood glanced up, the look exchanged between them saying much their words could not. 'She will be at White's next week. For the awards.'

'You are sure?' Razeby felt his heart beat quicker at just the prospect of seeing her there.

'My father is on the committee. Alice is the new darling of Covent Garden. The theatre has gone from barely making ends meet to being practically sold out every time she steps on stage. White's know she will go down a storm with its members. They have offered Kemble, the theatre and Alice a substantial amount of money for her presence.'

Razeby gave a nod. 'Thank you for the warning, my friend.'

Alice stood in the small anteroom that adjoined the main banqueting room in White's Gentleman's Club in St James's Street.

A nervousness ran through her, making her palms

clammy and her stomach turn a few cartwheels, and she knew it was not down to presenting a few awards to some stuffy, rich old gentlemen. She knew Razeby was in there. She knew, too, that he would be in receipt of one of the awards. Kemble had warned her. And the fact that Kemble had felt the need to do so was all the more reason that she could not refuse the invitation to be here tonight.

Had she and Razeby never been, she would have accepted this opportunity without hesitation. It promoted both herself and the theatre, and it paid well. So she accepted it just the same now. Not letting Razeby dictate her actions. She was getting on. Making a success of herself. Refusing to avoid him. And maybe there were a few other reasons, too.

It gave her another opportunity to show him how much she was over him. And maybe even to rub his nose in what he had given up just a little more. She smiled at that thought.

She was a successful actress. She earned her own money. And she really was over Razeby.

Alice took a deep breath and smiled.

The men were seated around the table in the banqueting room of White's Gentlemen's Club.

The dinner had been eaten. Their glasses were filled with port, cigarillos were being smoked, snuff boxes being opened and offered.

Mr Raggett, the proprietor of the club, had come in person to host the dinner and awards.

'And now, gentlemen, we come to the purpose of this, our annual awards ceremony. The giving of awards for services we, within our little club, consider outstanding in the past year. Services to our gentlemen's community, to the general well-being of the city of London, those in support of charities, and of the arts. And those a little less serious in nature…' He smiled and everyone in the room smiled, too, at what was coming. 'The member who has won the most entries in the betting book, and the least. The member who consumed the most bottles of port and still left standing, and he who holds the record for sleeping the longest in the drawing room.' Everybody looked at old Lord Soames.

'Speak up, young man,' Soames said in a loud voice. 'Can't hear a word you are saying.'

A chuckle rippled round the table, all the more so given that Raggett was sixty if he was a day.

'Every year we invite someone special to present the awards to each of our gentlemen and this present year is no exception. I guarantee you will not be disappointed. Gentlemen, please put your hands together and welcome straight from the stage of Covent Garden's Theatre Royal…'

Razeby knew what was coming yet he felt the anticipation of just hearing her name spear through his blood.

'…the delightful Miss Alice Sweetly,' finished Raggett.

Every man at the table got to his feet and applauded as Alice swept into the room.

She was dressed in the same pale-green silk evening dress as he had seen her wear a hundred times. A dress that complimented her fair colouring. The bodice was low, but not indecently so, fastened in the centre with a line of pearl buttons that he was most adept at unfastening.

The light from the overhead chandelier cast golden

tones in the dark blonde of her hair. She had not followed the fashion, trying to curl her hair and wear it
up in a mass of flowing ringlets. She had told him so
many times that her hair defied all attempts to hold
a curl, no matter how tightly she tied the rags in it or
how long she left them in place. She wore it in its usual
simple style, caught back in a simple chignon. And tonight she would pluck those pins from it and uncoil
it to hang loose and free down her back in long silky
straight lengths. With deliberate control he turned his
mind away from that image.

Raggett announced each award in turn, then read
the name of the winner from the list, before passing the
appropriate small silver cup to Alice. It was Alice who
presented the cup to each winner, brushing a light kiss
against each man's cheek.

He felt his stomach curl with anticipation. He tried
not to think of it. It was just an award. Alice had been
his mistress, nothing more. The sex had been amazing.
She had been amazing. But that was over, done with.
Or so he told himself. And he was taking Miss Longley
out in his curricle in the morning. Doing what had to
be done. He should just propose, move things on faster.

'The Marquis of Razeby.' Raggett's voice brought
him back to himself.

He got to his feet, walked the length of the table to
where she stood. And he couldn't take his eyes from
her. She was so self-contained, so radiant and golden,
exuding that same strange paradoxical play of shyness
and confidence that had enticed him right from the very
start. And as he walked towards her, her eyes watched
him with that same calm which did not quite cover the
teasing playfulness he knew lurked beneath.

'Congratulations, Lord Razeby,' she said in that sweet, soft, sexy voice. It stroked against his ear, rippled down the length of his spine, straight down into his breeches.

'Miss Sweetly,' he said in a voice that was nothing more than polite, but the hint of a smile played about his lips as much as it played about hers.

She knew what she was doing to him. Her smile broadened as she passed the silver cup into his hands, the tips of her fingers so close to his that his own tingled as if she had stroked against them, when in truth they did not touch. He could smell her perfume, the familiar clean scent of her, making his heart beat faster and stoking the heat all the hotter in his blood. Triggering memories he could not stop: Alice in his arms, Alice naked beneath him on the bed.

She had kissed all of the others. Her eyes held his with that hint of mischief and he knew that she was going to kiss him. And, God help him, he wanted it so much, even standing there while half the members of White's looked on.

She leaned closer, tilting her face up to his, her eyes holding his all the while. And he could feel the speed of his heart and the driving urge to move his mouth and take hers with all the force of what was crackling between them. She smiled as if she knew exactly what he was thinking.

Her breath was warm against his cheek, the brush of her lips soft and hinting at so much more. All of which he knew, all of which he longed for.

His fingers tightened around the cup. 'Miss Sweetly,' he said in a low husky voice.

He saw the way her smile deepened and he smiled,

too. Sharing this moment. Like so many they had shared before. As if there were only the two of them in the room. As if nothing else mattered. As if there were only light in his life.

It was with a supreme effort of willpower that he managed to turn away and give his thanks to those assembled in the room before resuming his seat. But after it was done he kept his eyes on her for every last moment, until she walked from the room with that sexy little wiggle he knew too well.

Alice Sweetly, you minx! And he smiled again and felt a glow in his heart.

'Razeby was at Almack's again last night.' Within Alice's little parlour two days later, Sara announced the fact without so much as a glance in Alice's direction.

Alice should have been glad of it because it meant that she really was fine over Razeby and all of them knew it. But the words did not engender gladness. Rather it felt like a hand had tightened around her heart.

'Was he?' She concentrated on pouring the tea. Part of her did not want to hear how Razeby was getting on in his search for a woman to marry and part longed to know every damn detail. She did not ask the question but Sara told her the answer any way.

'He danced with Miss Penny, Miss Lewis, Lady Persephone Hollingsworth.' She counted the names on her fingers as she rhymed them off. 'Miss Jamison, and twice with…' she paused for effect '…Admiral Faversham's daughter, who is quite considered the catch of the Season.'

'Was Fallingham there,' Ellen asked, all sweetness, 'making a list of Razeby's partners for you?' She sipped at her tea, a picture of innocence, but Alice was not fooled. It both gladdened and worried her.

'Only because his crowd were all there. It's not as if he's bride hunting. He'll not be looking to settle down for ages yet.' Sara could not quite keep the defensive tone from her voice.

'You hope,' murmured Tilly beneath her breath.

'What was that?' Sara snapped. 'I didn't quite catch what you said.'

'I didn't say nothing, it was just a bit of wind. Tea don't half make me burp.' Tilly shot a smile at Alice.

Alice shook her head and barely suppressed the grin.

'They're saying that Miss Faversham has quite set her mind on him.'

'She ain't got a chance in hell,' said Tilly.

'She's an heiress,' retorted Sara.

'She'd have to be,' said Ellen. 'She's got a backside on her the size of a horse and a face to match.'

Tilly sniggered.

'He'd have to be blind to go for her,' Ellen said.

'It's about breeding and money,' protested Sara.

'Just like a horse,' said Tilly with a giggle.

'Enough, girls,' Alice said with a chuckle.

But when her friends finally left and the maids came in to remove the used tea tray, the image of Razeby dancing with all of those women, one of whom would be his wife, lingered.

For all the teasing and the jest, she knew what Ellen and Tilly had been doing—trying to protect her. As if she needed protecting! As if she were hurting from the split with Razeby! She felt mortified just at the thought, and a determination to prove to them otherwise, that it was just as she said, Razeby had never meant anything serious to her.

A vision of him sneaked into her mind. Standing before her at White's, with those smouldering brown eyes that sent spirals darting through her body. And it was as if she felt again the rasp of his cheek beneath her lips and smelled the scent of him in her nose. And felt that sense of heady power. And despite everything, she smiled at the memory. She could not help herself.

It was a very dangerous line she was walking. A knife edge, just like being on stage at the theatre. Avoiding avoidance. Temptation—for him and maybe even for her. Showing him what he could not have. But she could not turn back from it. Not when there was still clearly work to be done.

Chapter Ten

Within Lady Hadley's stifling ballroom a few days later, Razeby and Linwood were standing by the glass doors that led out into the back garden, breathing in the draft of cool air.

'How goes your search?' Linwood asked.

'Well enough.'

'Almack's, matchmaking, picnics and balls… You have been busy.' Linwood paused. 'And yet you do not appear to have narrowed down the field.'

'Keeping my options open.' Razeby took a sip of champagne.

Linwood gave a nod of understanding. 'White's betting book has Miss Faversham as the favourite.'

Razeby said nothing.

'With Lady Esme Fraser as a close second.'

'There are better alliances for Razeby out there.'

'Maybe, but it seems you find a reason to reject every suitable woman who comes your way.' Linwood held his glass up to the light and examined it.

Razeby felt the slight tension in his jaw. 'Nonsense.'

'Indeed, one might almost think that your heart was not in it, Razeby.'

His heart…? Razeby thought of Alice at White's. Of the mischievous look in her eyes, of the caress of her breath and the warm tease of her lips. He thought of her in Dryden's and of that heart-stopping moment in Hyde Park. All the tension that rippled between them. And the way he felt when he saw her, when he was with her, when he touched her. He pushed the memories away, crushed the feelings that were coursing through his mind and body, knowing they were something he could not allow.

'What has heart to do with it?' he said grimly. 'It is about consolidating positions, about power and money, and safeguarding the future. Duty, my friend, nothing else. We all know that.'

'And Alice?'

'Alice has nothing to do with it.' He said it too quickly. 'It is over between us.' If he said it enough times maybe he would come to believe it.

'So you keep saying,' said Linwood. 'But from where I was sitting in White's the other night, it looked anything but over.'

'You are mistaken.'

Linwood said nothing, just looked at him.

'We are both adults. We both understand how these things work. '

Still Linwood said nothing.

'Hell, Linwood! We still move in the same circles. What do you expect? That we should snub one another? Alice is not like that. I am not like that.'

'So it would seem.' Linwood raised his eyebrows by

the tiniest degree. 'And you do get to forgo Almack's tomorrow.'

'I am the charity's patron, for heaven's sake! I can hardly miss their benefit ball. It is just unfortunate that it happens to coincide with Almack's.'

'Most unfortunate,' agreed Linwood with his usual deadpan expression, but Razeby knew exactly what his friend was thinking.

And the problem was Linwood was not far wrong.

'Are you sure about this, Alice?' Venetia set the fan back down upon the dressing table in Alice's bedchamber.

'Frew has invited me and it's for a very good cause.' Alice pushed the last hairpin into place and turned away from the peering glass to look at her friend. 'The Benevolent Society for the Assistance of the Unfortunate and Homeless of London.'

'You do know that Razeby is their patron.'

'Of course I know.'

'And that as such he will be there tonight.'

'I can't let that stop me. If I avoided every place I thought he'd be, I'd never set foot outside the door.'

'Alice...'

'What?' She tried to look all innocent. 'It's the truth!' And it was, just not all of it.

'You do not have to do this.'

Alice met her friend's eyes directly. 'Yes,' she said firmly. 'I do, Venetia. If I avoid him, what message does it send all of London? I'll not turn away from a single situation.'

'Proving to the world that he did not hurt you?'

Proving to herself. Proving to him. That was what this was about.

'Or punishing him by showing him just what he has lost?' Venetia asked.

'Maybe a bit of both. I'm not afraid to face him, Venetia.'

'You are not afraid of much, Alice Flannigan.' Venetia's eyes held hers. 'I heard you beat him at Dryden's.'

'I beat them all,' Alice said carefully.

'At *vingt-et-un,*' pointed out Venetia. 'Razeby's game.'

'So?' Alice gave a shrug, but she knew Venetia understood something of the game's significance between them.

'You are playing dangerously with him.'

'We always played dangerously, me and Razeby.'

'Such games do not always turn out the way we think.' Venetia's warning, though veiled, was unmistakable.

'Maybe not, but sometimes for the sake of our pride we have to play them,' Alice said and met Venetia's gaze. 'I'm getting on with my life, Venetia. I'll not let Razeby get in the way of that. And if, along the way, he's made to feel just a tiny bit of regret, is that such a very bad thing?'

'As long as you know what you are doing, Alice.'

'I do, trust me. I'll flirt with him just the same as the others. But it doesn't mean anything. Honest.' She gave a grin. 'Well, maybe I'll flirt with the others just that bit more to annoy him!' She pressed a swift kiss to Venetia's cheek.

'Alice Flannigan, you are an incorrigible woman.'

Alice laughed. 'I'll say it now because I can't say

it once we're at the ball. Enjoy the evening. Dance with Linwood until your head's dizzy. It really is for a good cause. Had there been a similar charity in Dublin years ago, it would have saved my mam a lot of trouble. Being homeless with thirteen mouths to feed isn't much fun.'

'I hope you enjoy yourself, too, Alice.'

'Oh, I'll be doing that, all right. You needn't worry on that account.'

'Will you be all right with Frew?'

'I know how to deal with Frew. He'll be getting a few dances and not a thing more.'

The two of them laughed, knowing that Alice could more than handle herself.

The ballroom was crowded. Alice caught sight of Venetia and Linwood standing talking with Linwood's parents, Lord and Lady Misbourne, and Venetia saw her, but they could not give any acknowledgement, or even appear to notice one another. *Ton* and *demi-monde*. Two different worlds indeed, even if they were standing only a few yards apart in the same room.

Alice was wearing a new dress from Madame Boisseron. It had cost a small fortune, much more than Alice would ever normally have paid for a dress, but she had bought it, and a few others, with the winnings from her card game. The skirt was plain ivory silk, the bodice was gold silk, suggestively cut and fitted, but without even a hint of cleavage on display. The dressmaker had said that it would make every man that looked at it unable to take his eyes from her, which, judging from Frew's reaction, seemed to have been an accurate prediction.

It had small gold sleeves that were really just two bands of silk framing her fully exposed, naked shoulders. She wore not so much as a ribbon or a necklace, neither a bracelet nor a ring, and yet Madame Boisseron had been right to say the dress was designed to be worn this way, without a single item of adornment. Alice had known it the moment she looked at herself in the peering glass. And she knew it now from the way every gentleman in the room was looking at her. And the way Venetia raised her eyebrows and sent her a secret smile.

Razeby was dancing with some respectable young lady across the dance floor. Alice told herself it did not matter. Every man in Razeby's position had to do the same, eventually. It was just as he had said—he had a duty to marry and provide an heir. She ignored the stab of jealousy and moved her mind to more pleasant thoughts.

She glanced across at Frew, and the fact that he so clearly thought himself so handsome and a gift to all of womankind made her want to chuckle; he set not a single firework alight in Alice's arsenal.

'You are looking especially beautiful tonight, Miss Sweetly,' he said.

'You're too kind, Mr Frew.'

'My given name is Edward.' His eyes stared deeply into hers, affecting a smoulder that at best appeared contrived, and at worst as if he had contracted an ocular complaint.

'How interesting, Mr Frew.' She smiled.

Razeby would have laughed at the response. Frew just looked slightly aggrieved.

She refrained from teasing him further and resigned

herself to a very dull evening in his company. 'So what was that poem you recited in the Green Room the other night?'

'I wrote it just for you, Miss Sweetly.' Frew began to recite the flowery words again, but Wordsworth had nothing to worry about. After two verses she knew that if Frew made one more reference to long thrusting swords and softly dewed maidens she would not be able to keep a straight face.

Halfway through the dance his hand took hers and their steps led them to exchange places. It was the point she had been waiting for. She glanced again towards Razeby, whispering his name in her mind as if to call him.

Razeby's eyes moved to meet hers, as if answering her call. She watched his gaze drop to her dress and sweep over it before coming back up to her face. She held his gaze, gave him a small teasing smile. *Nice?* it asked.

Very nice, indeed! His eyes answered with an unmistakable interest.

She gave him a naughty arch of her eyebrows, knowing full well what it would do to him, before she turned back to Frew.

She leaned her mouth closer towards Frew's ear, let him hold her that little bit closer than respectability decreed. 'Tell me that last line again, Mr Frew. You do have such a way with words.'

Frew positively puffed out his chest, and, looking like a man that thought his luck was in, he obliged.

By the next time she could glance in Razeby's direction she saw he was watching Frew with a distinctive glower.

She drew Razeby an admonishing look.

He put on his innocent face.

She gave that smile that told him she was not fooled for a minute by his protested innocence.

He grinned an admission.

The dance took them away from one another. She did not see him again, only Frew. And she could not help feeling a little deflated at that. But not as disappointed as Frew at only being allowed a chaste kiss of her hand when he delivered her home.

When she lay in bed that night it was not Frew she was thinking of or his terrible poetry, but Razeby.

No one could accuse her of avoiding him. Not after Dryden's. Not after White's. And not after tonight. She smiled because it felt like her plan was coming together. And she smiled just because she had enjoyed the little exchange with him and it made her feel warm and dangerous and excited. In the back of her mind she heard again the whisper of Venetia's warning. There was a truth to it, she acknowledged, because as surely as Alice dangled an enticement before Razeby, she felt the pull of him. There was a rapport and an attraction that existed only with him. And that was a very dangerous thing. Venetia was right; she should have a little more care in her dealings with Razeby.

'You know you are more than welcome to come, Razeby, but do you really think it is a good idea?' Linwood asked his friend as they sat together in the drawing room of Linwood's home a few nights later. He got up and poured two glasses of brandy from the decanter that sat on the nearby desk, passing one of them to Razeby.

'A man is entitled to one night off.' Razeby accepted the brandy with a murmured 'thank you'. He knew what Linwood was saying was true. Going to watch Alice in one of her plays in the company of Linwood and his wife was the worst idea in the world. He knew it and yet here he was sitting in Linwood's drawing room, suggesting the idea. 'Besides, I have a wish to see the play.'

Linwood raised a single, dark, sceptical eyebrow. 'Or a wish to see Miss Alice Sweetly.'

'Maybe,' he conceded. 'She *is* the most talked-about actress in all London. Her reputation as a serious actress on stage challenges both Venetia's and Mrs Siddons's. Maybe I just want to see how her performance has developed.' And part of that was true. But only part.

Linwood did not look convinced. 'Your presence will not go without comment.'

'Because Alice was once my mistress? Am I never to set foot in the Theatre Royal again?'

'No one is saying that.' Linwood met his gaze. 'But what happened to the clean severance?'

'The severance was clean. Alice understands the situation as well as I do. There is nothing between us save for civility.' But he was lying. There was something very much more than civility between them. Something that was driving this compulsion he felt to see her.

'It is not as if I have lost sight of what I am doing. I will be at Almack's tomorrow.' There was no harm in just seeing her. He drank the brandy down and glanced away towards the window. It changed nothing, save made him feel better. 'I will have myself a wife before the Season is done, Linwood. I have to. There can be no two ways about it.'

'I understand that it is "over" between you and Alice,

but have you considered that when it comes to finding a wife there is always next Season?' asked Linwood.

Razeby smiled and met Linwood's eyes. 'No, my friend, there is not,' he said quietly. It was as close to telling him the truth as he could come.

Linwood's eyes searched his as if seeking to glean the answer that was there. But Razeby held his gaze, steadfastly refusing to give away anything more, until at last Linwood, with a tiny incline of his head, acknowledged defeat and dropped the challenge.

Linwood topped up their brandy glasses. 'Well, in that case, Razeby, you had better spend this evening in the company of an old friend at the theatre.'

Alice stepped out on to the stage that night. It was another full house. The part came naturally to her. She closed off her mind to all of real life and just let herself be this other woman. She acted. And it was almost as exhilarating as teasing Razeby across a room, but nowhere near as dangerous.

His box was empty, just as it was empty every night. But her eye caught a glimpse of figures in Venetia's box. Alice slipped her gaze to her friend and saw not only Venetia and Linwood. Her heart skipped a beat at the sight of Razeby sitting there with them. She turned her eyes away, careful not to allow herself to be distracted.

It meant nothing, she told herself, but her heart quickened all the same. He had just come for an evening at the theatre. But following on from Dryden's and White's and the benefit ball, she knew that was not the case, that really his presence here did mean something. Alice just did not want to think precisely what.

* * *

He would not be in the Green Room. He would not dare. She knew it, yet the first thing she did when she walked in there was to look for him.

But Razeby dared.

'Miss Sweetly.' He bowed.

'Lord Razeby.' She curtsied. Her heart leapt at the sight at the sight of him, her nerves shimmered in delight. She could not stop herself from smiling.

All attention in the room was upon them for all it feigned otherwise. Every conversation was conducted with half an ear on theirs.

She could not avoid him. Could do nothing other than treat him as if he were any other man.

'I trust you enjoyed the play, my lord.'

'More than I could have imagined,' he replied.

'Then perhaps your imagination is a little lacking.'

'On the contrary, Miss Sweetly, my imagination is most excellent. I have often been complimented upon it.' She saw the message in his eyes.

She was the one who had complimented him on it... when they were making love.

Something exciting and bold and deliciously dangerous whispered between them.

'Your acting talent has blossomed and taken on a new and vibrant dimension.' He smiled.

'Mmm,' she said, sharing the smile. 'I think I've heard that somewhere else. And there's you laying claim to a most excellent imagination.'

'You wish for originality in the compliments to be paid you?' He raised an eyebrow.

'I'd settle for truth,' she returned.

He leaned closer, lowered his voice slightly. 'Then the truth is, Miss Sweetly, that you were wonderful.'

The same words he used in this same Green Room a lifetime ago. The same words he had whispered in their bedchamber every time he had come to take her home after those occasional stage appearances. The world seemed to shift and detach around them.

'And you're as much a flatterer as ever,' she said softly, her eyes tracing his.

'Never that, Alice,' more softly still. He was smiling that smile of old, making everything seem so right.

Their eyes held, stretching time, making the Green Room and its people disappear. She could feel the beat of her heart and sense his beat in time. Between them was that same connection there had always been.

'Ah, Razeby.' Hawick's voice interrupted. 'How goes the bride search?'

The words crushed the moment, dragging them both back to the reality of what could not be.

'Well enough, thank you,' said Razeby. He smiled politely at Hawick, but there was nothing of a smile in his eyes when he looked at the duke.

'You were supreme as ever, Miss Sweetly,' said Hawick, lifting her hand and pressing a kiss to the back of it.

'You're too kind, Your Grace,' she replied, easily enough, but she was acting. And beneath that bright surface it felt like the dark hidden depths of a pool had been disturbed.

'If you will excuse me. Your servant, Miss Sweetly.' Razeby bowed and walked away.

Such perilous, glittering allure. Alice knew she was playing with fire. But she could not turn away from the path she had chosen to walk, as if there had ever really been anything of choice in it. She could not turn away

from Razeby, for the sake of her pride and her live-
lihood. And more than that she could not turn away
from Razeby because, even knowing what she did, she
wanted to see him. It was a disquieting realisation. And
one which she sought to distract herself from with a
shopping expedition in the company of her friends the
next day.

The four of them sauntered along Bond Street laden
with parcels and boxes. Alice had allowed herself to be
persuaded into buying too many fripperies, but she had
to admit, it did make her feel good, even if the parcels
were cumbersome to carry and her feet were aching
from too much walking in shoes that were stylish and
new, but less than comfortable.

They had just left the milliners when Sara asked
the question.

'You did say you cleared out everything you could
from Hart Street, didn't you, Alice?'

'What do you mean?' Alice glanced across at her,
a sudden panic drumming in her breast that Razeby
might have revealed something of just how much she
had walked away from.

Ellen drew Sara a look of daggers.

'I saw that look, Ellen Devizes,' Alice chided.

'Lord, Sara, but you have some size of mouth on
you.'

'What do you mean?' Sara looked hurt. 'She's fine
about Razeby.'

'Even so,' countered Ellen.

'What aren't you telling me?' Alice asked.

There was a resounding silence.

'Out with it,' she said.

'Razeby's kept the house on,' said Ellen at last.

'That can't be right,' Alice murmured before she could stop herself.

'It is,' insisted Sara. 'He's been seen there.'

'Why on earth would Razeby do that?' Alice asked, her pace subconsciously slowing.

Sara raised her brows, widened her eyes and gave her that look that brought a blush of embarrassment to Alice's cheeks.

It was Tilly who finally told her. 'The rumour is it ain't just a bride he's looking for, Alice, but a new mistress. We thought you knew.'

Alice felt the words hit her hard. She glanced away to hide her shock. 'Rumours aren't always true.'

They all looked at her in a way that made her regret saying the words aloud.

'Going in there late at night. Leaving early in the morning. A girl doesn't have to be a bluestocking to work it out,' said Sara.

'You know what men are like.' Tilly patted her arm as if to console her.

'I do.' And yet she thought Razeby different. Even now. Even after all that had happened. It could not be true. She knew Razeby. And what he was doing was about duty, no matter how much she disliked the way he had gone about doing it.

'It's always about what's in their breeches,' said Ellen.

'It is,' agreed Alice with a smile to mask how much she was still reeling from the revelation.

'But you didn't leave anything behind, did you?' Sara persisted.

Alice's smile broadened. 'I didn't leave one thing.'

But, in truth, she had left a lot more than a diamond bracelet and some expensive dresses.

'You don't want some other woman getting her hands on anything that's rightfully yours.'

Tilly and Ellen nodded in agreement with Sara's words.

Alice laughed. 'I don't think there's any danger of that.'

'Glad to hear it, girl.' Tilly slipped her arm through hers.

'Come on—' Ellen gave a smile '—I need some new stockings and Benjamin Preece has been advertising ladies' white silk hose made of real China silk for only 7s 6d a pair.'

'I could do with some stockings myself,' said Alice, denying the disquiet she was feeling. 'And then we'll go and have tea.'

'Like ladies.' Ellen raised her eyebrows and affected a posh accent.

They giggled like girls.

'Preece's it is,' said Alice and, with her arm still linked in Tilly's, the group made their way towards Preece's warehouse.

In all of the days that followed the shopping trip Alice could not stop thinking about Razeby keeping on the house in Hart Street. It worried at her, like a dog at a bone. She tried to push the thought out of her head, throwing herself all the more into her parts on the stage over those next few nights, and afterwards, in the Green Room, working the room with a charm and a control that would have done all of Venetia's best teachings proud. But none of it stopped her thinking. At night, in bed, the thought was there just the same.

She looked at herself in the peering glass. There were much prettier women out there. Women who put her ordinary looks in the shade. She sucked in her tummy, examined her teeth and scrubbed a finger against the faint freckles that marred the bridge of her nose. Maybe he really had just grown tired of her. Maybe he had lied and misled her because he did not have the courage to tell her the truth.

She shook her head, unable to believe it. Razeby had more integrity in his little finger than the whole of any other man she had known. And rumours were just that, she told herself. A fire of gossip over nothing.

But all rumours started with a grain of truth, the little sharp thought countered.

And then pricked away at her relentlessly. Even if it was true, what difference did it make? she demanded.

But it did make a difference. Alice knew that, no matter how hard she tried to pretend otherwise. And because of that she knew she was going to have to discover the truth for herself.

She rose much earlier than normal the next day.

'Shall I fetch you a hackney carriage, Miss Sweetly?' the youngest maid, Rosie, asked.

Alice shook her head. 'It's a fine morning. I've a mind to walk and take the air.'

'I'll just fetch my cloak, ma'am. At this hour of the day it's still a bit chilly out there.'

'Don't bother yourself, Rosie. I've some lines to think through, it's best if I walk alone.'

'Very good, ma'am.' The maid bobbed a curtsy and opened the door for her.

The hour was still early enough that the streets were quiet. The ground was damp with rain that no longer fell, and, as the maid had warned, the morning was still cool with the night's chill. But the sun was out and the air was bright and clear, just the way she liked.

She walked slowly, breathing in the damp freshness of the air, while all around her London stirred. Carts with animals and vegetables come up from the country for the market rolled by. Milk maids leading cows by a rope, a gaggle of geese still wearing the little shoes to save their feet from all the miles they had walked. Alice walked, too, down Mercer Street and along Long Acre, crossing over to walk down Banbury Court. And, finally, onto Hart Street.

She strolled as if it were just a street like any other. Pretended not to even look at the house in which she had lived with Razeby. She deliberately stayed on the other side of the road. But her feet trod slower and her heart beat faster, and as she came closer her eyes fixed upon the building that had been her home for half a year.

It looked just the same as when she had left it. As if she could walk back in there right now and turn back time to be what it had been not so long ago. But then the fittings and furniture came with the house when Razeby had rented it, just as hers had come with the new rooms in Mercer Street. It did not mean that the house was not in other hands. It was just a damn rumour and she was a fool for even being here.

But at the very moment she chided herself with that thought, the black glossy front door opened. And Alice's heart jumped at the prospect of being caught here spying. She ducked out of sight behind a tree. Her fingers held hard on to the wide gnarled trunk as she watched while a tall, dark-haired handsome man she recognised too well emerged.

The breath caught in her throat. Her stomach gave a somersault before her heart stampeded off at full tilt.

The expression on his face was serious. He was not smiling. Indeed, there was nothing of his usual good-natured manner with which she always thought of him. He walked off at a brisk pace in the opposite direction, not glancing back at the house once.

Her heart was thundering and she felt shocked, and all she could hear in her head were Tilly's words: *The rumour is it ain't just a bride he's looking for, Alice, but a new mistress.*

And he must have himself a new girl, or why else would he have spent the night there? She stared at the windows. All the blinds and curtains were opened, but there was no movement, no hint of a woman's face watching him leave.

She waited until he was almost out of sight before stepping out from behind the tree and making her way back to Mercer Street.

Chapter Eleven

Razeby was at Almack's again. So many times, going through the same motions. All with one purpose that was contrary to that which he desired. It was bad enough being here without his friends turning up to witness it. Linwood was different, because, despite all of Razeby's denials, Linwood knew something of the truth and he understood, in part.

'Came to give you a bit of support, old chap, in the old bride hunt.' Bullford beamed.

'How considerate of you all,' said Razeby with an irony that sailed right over Bullford's head.

'Well, we couldn't abandon a brother in need. You seem to be struggling, so we thought we'd better step in and help.' Fallingham sipped at his champagne.

'Struggling?' Razeby raised an eyebrow.

'Dragging it out,' Devlin explained.

Razeby smiled because the barb was dangerously close to the truth. 'I am merely being selective in my choice.'

'Selective? That's a good one,' quipped Monteith. 'I

must remember "selective" when it comes to deferring putting my head in parson's trap.'

'What's to select?' asked Fallingham. 'There's only three criteria to be considered: how well connected they are, how much money they bring to the deal, and how far they can open their legs.'

The men laughed at Fallingham's crudity. All except Razeby and Linwood.

Razeby glanced round at his friends—the group of society's most disreputable gentlemen. 'One glance at the company I'm keeping and the duennas won't let me near their charges.'

'We could always take care of the duennas for you, Razeby,' Monteith said. 'There's much to be said for the older, more experienced lady.'

'There's a truth in that and no mistake,' agreed Devlin. 'I heard a story about the widowed Mrs Alcock—'

'We've all heard the story of Mrs Alcock and if you repeat it in here you'll have us all thrown out, and then where will Razeby be?' said Bullford.

'Push off, the lot of you,' said Razeby as if in jest, but meaning it. 'Before Lady Jersey sees you.'

'There's gratitude for you,' drawled Monteith.

Razeby gave an ironic smile.

'You know where we'll be.' Fallingham finished the contents of his glass in one gulp and waved a farewell.

His friends moved off, all except Devlin and Linwood.

Razeby met Devlin's eye. 'I really have heard the story of Mrs Alcock, Devlin.'

'Wanted to speak to you,' said Devlin. 'Slightly sensitive subject.'

Razeby felt a sudden uncomfortable premonition of just what that 'slightly sensitive subject' might be.

'Not like you to be bashful,' he said and waited to see what Devlin would say.

'I just wanted to ascertain the situation. Regarding you and Miss Sweetly.'

Razeby's heart beat harder. 'I am looking for a bride, Devlin. Does not that say it all?' He forced his muscles to stay relaxed.

'I thought perhaps you and Miss Sweetly might still have something going.'

'We do not.' The words were curt. He kept control.

'I am glad to hear it.'

Razeby's gaze sharpened on Devlin. But Devlin did not seem to notice.

'The thing is, Razeby…' Devlin cleared his throat. 'There's something I've been meaning to ask you. Now that you and Alice are no longer together I thought I might ask her out. You wouldn't have any objection to that, would you?'

'Why would I possibly object?' he said drily. But inside he could feel the thud of his heart too loud and hard in his chest and the cold prickle of his skin, and something primitive and menacing snake through his blood.

'Thank you, Razeby.' Devlin gave him a nod. 'I had better catch up with the others.'

'You had better,' said Razeby in a voice that barely concealed the warning. He stood there and watched Devlin leave with a jaw clenched so tight it was painful, only shifting his gaze to Linwood once Devlin had disappeared through the door.

The two friends exchanged a glance.

'You are over her, remember,' Linwood said quietly.

'I remember,' Razeby replied grimly. 'Remembering is all I do.'

Alice slipped the cloak hood from her head as the Linwood butler ushered her into the hallway of Venetia's rooms.

'Alice.' Venetia came hurrying out of the drawing room to see her.

'You don't have anyone in, do you?' Alice asked, darting a cautious look over at the drawing room.

'No one. I am just writing some letters while Linwood is out this evening.' She made no mention of exactly where Linwood had gone. She did not need to. Both women knew that there was a matchmaking ball at Almack's tonight and that Linwood would be there with Razeby.

'Is something wrong?' There was a look of concern on Venetia's face that made Alice feel guilty.

'Nothing,' Alice lied. 'I just fancied a chat, that's all.'

'Come on through. A chat sounds much more inviting than dealing with a pile of business letters.' Venetia ordered a tray of tea with crumpets and jam.

The drawing room was cosy, the curtains drawn against the darkness outside. They drank the tea and ate the crumpets, even though Alice was not one bit hungry. The scene reminded her too much of the dark winter nights when she and Razeby had toasted crumpets by the fire and spread thick butter on them to melt and drip down their chins and all over their fingers as they snuggled together beneath a blanket. She pushed the memory away.

They talked of the theatre, of how much Venetia

missed it, of the current plays, of Kemble and people they knew in common—indulging in a little gossip and laughing together.

'Talking of gossip,' Alice said and it sounded a little contrived even to her own ears, 'I was wondering...' She hesitated, then, taking a breath, asked the question that she had come here to ask. 'Have you heard any rumours concerning Razeby?'

'What kind of rumours?'

'About Hart Street.' Alice swallowed. 'It seems he's kept the house on.'

'I had not heard.'

Alice looked at her friend, wondering if she was telling the truth, or just sparing her feelings.

'I am sure if it is true there is a perfectly good explanation behind it.'

'It's true all right,' Alice muttered and then blushed when she realised just how much that reply revealed.

Venetia did not question her on it. 'Whatever Razeby's reasons, I doubt very much they stretch to what the gossipmongers are saying.'

'I thought you hadn't heard the gossipmongers saying anything about him.'

'And neither I have, Alice. But I can well imagine.' Venetia raised an eyebrow. 'I know what you are thinking.'

'Do you?' Alice looked into her eyes.

'Do you really think he is interested in another woman as his mistress?' Venetia asked quietly.

'No. Maybe.' Alice closed her eyes and shook her head. 'I don't know what to think any more, Venetia.'

'Whatever is going on with Razeby, I think you may rest assured it is not that.'

'You're probably right.' Alice gave a sigh. 'It shouldn't matter a toss, even if he's taking a different woman back there every night of the week. But a woman has her pride.' But pride was only part of Alice's problem.

Venetia gave a nod of understanding.

'I best be away.'

'You will not stay for some more tea?'

Alice shook her head. 'Thank you, Venetia.'

They both knew it was not the tea Alice was thanking her for.

Alice tried to put Razeby out of her mind and get on with her life. The prospect of seeing him worried her, because she felt like something had changed in her and she knew it was more important than ever that she maintain a façade of normality. But she had to see him again, and she did, only two days after speaking to Venetia.

The musicale in Mr Forbes's drawing room was in full swing, the formally arranged rows of chairs filled completely. Some gentlemen were standing against the walls at the back of the room and some at the sides. Forbes was a personal friend of Kemble's. He was a wealthy man, but not exceptionally so. Precisely how he had managed to secure the talent of Angelica Catalani to sing for them tonight was a coup that had everyone asking the question. The soprano was famously difficult in temperament and her fee was reputed to be beyond the reach of all but the richest in the land. But when she opened her mouth and sang, it was the most beautiful sound in the world. She had a voice with true clear clarity, a voice that made Alice think of crystal and purity and perfection.

Alice was here with Kemble and his sister, the famous tragedy actress Sarah Siddons. Their seats in the middle row meant they had a good view of Madame Catalani, and were the optimal distance to appreciate the music. Alice was trying very hard to focus herself entirely on the singer. Trying to block out the knowledge that Razeby was sitting at the back of the room with Miss Althrope, who accompanied him this night.

The programme for the evening, neat and nicely printed, was lying open on her lap. Before the music had started she had pretended to read it, and chatted with Kemble and Mrs Siddons. As she had suspected, Kemble could not help himself running through the scheduled music and discussing each one. Alice had smiled and listened and added in her tuppence, conscious that Razeby could see her and her every reaction. It was important that she look as if she were having the best time in the world. Without him.

It should have been easier once Madame Catalani started singing. All Alice had to do was sit there, looking serenely engrossed in the music. But it grew strangely more difficult.

Madame Catalani's voice was so haunting and melodic that it made Alice feel emotional. Emotions were dangerous. Especially emotions of the sort that were seeping into her chest. She glanced away from the soprano, seeking to distract herself, but all she could see were the fashionable red-painted walls around her. Red—pray God that they had been any other colour!

The applause sounded. Kemble glanced at her, applauding for all he was worth, nodding at her and smiling his enjoyment. She made herself smile back and clap all the harder. But then Madame Catalani began to sing again, a piece so devastatingly haunting that it had the power to pierce through all the armour Alice had donned. It moved her. It made her think of things of which she did not want to think. The truth of feelings and pretences.

It made her think of Razeby.

She dropped her gaze to rest on the programme lying on her lap. But the beautiful voice sang on and inside of Alice all of her emotions seemed to be twisting and turning and welling dangerously high. And there, ever present, was that burning awareness of Razeby sitting behind her with another woman. It was like a burr, cutting into her. Or maybe it was just the haunting voice and that music, and those red, red walls. All of it pressing in on her. Suffocating her, until she did not think she could bear it for another minute.

She leaned closer to Kemble, whispered near his ear, 'If you'd excuse me for a few minutes, Mr Kemble. I'll be right back.'

Kemble gave a nod, barely taking his eyes from Madame Catalani.

Alice made her way from the row as inconspicuously as she could.

Razeby was not focused upon Madame Catalani like everybody else in the room. Rather, he was watching Alice leave alone, and a few moments later the sleazy figure of Quigley slip out after her. No one noticed. Madame Catalani sang on. The whole audience was transfixed.

Razeby whispered his excuse to Miss Althrope. And went out after them.

The hallway was empty. Not a footman or a maid

was in sight. Madame Catalani's voice was softer, more muted in volume out here. Beneath it Razeby heard the quiet footsteps on the staircase. He moved silently to follow, reaching the top of the stairs just in time to see Quigley's black-jacketed back at the end of the passageway disappear through a door signed as the ladies' withdrawing room. Razeby's eyes narrowed.

He made his way along the passageway.

Alice had no need to avail herself of the withdrawing room's facilities behind the modesty screens. She could still hear Madame Catalani's voice, even up here, but at least she was alone. And the walls were a cool pale grey rather than red. She could breathe. The sky was a clear blue through the windows, the afternoon sunshine lighting it brightly, but the sun was at the front of the house, and this room at the rear. It was cool in here, the fire unlit. And Alice was glad of it. It was just that aria, she told herself, and those red walls and the heat of the room downstairs. A few moments in here and she would be in command of herself once more. She took another breath just as the footsteps sounded outside the door.

Alice pretended to be smoothing down the skirt of her dress as the door opened behind her. She did not look at the reflection in the full-length looking glass, just lowered her eyes and turned to leave.

'Why, Miss Sweetly. There is no need to rush off, my dear.'

She stopped dead in her tracks, the sight of the lecherous Mr Quigley standing there making her stomach tighten in shock. 'Mr Quigley! What on earth do you think you're doing in here? This is the ladies' with-drawing room!'

'Yes. I am well aware of what room this is. But I wanted to have a little word with you, in private. And it is so very difficult to get you alone.'

'You'll understand if I don't oblige. Mr Kemble and Mrs Siddons are waiting down the stairs for me.'

'Now, you cannot expect me to believe that Mr Kemble and Mrs Siddons, or indeed any person in that drawing room, are not so engrossed in Madame Catalani's singing that they will miss you for a little while. And with you, I do only need a little while.' He licked a tongue against his lips as if he could taste her upon them and she could not suppress the shudder of revulsion that went through her.

She made to pass him by, but he caught hold of her wrist lightly with his little claw-like fingers.

'Now, my dear Miss Sweetly,' he began. He smiled in a leering sort of way, leaning in close so that she could smell the stench of stale wine upon his breath. 'I have had my eye on you for a long time. And now that Razeby is off the scene and you are left alone, without a protector, I thought I would do the chivalric thing and take you under my wing.'

'Honoured though I am by your offer, sir, I'm afraid I must decline it.' She said it politely but firmly.

'Come now, Miss Sweetly.' He put on a cajoling voice.

She looked pointedly at where his hand was fixed. 'If you'd be kind enough to unhand me, Mr Quigley.'

'Now, don't be like that, little Miss Sweetly. Such a stern tone does not suit.' His fingers tightened around her wrist and he dragged her close to him, sliding his hand round her hip and over her buttock to fasten there. 'Just one little kiss for an old man.'

'No!' She tried to push him off, but he was surprisingly strong for a man of his age.

Her eyes met his and she saw the lust that had always been in them when he looked at her and the new intent that lurked there. And the panic rose in her.

It happened so fast she was not sure what had actually taken place until she saw Quigley, face pressed against the wall, his arm up his back, held there by a tall dark figure she knew too well.

Quigley gave a little whimper of fear.

'What the hell do you think you are doing, Quigley?' Razeby's voice was quiet, but it cut through the sudden silence of the room like a whip.

She stared, unable to believe that Razeby was really here.

'I thought you were done with her, that she was avail—' Quigley gave a yelp as Razeby inched the older man's arm higher. 'I made a mistake. I'm sorry. Won't touch her again.'

'It is to Miss Sweetly you should be addressing your apology.' Razeby's face was like flint. She had never seen him like this.

'Apologies, Miss Sweetly.' Quigley's words were strained and urgent.

She nodded her acceptance, her eyes darting from Quigley's contorted face to the dark, dangerous expression on Razeby's.

Quigley gave another moan of pain.

'Let him go, Razeby. I think he's drunk.'

She saw the snarl on Razeby's lip. 'Stay away from her, Quigley,' he hissed.

Quigley nodded, his face powder white. 'Message understood, my lord.'

Only then did Razeby release his grip on the man.

Quigley picked up his hat, which had been knocked off in the process of being slammed face first into the wall, and disappeared through the door.

Alice did not move and neither did Razeby. They stared across the few feet that separated them. Her heart was thudding hard enough to break free of her ribcage. Her blood was rushing so fast she thought she might faint. But neither were because of Quigley.

'Are you all right, Alice?' His voice was quiet, but intense and loaded.

She nodded, not trusting herself to speak.

He moved slowly to stand in front of her, his eyes raking hers. 'He did not hurt you?'

'No.' She shook her head.

And all of the tension that was roaring between them had nothing to do with Quigley.

Their gazes were locked, unable to look away. Inside she was trembling so much she feared it would show.

'I am glad of that.' He reached his hand to hers and took hold of it, his fingers surrounding hers with warmth and strength and gentleness. 'You are shaking.'

'It's cold in here,' she lied.

He slipped off his tailcoat and wrapped it around her shoulders.

The scent of him enveloped her, bringing with it too many memories, too many conflicting emotions that warred and struggled within her chest.

'No!' She pulled his coat from her shoulders and thrust it back into his hands.

The silence hissed between them, the tension winding tighter.

And still she could not look away. And neither could he.

Their eyes held, conveying so many words, none of which could be spoken.

Her heart was thudding so hard she could feel each beat reverberate through her body. A shiver rippled down her spine and tingled across her skin. She was breathing faster now, more shallow, not knowing how much longer she could keep herself together.

He looked at her for a moment longer. Then he drew her a small incline of his head and walked away.

Through the open door she watched him pass the two young ladies who were poised on the brink of entering the withdrawing room.

'Ladies,' she heard him say politely as he calmly walked past them.

The two girls were giggling and gaping as they entered the withdrawing room. But they fell silent when they saw her standing there, their eyes growing wide with shock and speculation.

Alice held her head up, flicked some imaginary dust from her skirt, then sauntered out with all the dignity of a duchess, as if she did not give a damn that she had just been caught with Razeby in the ladies' withdrawing room.

When Razeby came back into the drawing room Quigley's chair was empty. Razeby returned to take his seat by Miss Althrope's side, who was far too well bred to comment upon a gentleman's absence. Whether she had noticed Alice leave he neither knew nor cared.

His blood was still pounding from the sight of her, his mind still focused and intent—with lethality towards Quigley and something else altogether for Alice. He could feel her in every beat of his heart.

It was not supposed to be like this. He was not supposed to feel like this. He knew that, but sitting there with Miss Althrope by his side, his eyes half on Madame Catalani, half on the door waiting for Alice to return, he did, and there was not a damn thing he could do to change it.

At last Alice slipped into the room, resuming her place beside Kemble once more. She did not so much as glance his way. Just sat there seemingly quietly intent upon Madame Catalani's performance. But she did not need to look at him. He was so damned aware of her that Madame Catalani could have missed every single note and he would not have noticed. He could feel the sense of Alice thudding through his chest, feel the knowledge of what was between them in his blood and in his bones. He stared straight ahead, as if watching the soprano, but he was watching Alice for every minute of that concert. And he could not look away.

Chapter Twelve

Alice did not know how she got through the rest of that musicale. Her hands were still trembling when she got home. She told herself it was because of Quigley, but she knew it was not.

It was wrong on so many levels. Razeby had rid himself of her without the slightest regard for her feelings. What had been between them was nothing more than sex. He was actively searching for a woman to marry. And yet this afternoon in that ladies' room made her think she had got it all wrong. It was preposterous. Downright ridiculous. But that look in his eyes, filled with meaning, piercing, as if he could see right through to her very soul. As if he felt, really felt, the same as her. The whole experience had shaken her more than she wanted to admit, stripping all her denials away for the flimsy pretences they were.

And that realisation made her feel weak and out of control and afraid. Afraid that the mask was in danger of slipping, the threat of all that lay beneath exposed to the world.

Never let them see how much they hurt you.

The mantra came easily to her lips. She knew it by heart and had said it to herself a thousand times since that night with Razeby. And yet now she was panicking, gathering her armour around her all the tighter. Telling herself that she had been mistaken in what she felt and what she thought she had seen in his eyes.

He had taken all she had to give, used it and discarded it. She could never allow herself to forget. All she had left was her pride. She would not let him take that. She could not let him take that. She had no choice but to carry on.

'So, how was Madame Catalani the other day?' Venetia took a small sip of coffee and glanced across to where Alice sat on the sofa in Mercer Street.

'She's got a wonderful voice on her. Magical almost.' So magical that it could make a woman betray herself and imagine things.

'I heard Razeby was there, too.'

'Was he?' She tried to sound vague, but she could not meet Venetia's eye.

'Alice,' Venetia said softly, 'there is a rumour going around, about you and Razeby, at the musicale.'

'There are always rumours,' Alice said flippantly.

Venetia said nothing, just held her eyes, looking at her, knowing she was lying.

Alice closed her eyes and gave a sigh. 'It wasn't like that.'

'What was it like?'

'It was Quigley. He followed me into the ladies'. You know what he's like.'

'A lecherous old toad.'

'He made a pass at me. He's got a strength in him

that you wouldn't credit, Venetia. I thought he was just an old man. I never thought that he'd actually use force.'

Venetia paled. There was a look of horror in her pale eyes, even though she was trying to hide it and her voice when she spoke was calm. 'Did he…hurt…you, Alice?'

'No. He tried to kiss me. I don't know how far he really meant to go, but he got nowhere. Razeby stopped him.'

'And how did Razeby come to be in the ladies' withdrawing room?'

Alice glanced away. 'He was just passing.'

Venetia raised her eyebrows and Alice could see the scepticism in her friend's expression. 'Are the two of you back together?'

'No.' Alice closed her eyes with a weariness. The confusion milling in her brain since that day seemed like it was sapping the very life from her. 'How could we ever be back together? After all he di—' She caught back what she had been about to say and stopped herself. 'He's searching for a bride. He was there with Miss Althrope.'

'You still have feelings for him, don't you, Alice?'

'Yes. No.' She glanced away. 'How could I?'

'We feel what we feel, Alice, regardless of sense or logic.' Venetia paused. 'I know you have no wish to avoid him, but maybe you should, just for a little while.'

'No. I can't.' She shook her head, feeling more afraid than ever. 'I won't, Venetia.' Because to do so would be to admit the truth. *Never turn your face from the thing you fear. Be bold and brave. And never, never let them see how much they hurt you.* 'In fact, what I need to do is the very opposite.'

'Alice…' Venetia cautioned softly.

'He saved me from Quigley. But it doesn't change anything,' Alice said. 'I mean, I'm grateful for his intervention, of course I am. But—' Her heart was beating faster even at the memory of his eyes staring down into hers, of all that had strained and trembled between them. And the dreams and nightmares that had made sleep impossible. And the thoughts that jibed at her all night and whispered in her ear every day. 'It changes nothing,' she said again, more firmly. 'I have to get on with my life. I have to show them all Razeby doesn't matter to me. I have to show *him* he doesn't matter to me.'

There was a small silence.

'Then be very careful, Alice.'

'I will,' she replied softly.

The doors of her wardrobe were wide open. Alice stood before them, looking in at the line of new silk evening dresses hanging there. They were both beautiful and expensive. They were her fresh start, bought with the money she had won at Dryden's that night.

Her eyes moved to the emerald silk dress at the very end of the wardrobe, hanging slightly separate from all the others. The one dress that she had taken from the house in Hart Street. The dress she had had made with Razeby in mind. The dress that he always swore he could not resist her in.

She reached out and lightly touched her fingers to the long flowing green silk of the skirt and the images flashed in her mind—vivid and real enough to make her gasp: Razeby's mouth on hers, his hands peeling off the bodice to expose her breasts naked and aching for his touch. Her rucking up the skirt and straddling

Razeby in his town coach because they could not wait until they got home. Making love across the desk in his study, on the sofa in the drawing room, on the Turkish rug before the drawing-room fireplace. And the time on the staircase and then again on its window seat before they had made it into the bedchamber. The razing intensity of the memories had her shivering. She snatched her hand back as if the cool silk had burned her.

She forced herself to breathe, to still the tremor that was racing all through her body and deny those feelings that were threatening to escape from the dark place in which she had locked them, grasping at anything to shore up the cracks in the walls of her defences.

It was just sex. It had always been just sex, and nothing more, for Razeby. And for her. She needed to prove that to herself, once and for all. And she knew the very way she could do it…if she was brave enough.

Alice took another breath and turned her eyes to the emerald-green silk once more.

Wearing the emerald-green evening dress had seemed such a good idea at the time, but standing here on the threshold of the Brewer Street Rooms, with Devlin looking at her with desire so blatant in his eyes, Alice was not so sure.

'That dress, Miss Sweetly…' Devlin's eyes dropped lower to the pale swell of her breasts over the tight green silk of her bodice. He leaned a little closer and lowered his voice for her ears only. 'You look positively irresistible.'

Irresistible. The same word Razeby always used. She did not want to hear it on Devlin's lips. It felt wrong. As wrong as wearing this dress in any man other than

Razeby's company. But that was all the more reason to wear it. To take away its power. To take away *his* power over her. To prove once and for all there was nothing left between them, that there never had been, no matter how he looked at her.

'You certainly know how to make a woman blush, Lord Devlin.' She smiled.

He held out his elbow to her in invitation.

She ignored the unease that stroked like a feather against her skin, closed her ears to the doubts and the discomfort, and the nervousness that was jittering in her stomach. It might feel wrong but it was the right thing to do, she reassured herself. Besides, it was too late to change her mind. She had better just get on with it. Everything would be fine. This was not the place a marquis came to find a bride. With a smile she rested her fingers lightly against his arm and, holding her head up high, let Devlin lead her into the room from which the music was playing loud. Everything would be fine, she told herself again.

But the minute she walked through those doors she knew it was not.

On the opposite side of the dance floor stood Razeby.

Alice felt a sudden panic well up and threaten to spill over. The urge to turn around and run right back out that door almost overwhelmed her. She swallowed, forced herself to breathe, reined herself back under control.

It should not matter if he was here. It should not make the slightest difference. Indeed, maybe it was even for the best. That he would witness this ultimate show of denial. Denying her feelings. Denying him. Maybe he even deserved it, that taunt of what he had so thoughtlessly cast aside. She had almost convinced herself of it by the time Devlin led her over to him.

'Razeby.' Devlin bowed. 'Did not think you would be here.'

'Change of plan,' Razeby replied and there was a coolness to his voice that stroked a warning down her spine.

Too many women, young, old and in between, were eyeing Razeby with a barely concealed interest. But Razeby seemed unaware and, notably, Miss Althrope was not by his side this evening. Indeed, there was no sign of a woman. Only Linwood.

Devlin's smile was slightly stilted. 'Not your usual scene.'

'Nor yours,' replied Razeby. He smiled, but there was something in the way he looked at Devlin, something almost threatening.

Devlin's smile faded. 'Miss Sweetly and I can certainly vouch for the quality of the champagne.' He took a sip from his glass.

Alice said nothing. Her glass was still brimful, not one drop had passed her lips, even though her mouth was as dry as a bone and her pulse was thrumming in her throat.

It was just a dress, she told herself. But it was not.

She knew that.

And so did Razeby.

There was nothing of Razeby's charm this evening, only a veneer of politeness so thin as to barely conceal a darkness and an intensity that made Linwood look positively light in comparison. She could feel the strain of the atmosphere between Razeby and Devlin, heavy with things that had nothing to do with friendship.

Devlin slid an arm around her waist, making her jump at his touch. 'Does not Miss Sweetly look charming tonight?' Spoken so politely, and yet there was that sense that he was deliberately baiting Razeby.

Razeby finally moved his gaze to her, letting his eyes wander from the green sparkle of her slippers, slowly up the silky green skirt, over her bodice and her breasts, until it finally met her own. Her heart was hammering harder than a blacksmith's hammer against an anvil, her pulse pounding so fast in her throat that she felt sick.

His gaze was long and cool, his mouth unsmiling. 'Charming indeed. But it is not the word I would use.'

Irresistible. The word whispered between them, and all that had passed between them while she was wearing this dress was there in the room, making the nerves flutter all the more wildly in her stomach.

She tore her gaze away. Swallowed. *Oh, Lord!* She quailed at the challenge, longed only to walk away. But she knew she could not do that. So, instead, she breathed and she stood there.

'Shall we dance, Miss Sweetly?' Devlin smiled.

'I thought you'd never ask,' she said and she meant it. Anything to get her away from Razeby and that terrible sense of something brewing, and the feeling that she could not have got this more wrong. She forced a tight smile and let Devlin lead her onto the floor.

Devlin did not return them to Razeby and Linwood. And she did not look at Razeby again, just got on with the evening. Danced two dances with Devlin. Drank half a glass of champagne. Smiled. Pretended she was interested in what Devlin was saying, that she was not conscious for every second of Razeby and the fact that he did not once dance.

* * *

Razeby saw Alice the minute she came into the room. He saw the evening dress she was wearing—the emerald silk—and he understood her message too well.

By his side he knew Linwood was watching her, too. Every man and woman in the room was. How could they fail to? She was the celebrated Miss Sweetly and looked golden and radiant and downright irresistible.

He thought of the rows of fine silks and satins she had left hanging in her wardrobe in Hart Street, and of the diamond bracelet and cheque that she had turned her back on. He had not understood it at the time. But now he did. She had chosen her weapon well. Saved it. And now she wielded it, pointed and sharp as a stiletto blade.

Linwood murmured something, but his friend's voice went as unheard as the music that played.

He watched Devlin lead her out on the floor. He knew he should go and claim a woman to dance with. Any woman. It would not matter. But he did not. He just stood there and watched Devlin handle her upon the dance floor, wearing that dress.

He could hear the beat of his own heart, the rhythmic thump so hard that it seemed to reverberate in his throat, through his bones, deafening in his ears.

She did not look at him. She did not need to.

And all of the past was whispering through him, taunting him as surely as she was.

Something inside of him felt dangerously close to snapping.

Alice sipped her champagne and let herself relax a little. They were halfway through the evening. She had got this far. She could manage the rest of it. Just about.

The notes of the next piece of music began, just those first few notes and her stomach sank and her blood turned to ice. And she was gripping the glass so tight that her knuckles shone white.

Fate could not be so cruel. *Please God, let her be mistaken.*

But the notes played on, blossoming into music, and there could be no mistake. She knew that music, knew that dance. The *Volse.* Their dance. Hers and Razeby's.

Her heart faltered, stumbling over its beats.

'Shall we dance, Miss Sweetly?' Devlin's voice was warm and close.

She felt frozen with horror. *No!* she wanted to say, categorically, unreservedly. *No!* It wasn't supposed to be like this. 'I'm only halfway through my champagne, Lord Devlin. We'll dance the next one.' She forced the smile to her lips.

'Come, Miss Sweetly,' he chided in a teasing tone. 'Leave the champagne. I'll buy you a bottle of the stuff when we come off the floor.' And then to her horror he held his hand out in a gesture that was an obvious invitation on to the dance floor. Anyone that was looking would have known that he was asking her to dance.

Her heart felt like it was about to give way. She swallowed. Wetted her suddenly dry lips. Maybe he was not watching. Maybe he had not seen. She glanced over at Razeby.

But Razeby's dark watchful gaze was fixed upon her. And so were too many other eyes.

Her blood was rushing so fast, twisting and turning in such a torrent that she felt dizzy. Beneath her arms prickled with sweat, but her fingers felt chilled through to their bones.

She knew what she was going to have to do. Knew there was no way out without losing face, without admitting the truth—that this music, this dance meant something to her. That Razeby meant something to her.

She turned her face from Razeby's. Laid her fingers on Devlin's waiting hand. And let him lead her on to the dance floor.

Her steps in the dance were perfect. The dance she had been so nervous about, the dance Razeby had taught her, the dance they had practised together so many times alone in the drawing room of the house in Hart Street. Their very first public dance as a couple. When Alice had worn this dress just for him. Their dance, their music, their dress.

She brazened it out the best she could. But there was a cold sick feeling in the pit of her stomach. And the smile she wore felt like it was tearing her face apart. She could not look at Razeby. Not at all through the dance. Until the very end, when it was finally over. And then she could not stop herself. Her eyes moved to the spot where he had stood. But Linwood was standing there alone.

She scanned the room for him, her eyes raking the crowd to find him. But Razeby had gone.

'Now for that champagne.' Devlin smiled as he led her from the floor and she felt the small intimate stroke of his fingers against her wrist.

It was done. She had done it. Worn the dress. Danced the dance. Denied him.

'Are you all right, Miss Sweetly?' Devlin sat her down in her chair. 'You do not seem to be your usual self. Your cheeks have gone quite pale.'

'If you would be so kind as to take me home, Lord Devlin.' She swallowed. 'I'm feeling a little unwell.'

'Of course. I will summon my carriage at once.'

Devlin's coach rolled away along the road.

Alice was walking up the steps to her front door when Razeby stepped out of the shadows.

'Razeby,' she whispered his name through the darkness. 'What are you doing here?'

She saw his gaze lower pointedly to the green silk of her skirt that peeped, so vibrant and taunting, from beneath her cloak, even in the yellow glow of the nearby street lamp, before coming back up to her face.

'Are you deliberately trying to torture me? Because if so, it is working.'

The breath was shaky in her throat. She opened her mouth to speak, but the look in his eyes made her rapidly close it again.

'Does that knowledge make you happy?' he demanded.

She stopped in her tracks, glanced round at him, told him the truth. 'No, Razeby. It doesn't.' She turned away, moving towards the steps that would take her up to her front door.

'Damn it, Alice! Do you think that you can just walk away from me?'

'Like you did to me?' She swung round to face him. 'What did you expect, Razeby?' She had spent all these weeks denying it, everything she had done had been to hide it—from the world, from Razeby, and most of all from herself. But his words, his being here, the whole night... All of the walls she had spent these weeks building, higher and wider and deeper, exploded apart.

The anger, the hurt, the pain—all of it surged up in a great wave to rush through her.

'That you would understand.' His expression was one of torment.

'Understand?' She walked right up to him and stared into his face. 'Oh, I understand too well! You cast me aside like I was a piece of clothing that you were done with. Quickly, easily, without a single consideration for my feelings.'

'It was not like that!' All denial and shock.

'No? One minute we were in bed making love. The next minute you were coolly dismissing me. Am I making that up?'

'Alice…' He raked a hand through his hair.

'Don't you *Alice* me! You could have said something before. You could have had the decency to give me some sort of warning. All that time you were planning it. And not one word did you utter.'

'You are wrong. I never planned any of it. That is part of the damn problem. Atholl—'

'Atholl was an excuse!' She shouted it.

'No!'

'Do you think I didn't know that you were brooding on something all those weeks and months? When you thought that no one could see you.'

He glanced away.

'Oh, yes, Razeby, I saw. And do you know something? I was worried about you. Not about us—I thought we were happy together. About you.' She poked her finger hard into his chest. 'When all along you were planning to be rid of me. Bastard!' She was breathing hard, shaking with the force of emotion rolling through her.

'I have already told you there was nothing of planning with you.'

'I don't believe you.'

'I have a duty to do. I cannot walk away from it, Alice. No matter how much I might want to!' There was an agony in his voice.

'Yes, you do. I never denied that. But there's a way of doing it, Razeby. A man might do his duty and retain something of a heart in doing so.'

'I am not without a heart, Alice.'

'Aren't you?'

'Hell, Alice. I did what I had to do.'

'In a cruel and callous way. You hurt me, Razeby!' she shouted. The words were out and there was nothing she could do to call them back. The echo of them resonated in the silence between them.

He stared down into her face, a look of horror in his eyes. 'Alice…'

'You hurt me,' she said again, more softly this time. 'I just wanted—'

'To hurt me back,' he finished quietly.

'No.' She glanced down at the small puddles that glistened on the darkness of the pavement beneath their feet. She had never meant for it to be like this. It was not supposed to be about hurting him, but denying that he had hurt her. About salvaging her pride and protecting herself. But there was an element of truth in what he said. 'I suppose I did, a little bit.' She swallowed and her throat felt dry and tight. She looked directly into his eyes. 'But you deserved it. You made me believe there was something more than sex between us. It doesn't come much more callous than that.' She turned to walk away.

He moved so fast. One minute he was standing there, the next he had her in the shadows and backed against the wall, his body so close she could feel his heat, smell the heartachingly familiar scent of him.

'You think I do not have feelings for you, Alice?' His voice was so harsh with passion that she trembled to hear it. 'You think that being apart from you is not tearing me apart?'

Her breath was as ragged as his. All she could see in the darkness was the glitter of his eyes, but she could feel the razing intensity of his stare.

'There are other factors at play, Alice. Things I could not tell you. Things I still cannot.'

'Things like you were tired of me and that it was time to move on. I saw you leaving Hart Street the other morning, Razeby.'

His eyes narrowed with both incredulity and anger. 'And you think I am keeping another woman?'

'It's what they're saying.'

'Then it must be true.' His tone was cold.

'Why else would you have stayed there overnight?'

'Why else, indeed?'

He leaned his face so close that she felt the caress of his breath against her cheek, so close that she thought he was going to kiss her.

His whisper was low and intimate, and dangerous. 'If you honestly think that, then you do not know me at all.' He looked at her for only a moment longer, then he released her and walked away into the darkness of the night.

Alice was shaking so badly that it did not matter how hard she bit upon her lip, she could not stop it. She watched him go and could not move. She stood there alone in the darkness, feeling the light patter of the rain against her hair, feeling its dampness mingle with the tears that wetted her face, as the chill of the night air seeped through her bones.

All of her defences lay in ruins around her. There could be no more denials. No more lying. Alice finally admitted the truth to herself. And with the truth came a pain that was hard to bear.

She loved Razeby.

She loved Razeby and he had broken her heart.

Chapter Thirteen

Alice was sitting exactly where Razeby had thought to find her. On the marble bench positioned in the furthest corner of the room, staring at the painting opposite. Three days had passed since that night outside her rooms, and he had come here to the Royal Academy's Exhibition Room on every one of the mornings since to look for her.

The Exhibition Room was quiet, only one or two more committed visitors having risen so early to come and study the artworks without the press of the usual crowd. The night's rain had given way to sunshine, but little of it reached in here. The light from the softly arched ceiling windows was soft and muted, illuminating only the central portion of the floor so that the richness of the paintings hanging upon the surrounding walls would not fade.

His footsteps were quiet against the wooden floor as he made his way across the gallery and sat down at the end of the bench, as if he too were studying the Canaletto's painting of Venice's Grand Canal.

She glanced round at him briefly before returning her gaze to the painting.

'How are you, Alice?' He spoke quietly, for her ears only.

'Grand.'

A pause.

'It has gone far beyond the stage of pretence, Alice. How are you really?'

'Bearing up.' She met his eyes. 'And you?'

'I have been better.'

She smiled at that, but it was a sad smile. She took a breath and returned her gaze to the painting.

'I have been sleeping alone at Hart Street because I can still smell you on the sheets and still feel your presence in the rooms.'

He heard the way she caught her breath. 'Razeby...'

'You did not really believe otherwise?'

She shook her head, but did not look round at him. 'Not in my heart.'

'I am sorry that I hurt you. I am sorry for the way I told you and for the suddenness of the parting. But clean and quick is supposed to be the best way of severing something that one has no wish to let go. I thought it was the best way for us both. I see now that it was not.'

'I'm sorry, too. I never meant to hurt you that night, Razeby. With the dress, and the music and the dance.'

'And Devlin,' he said.

'You looked as if you might be about to lynch him.'

'I came seriously close.'

She was still looking at the painting, but she smiled another smile tinged with sorrow. 'It was all as much a torture to myself.'

There was a small peaceful silence.

'How did you know I would be here?' she asked.

'Just a gut feeling.' He let his eyes sweep along the yawning turquoise of the Venetian sky upon the canvas. 'You always said this painting took you to another world. I thought we could both do with another world just now.'

Her hand lay flat upon the bench they shared. He rested his own beside it, feeling the marble of the bench cool beneath his palm. The edge of his little finger just touched against hers.

'If only.' Her expression was composed, relaxed even as her eyes rested upon the painting. 'It looks so beautiful, doesn't it? The detail of the architecture. The colour of the sky. The way the light shimmers on the water. I've never seen a sky that colour.'

'Riches for the eyes,' he said.

She gave a little laugh, but there was an unbearable sadness beneath it. 'Is Miss Althrope the one?' she asked softly.

'Not Miss Althrope. I found the one over half a year ago. I just cannot marry her.'

She closed her eyes. 'Don't.'

'Why not? It is the truth, even if it has taken me this long to realise it.'

'It'll only make it harder.'

'It could not get any harder.'

'You shouldn't be here with me, Razeby.'

'No, I should not.'

They sat in silence, their eyes fixed only on the Canaletto and another world.

And then he got to his feet and walked quietly away.

Alice kept on going. One day at a time. Acting upon the stage most evenings. Rehearsing most afternoons. Sparkling and enticing within the Green Room because that was part of her job as much as the acting, the promotions, and all the other little things that had to be done. She kept on smiling, kept her chin up. But inside she felt hollow, as if everything of any worth had been emptied from her. She kept on going, because she had to, and because she did not know any other way to be. But when no one was looking, when she was alone, it was difficult to bear.

It had been four days since he had come to the Exhibition Room. And she had taken care to avoid him on each and every one of them. Only four days and already it felt like a lifetime. She wanted to see him so much, to hear the sound of his voice, just to look into his eyes, and to see his smile. But it was better this way, she told herself, for them both. She no longer cared if the world knew she was avoiding him.

The letter arrived the following week.

Lots of men sent her letters. Alice never opened a single one, just burned them as they were. But she did not burn this one. She recognised the rich black scrawl of pen on the front before she even turned it over to see the impress of Razeby's crest in the seal. Her heart was beating too fast, her hands trembling as she cracked the thick red wax and unfolded the letter, trembling as she traced her index finger along each line of patterned ink. But it did not matter how long she stared at them, or how hard her eyes strained, there were only two words upon the page that she could read, one at the start of the letter, and the other at the end—*Alice* and *Razeby*.

She wished she had told him now. She had told him everything else. About her secret life in Mrs Silver's. About her family in Ireland. Truth and conversation had always flowed easy between them, even from the very start. And yet she had not been able to admit that

Miss Alice Sweetly, star of the stage, whom all of London thought could read and write, could do neither; that she had learned her parts only through Venetia. Being an actress was the only proper good thing Alice had ever done in her life. She could not bear to have that one achievement stripped away and be exposed as a liar, not before Razeby of all people. But standing here with Razeby's letter in her hand, she would have done just that to know what it said.

She could hardly ask a stranger to read it to her. Nor could she take it to Venetia—the letter felt too intimate, too private for that. So Alice refolded the letter very carefully and hid it in the bottom of her travelling bag next to the most precious of her possessions, the engraved pen that he had given to her. Maybe not today, but one day, in the future, she would be able to read it.

Another week passed and it felt like a month to Alice. She sat alone in the fine, gleaming new black carriage that Kemble had sent to take her to the charity auction, wearing the new dress she had collected only the day before from Madame Boisseron. Using up yet more of the money from her savings, but she knew this was something she needed to do. The neckline, high as a débutante's, would have them all talking, but Alice did not care.

The carriage rolled to a stop and the door opened. She took a deep breath, summoned up a smile and the protection of her persona, and, taking the footman's hand, let him help her down to step outside.

A crowd had gathered to watch society's richest and most famous turn out in force. Newspaper artists were sketching in a frenzy. Reporters were scribbling notes.

Voices in the crowd were shouting her name. 'Miss Sweetly!'

'Is it true that a dance with yourself is to be auctioned, Miss Sweetly?'

'Now that would be telling.' She smiled. 'You'll have to wait and see, gentlemen.'

'I'd pay me last farthing for a dance with you, Miss Sweetly,' an old man at the front of the crowd shouted. He looked poor, his face lined from a hard life.

'Then you're a very generous man, sir.'

The crowd laughed.

She walked right up to him. 'And I like a generous man.' She smiled and kissed his cheek.

The old man beamed. 'God bless you, Miss Sweetly.'

The crowd erupted in a roar of astonishment and delight, then took up the old man's chant. 'God bless you, Miss Sweetly.'

She smiled and made her way up the red carpet that lined the stone stairs up into the fine mansion house.

The light of a thousand candles magnified through the crystal drops of the chandeliers and wall scones blazed as bright as daylight dazzling her eyes. She paused for just a moment on the threshold of the ballroom, collecting herself and letting her gaze drop down to the skirt of her dress, the silk of which was newly imported from India. Its colour was a highly unusual pale-green aqua that reminded her of Canaletto's sky. It made her remember the words Razeby had uttered so quietly at the Royal Academy.

Alice took a deep breath, and Miss Sweetly, with her head held high, walked into the ballroom.

Within the charity auction ballroom, Razeby was standing with Linwood and Venetia. He had heard the crowd outside chanting Alice's name. When she walked through the door, the sight of her took his breath away. The dress she was wearing was pure, innocent almost, and yet sensually beguiling in every sense of the word. The colour made it a secret message that only he would understand.

He had thought it hard seeing her when he knew that he could not have her, hard being tortured by watching her dance with Devlin. But these past days of not seeing her were worse.

She smiled and sparkled as if nothing was different. But everything was different. It was so palpable that he wondered that everyone else could not feel it, too. She moved around, circulated, talked to those who had only bought their tickets to come here and see her. But she was very careful to keep her distance and more than careful not to look at him, not once. And by that small tell he knew that she was aware of his presence.

There was a little dancing, and then a light supper before the auction.

He drank champagne and chatted with Linwood and with Venetia, and he watched Alice. On the surface she seemed as she always did, that quiet contentment, that glow of slight innocence. But he could see beneath the façade to the real Alice and it was not happiness that he saw, but a pain and longing that mirrored his own.

On every other occasion she had danced. Tonight Alice stayed away from the dance floor. For the sake of the auction and the dance she was selling, so the whisper of explanation went.

Razeby should have been asking Miss Althrope or Lady Esme Fraser up on to the floor, but he made no move.

When it came to supper, Alice's plate held a selection from the dishes spread out within the supper room, but she ate not one single bite.

Razeby did not bother to go through the pretence of the supper.

He willed her to look at him.

But she stubbornly refused.

And then, at last, it was time for the auction to begin.

The Foundation for the Support and Education of Orphans had engaged John Philip Kemble himself to play the part of auctioneer for the evening. Kemble's noble bearing and great acting experience meant he knew exactly how to drum up interest, to create drama and effect and play a crowd. The Foundation wanted as much money wrung from the audience and Kemble was the man to do just that. He auctioned a glass of champagne with Prinny, a promenade around the room with Sally Brooke, a session of secrets and advice from the lady patronesses of Almack's on how to land your desired catch from the marriage mart—his mother had told him to bid on that one—a personal poetry recital by Lord Byron, and, at last, the one that had generated the most interest, the one for which almost every man in the room had been waiting for—a dance with Miss Alice Sweetly, the sweetheart of Covent Garden.

Kemble introduced her and Alice, clad in the Canaletto silk, walked out to stand before them all. She smiled in that slightly shy way of hers. She was not sophisticated or polished. There was nothing contrived about her in the slightest. She was uncomplicated, beautiful, honest and the warmth in her heart and her soul showed in every glance from her eyes, in her every aspect. She did not think herself some beauty, even though she was. She did not pose or pout. But that indefinable quality shone out of her brilliant as a flame in the darkness. And Razeby knew that every man standing there was helpless as a moth before its pull.

'Gentlemen, the dance for which you are bidding is…' Kemble paused for effect '…the *Volse*.'

Razeby felt the muscle of his jaw tighten.

He saw the way Alice's eyes widened ever so slightly, the hint of frozenness in her expression before she covered it with a smile. She had not known.

The hum of excitement moved through the room. The *Volse*. It was a dance of courtship and of wooing, for them at least. A scandalous dance that allowed something of an intimacy of both touching and conversation. It was a dance that belonged to Razeby and Alice.

The bidding opened up and there was so many tipping of programmes, so many nods of heads and raised hands that Razeby lost count. Like the rutting of stags, there was an undertone of competition and of pursuit. And all the while Razeby stood there and watched it, until the mêlée faded, brought low by the fierceness of the bidding and the enormity of the sums offered. Until it came down to two of the richest men in the room—Hawick and Monteith.

'Two thousand pounds,' Monteith offered.

'Two thousand one hundred,' Hawick came back.

'Two thousand, three hundred.'

Quick as a flash, Hawick replied. 'Two thousand, four hundred.'

'Two thousand, five hundred?' Kemble enquired of Monteith. But Monteith shook his head with the graciousness of the defeated.

'Two thousand, five hundred anywhere in the room?'

Razeby saw the smile that slid across Hawick's face, the certainty that he had won.

'Going,' said Kemble.

Hawick's eyes turned to claim Alice, as if she was already his.

'Going.'

Those surrounding Hawick were already shaking his hand.

'Five thousand pounds,' Razeby said in a lazy tone.

The gasp that went round the room was audible.

He saw the way both Linwood and Venetia stared at him, even their usual composure ruffled.

'Your Grace?' Kemble enquired of Hawick.

Razeby could feel the beat of his heart and hear the hiss of the collective silence within the room. It was the longest few seconds of his life.

'My congratulations to Lord Razeby,' Hawick said, but the look that he shot Razeby was a deal less friendly.

'Going.'

'Going.'

'Gone.'

Only then did Alice look at him.

'The dance is sold to Lord Razeby for the most generous sum of five thousand pounds.' Kemble was still talking, but Razeby's focus was fixed on Alice.

Chapter Fourteen

Alice's hand was in Razeby's and it did not matter that all of London was watching them, the sole couple on the dance floor—it made everything feel right. It warmed the coldness. It filled the void. It lit the light within her heart, just to be with him for these few moments.

Their steps were perfect, their bodies moving in perfect time, each a perfect complement to the other. It was their dance. And as the music, so sweet and melodic, played on she knew that she would never dance this dance with anyone else.

She looked up into his so-beloved face. 'You have created a scandal,' she said, but she could not stop herself from smiling.

'All for a good cause.' He smiled, too, that same smile of old.

And that attraction, that same connection that had existed between them from the very start, bound them stronger than ever.

'You have been avoiding me, Alice.'

'It is for the best, Razeby.' Their eyes held and the

dark liquid warmth and tenderness that she saw in his sent a thrill right through her body to her heart.

'You admit it, then?'

'I admit nothing.'

'You did not answer my letter.'

'What letter?' she said teasingly, but her heart missed a beat and her stomach gave a little somersault.

'You know very well, Miss Sweetly.'

'You must be mistaken, Lord Razeby.'

He smiled. 'Over many things, but not this.'

'I get so many letters.'

'I am sure you do.'

'Refresh my memory. What did the letter say?' She bit her lip while she waited to hear.

He lowered his voice so that it was soft and dark and smooth as black velvet. 'Do you really want me to say it aloud, Alice? Here?' The smoulder of sensuality in his eyes stroked a shiver down her spine.

She felt a faint blush warm her cheeks. 'Maybe not here,' she conceded.

They danced on.

'I know why you did not take the dresses from your wardrobe.'

Her heart skipped a beat at his words. 'Because I wanted a new wardrobe,' she replied smoothly.

'Really?' He arched an eyebrow.

'Now that I'm a famous actress I've got to be keeping up with the fashion.'

'And the diamond bracelet?'

'Diamonds are so passé. Didn't you know?' she teased.

'And the cheque?'

'Such an inadequate amount.'

'Why don't I believe you?'

'Because you've a mind that runs to suspicion.'

He smiled. 'I have another theory.'

'That I knew that you had taken to wearing ladies' dresses?'

He laughed. 'You did tell me that I looked good in your old polishing apron and nothing else.'

She couldn't help herself. She laughed, too.

And when the laughter died away and their eyes held, both were filled with the simple joy of just being together.

'No, my theory is a little different to that,' he said quietly.

Her smile faded. She swallowed, suddenly afraid. Her eyes clung to his.

'Do you not want to know what it is, Alice?'

'Not here, Razeby. Please.'

'Not here,' he said, soft as a breath against her ear.

They danced on together as all of London looked on.

Venetia sat beside Alice on the sofa of the little drawing room in Mercer Street.

'Last night, you and Razeby…' Venetia let her words drop away, but not her gaze.

Alice shook her head. 'We're not back together, if that's what you're asking.'

'It is what all of London is asking, Alice.'

She swallowed. 'Creating a bit of scandal is just a part of the job, isn't it?' But when Razeby had taken her hand in his, nothing of it had been about the job. 'And it was for charity.'

'It was. And that means that you can get away with it. But you only get to play that card once.'

Alice did not meet her eyes. She knew the truth in what Venetia was saying. They had got away with it this once. They would not get away with it again.

'Are you still playing your dangerous game with him?'

Alice shook her head. 'I never really was.'

'You have feelings for one another.'

Venetia's words were not a question but Alice nodded her admission, glancing down at her tea, knowing she could no longer pretend a denial.

'Oh, Alice,' Venetia said softly. 'What are you going to do?'

'Keep on going. Me in the theatre. Him finding a wife. There's nothing else we can do, is there?'

'No, I suppose there is not,' agreed Venetia, and gave her a little hug.

They drank their tea in silence.

Razeby was not faring any better.

His mother had come to call upon him at his house in Leicester Square with a rather obvious purpose in mind.

'You look tired, darling. Did you have a late night?' His mother touched a hand to his cheek as she scrutinised his face.

'No.' He did not elaborate.

She took her seat on the sofa and turned her attention to the tea tray. 'I took tea with Teresa Darrington yesterday.' Her focus was seemingly all on her tea-making ritual, but Razeby was not fooled.

'Did you?' He stood by the mantel, watching her measure out two rounded dessert spoons of tea leaves into the tea pot before carefully locking the caddy and pocketing the key. Alice refused to lock away the tea from her servants. *What harm does it do if they take a little to make a bit of extra money for themselves, as long as they aren't greedy?* she always said. It was typical of her attitude to life.

'The family are somewhat parochial—they come from trade—but a good alliance nevertheless,' said the Dowager Lady Razeby.

'Because Darrington is minted?' He wondered whether his mother had read the newspaper reports over him and Alice at the auction.

'There is no need to be so vulgar, James. But yes, if you wish to put it in such a fashion. He owns half the mills in Yorkshire and has vast investments overseas. And his lands...' She lifted the kettle from its small lagged box and poured the hot water into the tea pot.

'Run concurrent with Razeby,' he finished.

'Miss Darrington, his only child and heiress to the entirety of his fortune, is making her come out this Season. Perhaps you have already met her?'

'I do not recall.'

She gave the tea in the pot a stir and replaced the lid before turning over the small timer that still sat upon the tea tray to time the brew. His mother was very precise in the way she liked her tea. 'I thought to invite Miss Darrington and her mother to accompany us on our little outing next weekend.'

His eyes focused the grains of sand rushing too fast through the narrow glass of the timer. Rushing like all of life around him, when the only haven within it was Alice.

The ticking of the clock was loud within the quietness of the room. The timer was almost done.

He gave a nod, but it felt like there was an iron band around his chest that was growing only tighter.

'Splendid,' his mother pronounced. 'I thought you would agree. I will send a note round to Mrs Darrington today.' She smiled and, as the last grains of sand slipped through the timer, lifted the teapot to pour the tea.

Alice kept on going, just as she had told Venetia she would. Every afternoon she rehearsed on stage. And every evening she performed before a packed theatre. And just as ever, all the emotions that she was trying to hide were channelled into the parts she played. But it was growing more difficult. There was a sense that the boundaries between the roles and reality were beginning to blur.

She cut back on the promotions she accepted. She was afraid of seeing Razeby again and even more afraid of not seeing him. Afraid that he had guessed the truth in full. *I know why you did not take the dresses from your wardrobe.* The words haunted her.

He was searching for a bride. This could not be. She had to avoid him, to stay as far away from as she could, she told herself determinedly again and again. But what she felt in her heart was something else altogether.

She yearned to see him, longed to hear the sound of his voice, needed to feel the warmth of his eyes, the touch of his hand. It felt like part of herself was missing.

She filled every minute of every day with activity, filled her mind with lines and acting and everything she could, but none of it made any difference. Amidst all of the activity and the people who surrounded her she was lonely. Amidst all she tried to cram into her head he was still there in her thoughts. Always. As if he were a part of herself that she could not deny.

At night she could not sleep. In the mornings she could not wake. And in between she still put a smile on her face. With dogged determination she still kept going. She still sparkled in the Green Room. But it was becoming harder with every day that passed. In her ear was the whisper of his name. And in her heart was the beat of his. And she had the sense that something bigger than either of them had been set in motion that they were powerless to stop.

Time was running out as surely as the grains of sand in his mother's tea timer.

Razeby knew that every accusation about prevaricating, about making excuses and stalling for time over finding a woman to marry was true. When he stood in that ballroom at Almack's all he could think about was Alice. The dance at the auction had buoyed him, elated him almost, but now, as the days passed without a sign of her at a single function, the feeling had faded to be replaced instead with a sense of bleakness.

He needed to marry. Before his thinking had been so clear. Black and white. Now he saw only shades of grey. And what he thought about, what he dreamed about, what he could not get out of his head was not the future of Razeby, not the days that were ticking down to his thirtieth birthday, but Alice Sweetly.

'A little water clears us of this deed.' Within the empty Covent Garden theatre came the prompt for the fourth time that afternoon.

'A little water clears us of this deed,' Alice said.

'Everyone take a break. We will reconvene in half an hour,' Kemble ordered.

The stage cleared of everyone except Alice and Kemble. He walked over to her.

'I'm sorry for fluffing the line.' She smiled and gave a little shake of her head, trying to clear the thick cotton wool feeling from it. 'I must be a bit tired today.' She could not remember the last time she had slept the night through.

Kemble was both an acclaimed actor and a manager. And as such he had high standards, he pushed hard, expected much. The slip was not her first. There had been too many of late. All those lines she was holding in her head were becoming confused and slow to recall—Alice, whose memory had never been anything other than perfect. It was how she had managed to fool people for so long over her inability to read. She expected him to harangue her, but Kemble did not look angry, only worried.

'You look pale, Alice.'

'I always look pale when I've no make-up on my face.'

'You've been working too hard of late.'

'Not hard enough.' Razeby was still there in her head and in her heart.

'You need some time off. Some early nights. A rest.'

'I don't need a rest.' If she rested, she would start thinking more and she did not want to think, could not bear to think as it was.

'In my opinion, you do,' Kemble countered.

'No, I—'

He placed a fatherly hand on hers. 'I need you at

your best, Alice. I need Miss Sweetly to sparkle and be happy. We all do.'

'I am sparkling, aren't I?' she asked, suddenly afraid.

'You will be again, after a rest. Sort out whatever is going on in your life and come back in a week.'

She kneaded her fingers against the tight spot on her forehead.

'They will want you all the more for the absence. And I do not want to risk losing you.'

She took a breath.

'Will you get through tonight's performance all right, Alice?

'Of course I will. I'm fine, really I am.' But she was not fine. She knew that. And so did he.

He nodded and called over to a stage hand, 'Have a cup of tea taken to Miss Sweetly's dressing room.' Then, to Alice, 'Go and take your break. And then we will rehearse a little more before tonight.'

Razeby stood by the unlit fireplace in his study as Linwood took his seat in one of the nearby winged leather chairs. The morning light seemed harsher than normal, the ticking of the clock too loud.

Linwood's eyes moved to the empty brandy glass that sat upon the mantelpiece, although he made no comment upon it.

'Bad night, Razeby?'

Razeby glanced away. More an impossible night in which all that was happening haunted him and made sleep impossible.

'You did not go to Almack's.'

'No.'

The clock ticked louder.

'This is to do with you and Alice, is it not?' Linwood asked quietly.

Razeby raked a hand through his hair and did not deny it.

'You still want her.' Not a question, just a statement.

'I have never stopped wanting her.' Although want was not the right word. It was too petty and inadequate to describe what he felt about Alice. He gave a dry laugh and shook his head. 'I have never felt like this before, Linwood. Never felt what I feel for her for any other woman.'

Linwood gave a slight nod, as if he understood. 'It is hard when it happens.'

'I did not think it would be like this.'

'Does Alice feel the same?'

'We are stepping round it, Linwood, and I cannot blame her. She will admit nothing, but I believe the feeling is reciprocated.'

'You know that what is between the two of you—it is not going to go away, Razeby.'

'I know.' Razeby lifted the decanter and poured some brandy into his empty glass, before offering it to Linwood, who declined. He swallowed his own measure down in one go, but the burn and the strength of the alcohol did nothing to numb what he was feeling.

There was a small silence.

'Have you considered the unthinkable solution?'

'Were it that easy, I would make Alice my wife and all of society be damned.' He gave a bitter laugh. 'Just now she is their golden Miss Sweetly, but you, more than most, Linwood, know what they would do to her—what they did to Venetia, who is the daughter of a duke no less. And your family closed around her to ease her way. Alice has no such link to either nobility or gentility. You and I both know her past.'

'Few enough others do.'

'Even so.' He shook his head. 'Do you think my mother would take her to her bosom and protect her as Lady Misbourne does with Venetia?'

Linwood gave no reply, so Razeby told him the answer. 'I care for my mother, Linwood, but I am under no illusion as to her prejudices. She would feed Alice to the lions rather than have her in our family. Just now Alice is the *ton's* darling, but it would not be so were I to make her my wife. She would be ostracised, cast out, treated like a leper.' He rubbed a hand against his forehead. 'And I will not always be here to protect her.'

'You will be here long enough to—'

But Razeby held up his hand to stop him. 'I cannot marry her, Linwood.'

The silence hissed between them.

'The question is, feeling the way that you do, can you marry another?'

'I have to.' Every time he closed his eyes he saw the grains of sand slipping through that tea timer. 'There must be an heir for Razeby.'

'Then you had better stay away from Alice.'

'I know.' Razeby gave a smile that held nothing of happiness. 'It should be easy enough done. She is avoiding me.'

'Then it sounds as if she is doing the best that she can for you both.'

Razeby knew that. He knew he had to stay away from her.

He knew that he had to marry.

He knew what was coming.

And none of it made any difference. He still craved to see Alice with all of his heart.

Chapter Fifteen

Alice cancelled her engagements and stayed in her rooms for the next few days. She was no longer confident that if she were to see Razeby she would be able to hide from the world what she felt for him. Her sensibilities were running so wild that she felt like she was going mad. She needed to step back from it, to take charge of herself. Maybe Kemble was right, maybe she was just working too hard. Maybe she just needed to get some sleep. And then she would be able to don her mask once more, hiding the truth from the world, and from Razeby himself.

She did everything she could to make that happen. And she polished, polished for hours, polished for days. Polished until every inch of wood in those rooms gleamed and the air was sweet with lavender and beeswax. But none of it helped.

In the end she surrendered to the one thing that made her feel closest to him. She ran her fingers over the engraving on the barrel of the silver pen he had given to her, smiling a bittersweet smile at the message.

She took Razeby's letter from its hiding place at the bottom of her travelling bag and tried so many times to read the words he had written. It was useless, of course. There was no magical wand that made sense of the letters and words. And at the end of the day it did not really matter what he had written, for it did not change anything of the situation.

At night she dreamed that Razeby was making love to her. It felt so real that she could smell the scent of him, feel the warmth of his skin against hers, hear his voice calling her name and her body was welcoming his as she woke.

'Razeby,' she whispered his name as the dream slipped away and, in realising that it was just a dream, she felt the loss stronger than ever.

And so it went on, until her friends came to call.

'Where have you been hiding yourself, girl?' Tilly asked. 'We ain't seen you in an age and it's all over the newspapers that Miss Bolton is in your part at the Theatre Royal.'

'Kemble's just trying to stir a bit extra interest in the place. Making a mystery out of nothing to intrigue them.'

'He tell you to lie low, did he?' Tilly asked.

Alice gave a nod. 'Just for the week.' It wasn't exactly a lie, just slightly misleading.

'We were worried about you,' said Ellen, her gaze too shrewd as she studied Alice's face.

'I appreciate the sentiment, but there's nothing to worry about. Honest.'

'What you been up to then?' Tilly sat down beside her. 'Bet you don't know what to be doing with your time.'

'Catching up with some long-overdue sleep and letting my skin breathe; that stage paint doesn't half play havoc with my face.' It was an excuse for the shadows beneath her eyes and the pallor of her cheeks.

'We didn't like to say,' teased Ellen.

Alice smiled. It was the first time she had smiled in days. Already she felt better with her friends' presence.

'You're not being entirely honest with us, Miss sneaky Sweetly.' Ellen drew her a look.

Alice kept the smile on her face, but her heart skipped a beat. 'I'm sure I don't know what you mean.' She said it teasingly, but there was a sudden tension in her stomach.

Ellen gave a sniff of the air.

Tilly giggled. 'Your secret's out, Alice. The place is stinking of lavender and beeswax.'

Alice held her hands up. 'I admit it. I did have a quick little polish.'

All three women laughed.

'We've organised a night out at the theatre tomorrow with a few of the girls,' said Tilly. 'Hired a posh box at the side, with a good view of the stage. We know visiting the theatre's nothing special for you, I mean you're there nearly every day. But it'd be an experience to see it from the other side. To be one of the audience. And you'll be with us. It'll be a laugh. Say you'll come.'

'I shouldn't really.' But Alice was tempted.

'Staying in these four walls all day and all night until the end of the week will drive you mad, Alice,' said Ellen.

'Maybe you're right,' she admitted. Staying within them the last few days had not exactly helped.

Ellen smiled. 'You know we are.'

'All right then. Tomorrow night it is.' Alice smiled. Maybe a night with her friends was just what she needed.

Razeby knew he was being a fool, that still staying here alone in Hart Street was just torturing himself unnecessarily. But he had a perverse sense of needing to be here. Every room in the house held some lingering echo of Alice's presence. Within the bedchamber they had shared he stood by the window and watched the sun set, sipping his brandy and trying not to think of the night ahead with Miss Darrington and his mother.

Tilly had been right. It was a novelty for Alice to see the theatre from the audience's side. For too long she had only stood up there on that stage she knew so well. Tonight was different.

She had taken care with the rice powder and rouge to repair the shadows and the pallor that betrayed the truth upon her face. She wore the green silk, not to prove that she did not care, but to prove that she did. It made her feel connected to him. And she had been safe in the knowledge that he would not be at the theatre. But she had been wrong.

She sat in the box along with Tilly and Ellen and four other women, watching the players on the stage without seeing a thing of it. It was the dress that had brought him here, she thought. It had a magic all of its own. And she did not know whether to weep or to rejoice over it, because both those urges were vying in her breast.

'I'm glad we persuaded you into accompanying us.' Tilly slipped her arm through Alice's. 'We couldn't leave you in your rooms all alone, on a Saturday night, polishing furniture. I don't know why you don't get them maids of yours to do it.'

'I like wood polishing. It gives me a sense of satisfaction.' Alice did not tell them that she only polished when she was feeling anxious.

'I like polishing wood, too,' said Ellen. 'Just not the kind you're talking of.' She raised her eyebrows suggestively. Everyone laughed. Including Alice.

She was strong and resolute for such a long time, keeping her gaze fixed firmly on the stage below. Not once did she turn her head to look over towards Razeby's private box. But she knew he was there by the way Ellen's eyes turned too often towards it and the looks the women exchanged when they thought she would not see.

Tilly leaned closer to her and lowered her voice. 'We didn't know that he'd be here and with Miss Darrington, honest, we didn't.'

'Who's here?' she asked, as if there could be any other man in the world.

Tilly smiled. 'That's the spirit, girl. Sod him!'

Alice forced a smile. 'I hope not.'

They all laughed at the rude joke.

Then they all settled to watch the play—*All's Well That Ends Well*. A woman of low birth who was in love with a nobleman who was both beyond her and had no wish to be married to her. And then the low-born woman, Helena, spoke the words, 'T'were all one that I should love a bright particular star, and think to wed it.'

It was as if Alice could have spoken them herself of Razeby. They just seemed to reach inside her and touch the nub of all that was between them. It took so much effort not to flinch, not to tremble, not to show a single sign of it.

She dare not look away from the stage lest her eye found Razeby and Miss Darrington. And yet there was a lump in her throat that she could not swallow and the dangerous prickle of tears in her eyes. She managed through all of the first act and most of the second, before she knew that if she did not get out of this auditorium at that very moment she, who never wept, would disgrace herself by weeping in public.

'Please excuse me a moment, won't you? I'm away to the ladies',' she whispered to Ellen.

'Do you want me to come with you?' Ellen asked.

Alice shook her head. 'I'll only be few minutes.'

She escaped from the box and hurried out into the foyer, desperate for some small place to be alone. Just a few minutes in which to compose herself. Just a moment's relief from this torture of emotions. She could not hide from him for ever. It would get easier with time. It had to get easier with time, for she did not think she could keep going like this.

The foyer was quiet, not another soul present. Floating through from the auditorium she could hear the faint voices from the stage and, more loudly, the audience's reactions. She leaned back against the wall and closed her eyes, trying to find the strength to get through the rest of the evening.

'Alice.' At first she thought she was imagining his voice. Her heart missed a beat and then began to thunder. She opened her eyes to find Razeby standing before her.

'I saw you leave your box. Are you unwell?'

'I'm fine,' she said and tried to smile, but her lips would not curve to her will. 'I just needed a breath of air, that's all.'

They stared at one another. The faint noises from the auditorium and stage seemed very far away. Out here, standing with him, they might have been the only two people in the world.

'You have not been on stage for the past few days.'

'It's Kemble's idea of stirring more interest in the theatre.' She used the same excuse.

'When there's not a seat to be had at your every appearance?' He raised his eyebrows ever so slightly.

The silence hissed between them.

'Nor have you attended any of the dances or events.'

'I've just been taking a bit of a rest.'

'I know you are avoiding me, Alice.'

She shook her head, but her eyes never left his and she saw the shadows beneath them where before there had been none. 'You look tired, Razeby.'

'So everyone keeps telling me.'

'I'm sorry,' she said.

'So am I,' he said and she knew it was not the fatigue on his face that they were talking about.

'I should go back in. The girls will be wondering where I've got to.' But she made no move to leave.

'About those dresses in your wardrobe...'

'Don't, Razeby...please.'

'Not here, either?' He raised his eyebrows again but he was smiling and there was a gentle teasing in his voice.

'Definitely not here.' She smiled.

They looked at one another and there was such a depth of emotion between them that their smiles faded.

'I do know the reason, Alice.'

She closed her eyes. 'No,' she whispered and shook her head.

'I thought that seeing you and not being able to have you was a torture. But not seeing you is even worse.'

'I feel the same.' She clutched a hand to her forehead. 'But we can't be doing this, Razeby.

'I cannot stop, Alice.'

She stared at him. There was no teasing between them now. There was no smile, no laughter. Only dark intensity and brutal honesty and the agony of longing.

The silence seemed to roar.

He stepped closer, his eyes locked with hers. 'I miss you, Alice. So much.'

He was so close she could see every golden striation in the dark velvet-brown of his eyes, every dark lash, the first hint of blue shadow upon his jaw line. She could smell the scent of him that she knew each night in her dreams. And she could not stop all that was in her heart to swell and respond.

'I miss you, too, Razeby.'

A noise sounded somewhere in the near distance, someone leaving their box and coming out into the foyer.

Razeby reacted in an instant. He grabbed her hand and pulled her with him down the closest passageway that led from the foyer. Halfway along, he guided her along another passageway and then into another recess that led from it. He backed her against the wall, shielding her from view of anyone who might happen to pass. Except there was nobody else down this maze of passageways. No footsteps. Not even any noise from the auditorium. Only the sound of her breath too loud in her ears and the hard frenzied thud of her heart.

He was standing too close, his fingers still wrapped around hers. She knew she should not be here with him, that she should disengage her hand and walk away, but she did none of those things.

The touch of him, the feel of him… He rubbed his thumb against her fingers, in that small familiar gesture.

'We shouldn't be doing this,' she whispered, but her fingers entwined with his.

'We shouldn't,' he agreed as his free hand moved to gently cup her cheek. And in his eyes she saw all of what had always raged between them.

'Razeby,' she whispered. There was so much they could not say, so much tension, so much longing. She could feel it sparking in the air, like the terrible hush before the ferocity of a storm, feel it whispering across her skin and throbbing in her blood.

'Alice.' His eyes darkened. There was a fierceness to the handsomeness of his face, a torment that mirrored her own. She wanted him as she had never wanted him before. She needed him. It had been so lonely without him.

His hand slid round to the nape of her neck, then up into her hair, holding it firm. 'Alice,' he said again and his voice was hoarse and tortured.

Their eyes were locked only on each other, the moment stretched to a roaring eternity. And then, at last, he angled her face, and his mouth descended to crush hers.

Razeby. His name echoed through her mind, through her very being as she gave herself up to him, yielding to the fierce possession of his lips, giving all her heart had to give and receiving all of his in return.

There was nothing of the theatre. Nothing of shame or guilt or anything that was wrong. There was only this moment, this man that she loved with all that she was. He was the other half of herself. Her heart. Her very life. Here before her, like breath to a woman who had been slowly suffocating.

'Razeby.' This time the word escaped aloud, as her teeth scraped his chin, as her hands slid within his waistcoat and pulled his shirttails loose from his breeches that she might touch the familiar warm nakedness of his skin.

There could be nothing of resistance. The torrent that whirled between them was too strong. She surrendered to it, giving herself up to his kiss and all of the fury and passion and love that was in it. Against her thigh she could feel the hard press of his arousal and she longed for him, wanted him, needed him. She could not stop herself. Her hand slid to touch him there in that most private of places, feeling the large rigid bulge through his breeches.

He sucked in his breath, jerked beneath her fingers. 'I need you, Alice,' he whispered hot and harsh against her ear, biting gently at its lobe so that the fire in her thighs flared hotter and higher.

'I need you, too,' she admitted, and her voice was breathless as his.

All of time seemed to stop. Their eyes held for the expanse of the moment. They both knew it was inevitable. They both knew they were powerless against the force of what raged between them. In the silence all around the raggedness of their breath was deafening. Their gazes clung as the moment stretched beyond endurance. Trying to fight it and failing.

'Oh, Razeby,' she whispered. And then the last of their resistance, if there had ever really been any, crumbled. Razeby backed her against the wall and pulled her skirts up, sliding his fingers against her slick wetness.

Her fingers fumbled with the buttons on his breeches. His own closed over their tremble for a moment, looking deep into her eyes as he made short work of the buttons and freed himself from his drawers.

She moved her hand to stroke the silken length of him.

He wrenched her skirts higher.

She wound her arms around his neck as he lifted her up and plunged his heated length into her.

She gasped her relief, welcoming him back to the place where only he belonged.

'Do you want this?' he whispered. 'Do you want me?'

'You and no other, Razeby,' she replied with ragged breath.

'You and no other, Alice,' he said and thrust within her.

It was everything that was right, this mating, this coupling with the man that she loved. She needed him. She needed this physical joining with him, this reunification of two halves to make a whole. She met his every urgent thrust with the power of her own, groaning aloud at the ferocious intensity of it. So much need, so much love that she did not know if she could bear it. Their bodies strove together, rode together in unfettered abandon until they gasped aloud, rocking and exploding simultaneously in a union of utter love. And the glory of it was blinding. Alice ceased to exist. Razeby, likewise. There was starlight and sunlight and time itself seemed to shatter into a silver white myriad so that there was nothing, absolutely nothing save the merging of their two souls.

She cleaved to him and he cleaved to her.

'Alice,' he whispered and it seemed that every stroke of love that beat in her heart for him echoed in that one word.

'My love,' she whispered, unable to help herself.

He kissed her, and she could taste the salt of tears on her lips, but whether it was from his eyes or her own she did not know.

In the distance a bell rang, sounding the start of the interval.

Their bodies did not want to part.

There was the opening and shutting of doors, the hum of voices not so far away in the foyer.

And still he stood there inside her, their hearts beating in unison.

His eyes held hers.

She took his dear, dear face in both her hands, stroking his skin, staring into his eyes with all the love that she felt for him, her heart tender and aching. 'This is impossible, Razeby. You know that, don't you?'

'I know.' He closed his eyes and touched his lips to her forehead. 'God help us both, Alice,' he whispered.

Footsteps sounded, coming down the corridor. Yet still she could not move. It was Razeby who made them both decent, Razeby who shielded her from the view of whoever passed. The footsteps did not stop, just continued until they receded into the distance.

'There you are, Alice,' Tilly exclaimed and linked her arm through Alice's as she stepped alone into the now-crowded foyer. 'We wondered where you'd got to.'

Ellen was there, her perceptive eyes scanning Alice's face. 'Are you all right?'

Alice felt her cheeks warm beneath the scrutiny. 'Of course I am,' she said and turned her gaze back to the brash safety of Tilly.

After the interval was over they returned to the auditorium. And when the players were once more playing upon the stage and the lights had dimmed and the audience settled again within their seats, Alice's eyes found Razeby's box. He sat there, cool and dark and handsome. And across the distance and all of those people his gaze was not upon the stage or on the rich young woman who sat by his side, but on Alice.

God help them both, indeed.

After the theatre was over and the Darringtons and his mother delivered safely home, Razeby sat alone in the study of his town house in Leicester Square. An oil-painted portrait of his father, the seventh Marquis of Razeby, painted by Sir Joshua Reynolds, looked out at him from above the fireplace. A man so much like himself that it was like looking at his own reflection. The same dark hair, the same brown eyes, the same cleft in his chin. His father had been twenty-nine years old when the portrait had been painted. The same age as Razeby was now. A year later his father was cold in the ground. Dead at only thirty from a consumption of the lungs.

But he had done his duty and left behind a son to carry on the name and line. And Razeby had known his whole life that he must do the same.

'Was it ever the same for you?' he whispered and wondered for the first time at his parents' marriage. He did not think so. They had married young. His mother was the daughter of a minor baron. But he had never before thought to question whether his parents had been happy together. Whether they had been in love. Or if there had been another woman before her, a woman his father could not marry...a woman whom he loved.

He poured himself another brandy and drank it too quickly.

'Hell,' he cursed beneath his breath. Hell—for, in truth, that is what he felt he was in. Every time he closed his eyes it was Alice's face he saw, that shy and joyous smile that made his heart fill with a warmth, those beautiful blue eyes either teasing and playful, or dark blue as a summer midnight, half-closed in passion. There had been a bond between them right from that first night in the Green Room. She could tease him and beguile him. She could make him feel comfortable, at ease and excited all at once. He felt as though she understood him completely and that he understood her. And he missed that easiness, that natural affinity, that connection. In the meeting of eyes, in words, in a smile and in laughter. He missed just being with her. For him there had never been another woman like her. And there never would be. She was the one, in truth, just as he had told her that day in the Royal Academy.

He took a swig of the brandy. He had been under the same sentence his whole life, knowing what was coming. Knowing he would not live beyond thirty. And because of that he had made damn sure that he had lived his life. Squeezing every last drop from it, living every minute, taking it right up to the brink. But that had been before Alice.

Before Alice he had thought that living life to the full was about indulging himself, thrill seeking, hedonistic pleasures. That was what Alice was supposed to have been. An affair. One last blast in the dying light of the day. Something meant to last a few weeks until he got the lust and passion for her out of his system. But being with her had changed everything. Now he understood the difference between pleasure and happiness. Now he understood what it was to love.

He topped up the brandy glass and, sipping the rich heat of its contents, stood by the window watching the quiet darkness of the night. In his nose was the scent of Alice and on his body was the feel of hers. And he knew after what had happened between them in the theatre tonight that he could not marry another woman.

Love or duty?

Such a big question. A conflict that had battled within him since meeting Alice Sweetly. But after tonight there was no other choice he could make. He stood there and watched the dawn break through the darkness of the sky.

It had rained in the night, but this morning the sky was blue and the sun filtered in through the windows of the rented rooms in Mercer Street. Alice pulled the blanket tighter around her and thought of last night at the theatre. Her body felt alive, blooming from his touch. And yet her heart ached all the more. She was angry at her own weakness, but she knew now that the strength of what was between them was greater than all else.

She desired him. She longed for him. She loved him. And what had happened between them had been as natural as breathing. She could still smell his scent upon her, still feel the caress of his fingers upon her skin, still hear the whisper of his words against her ear. And if he came to her right now, even knowing that to love him was wrong and that it would only make things worse, she knew that she would do the same again.

She thought of rich Miss Darrington sitting beside Razeby in his theatre box. It did not matter that it was Alice who Razeby had made love to in the quiet corner of the theatre, it was Miss Darrington, or a woman like her, who he would marry. And that woman who would bear his children. And that thought served only to break her heart a little more.

In future she must avoid him completely, must walk out of the room when she saw him, no matter how blatant it was before all London. And never, ever be alone with him. It was the only way. Now that she knew she could not trust herself when it came to him.

It was late afternoon the next day that the maid came to Alice's bedchamber to tell her that Lord Razeby was waiting for her in the parlour.

She felt her heart skip a beat and her stomach give a somersault as she seemingly calmly set down the duster and jar of polish upon the dressing-room table. 'I told you that I was not at home to any visitors.'

The maid's cheeks coloured. 'He was most insistent, ma'am. I couldn't stop him.'

Alice gave a nod, knowing that she was being unfair; the girl would not have stood a chance against Razeby at his most determined. 'Tell him I'll be down shortly.'

But as she spoke the words there was a knock at the bedchamber door and she knew it was him standing there on the other side of it even though he made no move to open it.

A whisper of panic fluttered through her. She closed her eyes trying to control it. And knew she was going to have to fight not him, but herself, to send him away.

'It's all right, Meg, you may let him in and then leave us.'

The girl gave a nod and a curtsy, then did as Alice bade.

Razeby just stood there, leaning against the door frame.

'You shouldn't be here, Razeby.'

'I came to speak to you.'

'We did quite enough speaking last night at the theatre.'

'Not nearly enough.' His words made her heart flip-flop and her blood rush all the faster.

'What happened last night shouldn't have. We both know that. This is only making it worse. You have to leave. Now.' Before she yielded and made love to him again. 'I've got nothing more to say to you, Razeby.'

'But I have certainly got something more to say to you, Alice.'

Chapter Sixteen

Razeby paused. 'There is something I wish to ask you, Alice.'

'Then go downstairs and wait for me in the drawing room. We can talk there.' She was too conscious of the bed behind her and the way her body was already reacting to his presence, and the throb of her heart.

But Razeby's shoulder did not shift from where it leaned against the door jamb. His eyes dropped from her face, moved slowly over her body, before moving on to the gleaming polished surface of the dressing table, complete with its cloth and pot of beeswax and lavender polish, before returning again to her face.

'Are you feeling a little anxious, Alice?' he asked in a low velvet voice that stroked all the way through her. She shivered and he smiled.

Considerably so since his arrival. She glanced down at the plain worn apron still tied tight over her dress and blushed. Her fingers were trembling as she made to unfasten the tapes, pulling them into a knot in her fluster.

'Allow me.' He walked slowly to close the space between them. She closed her eyes as his fingers brushed lightly against the small of her back.

'You really shouldn't be here, Razeby.'

'So you have already told me.' He smiled again and the apron gaped free.

She swallowed and, after easing it over her head, paid unnecessary close attention to folding it into a small neat square.

Razeby took it from her fingers and slipped it into the pocket of his tailcoat.

'You aren't playing fair,' she whispered and turned to look up into his eyes.

'Fairer than you realise,' he said.

They looked at one another and she felt that same anguish and love vie in her heart.

'What do you want?'

'You,' he answered.

She sighed and closed her eyes. 'It's impossible,' she whispered beneath her breath. To resist him. For things to continue in this way. 'We can't do this. *I* can't do it. Don't you understand?'

'I understand too well.'

'Then why are you here?'

'For you.'

'I don't understand.' She shook her head, confused, hurt, both wanting him to leave and needing him to stay.

'I love you, Alice.'

'Oh, God!' she gasped and clutched a trembling hand to her mouth. 'What are you doing to me, Razeby?'

'Telling you the truth. Asking you to marry me.'

She gaped at him. Her knees felt weak. The blood roared in her head.

He caught her to him, holding her upright.

'This jest is too cruel,' she whispered and she was shaking like a leaf.

'It is no jest.'

She stared at him, wondering if he was drunk. 'Have you been at the brandy?'

'Not a drop has passed my lips today.' He smiled at her and inside her chest her heart felt like it blossomed.

'You can't marry me.' she said fiercely.

'Why? Won't you have me?'

'I'm an actress, Razeby.'

'I know what you are.'

'We're not like Venetia and Linwood. She might have been an actress, but her father was a duke. And Linwood's neck was in a noose. All of London understood why they married. And can forgive them because of it.' She swallowed. 'But it isn't the same for us. Look at me. I was born and brought up in a one-bedroom cottage outside Dublin, barefoot and lucky to have a single dress to my name. I was a whore in a bawdy house!'

He just held her gaze with steady brown eyes.

'I'd ruin you. And Razeby. All that your family worked so hard for. London would crucify us both were we to marry.'

'They would,' he agreed. 'And I would never leave you to face their wrath.'

'You're a marquis, Razeby. There's no getting away from that.'

'Is there not?'

She wrinkled her brow in confusion and shook her head. 'You've lost me.'

'I do not have to be a marquis.'

'If you haven't been on the brandy you've run mad.'

'I am thinking more sanely than I have done in weeks.'

'Then please tell me what you're talking of because I don't understand what you're saying.'

'It comes down to duty or you, Alice. And I choose you.' She stared at him, unable to believe the words he was saying. Like those of a dream, more than she could ever have hoped for or imagined.

'I do not have to be the Marquis of Razeby. I will give it all up for you; let Atholl run the place. He has a good head on his shoulders. And he will need something to focus upon when he returns home to England. He's not going to be going anywhere else for a very long time.'

'You can't just give up an inherited title, can you? I didn't think it worked like that.'

'It does not. But if I were to disappear, taking nothing more that the clothes I stood up in…' He raised his brows. 'We could run away together, Alice. Go abroad. After a certain amount of time had elapsed I would be declared dead and the title and estate and all that goes with it would pass to the next male in line—which is Atholl. And the seat of Razeby would continue in a fashion.'

'You're serious!'

'Never more so.'

She was reeling, shocked, hardly able to believe that he was willing to give up all that he had been born to, all that he cared for and loved, for her.

'I want you as my wife, Alice. And if this is the only way that I might have you, then it is what I shall do. So, Alice—' their gaze had not separated for a moment '—will you marry plain James Brundell?'

It seemed that her heart had swelled to fill all of her chest, and it glowed with a rainbow of glorious colour. He loved her. He wanted her for his wife. It was her heart's desire. He was her everything. *Yes!* she wanted to say. *Yes!* To yell it from the tree tops and press her mouth to his and kiss him with all that was in her heart. And if she did not love him so very much she would have done just that. She would have wrapped her arms around him and told him that she would marry him whatever name he called himself, if had not one farthing to it, and they had to live together in a one-room shack for the rest of their lives. But she did love him, and because she loved him she knew she could do none of that.

'What you're proposing is of such magnitude for your life, for your people, for all that you have been raised to be.'

'That is my decision to make.'

'You're talking about walking away from everything you are. From everything you love.'

'Not everything.' The look in his eyes was fiercely possessive.

'To be declared dead and have another man step into your shoes… I can't let you do that, Razeby.'

'We all die sooner or later,' he said softly, and there was a calm acceptance upon his face as he said those words.

'But to walk away from your duty would grieve you for every hour of every day,' she whispered.

He did not deny it. 'Not having you would be a worse death. I choose the lesser of the two evils. You shall not dissuade me from it, Alice. My mind is made up.' It was the truth. She recognised the stubborn determination in his eyes.

He was selling his soul to have her. And it really would destroy him. Maybe not today or even tomorrow. But the day would come eventually. And by then it would be too late to rectify. There would be no going back. And she could not let that happen.

'I'll come back to you. Move back into Hart Street as your mistress. Marry your Miss Darrington, or whomever you will. We can be discreet. I can bear it, Razeby.'

He smiled at her, and touched his thumb ever so gently to the centre of her lips. 'But I could not.' He looked into her eyes. 'It is you that I want, Alice, you that I love. I cannot marry another.'

She could have wept from joy and from sadness. Razeby, a man to whom honour and duty was everything. His love for her would tear him apart. Already she knew what she was going to have to do. There never really had been any decision to make, other than the way she must be sure to do it.

'I…I need some time to think, Razeby.'

'Not Razeby any longer. Just plain James.'

'James, then.' She smiled to soften her reply.

But he did not return the smile. 'What is there to think about?'

'Everything,' she said. And nothing. 'It's not every day a girl gets asked to wed.'

'I suppose not.' He smiled that glorious smile of his and gave a nod. 'Twenty-four hours, Alice. Not a minute longer. And I will be back for your answer.'

He kissed her fiercely with all the same passion and love that she could feel racing and throbbing through her own body. She clung to him and when he would have left she did not let him go, but held him to her and stroked his face, and kissed him more tenderly and with all the love that was in her heart.

'Let me love you, Razeby…' she said and did not speak the rest of the words. *One last time.*

He could not deny her, not when his body longed for hers and he wanted to climb in that bed with her and love her with everything that he was. A thousand times over and it would never be enough. He wanted her. All of her. For ever.

She unfastened the buttons of his breeches, pushed aside his drawers and freed his manhood into her hands. He was hard for her. Aching for her. She closed her hand around him and moved him within. Softly at first and then more firmly. He clenched his jaw to keep from losing control and caught hold of her wrist to stop her.

'On the bed. Now,' she whispered.

He peeled off his tailcoat, threw his waistcoat to follow and, pulling her into his arms, backed them both to the bed.

'I am yours to command,' he said as he gathered her skirts high and laid her gently down upon the covers. His gaze swept over her fair hair tumbling from its pins, at her kiss-swollen lips and the dark desire in her eyes, and the place between her legs that was so ready for him. He covered her body with his, their mouths clinging together, sharing lips and breath and tongues. But when he would have slid into her she inched her body just out of reach.

He groaned and made to capture her, but she stayed him.

'Not yet,' she whispered into his ear. 'I want to see you. I want to touch you. And taste you.' She stared down into his eyes.

Together they rolled on the bed so that she was on top and he beneath.

She unfastened his cravat and it was gone. She pulled the shirt up high to expose his chest. He peeled it over his head and threw it away.

'I want you naked,' she said.

'And I, you. I will take off the rest of my clothes only if you take off yours.'

'It's a deal.' She smiled, teasing him in that familiar way she had always done.

They stripped, and when he lay down on the bed again she came to him naked as the day she had been born, her straight pale-blonde hair freed from its pins to brush against her breasts, the pale rose tips nosing through its lengths. She straddled one of his thighs, kneeling there so that he could feel her warmth and moisture against him.

His manhood stood high to attention. She leaned over him, her long hair and her nipples brushing against his chest as she reached her lips to touch his. She placed one gentle kiss against his mouth. One on his breast against his heart. Then slid lower, to place another on his navel, dipping her tongue within to taste him there. Her mouth slid lower, following the line of dark hair, to the turgid thick length of his manhood. She kissed the tip of him and he almost came. She licked the length of him and he gasped aloud. She took him in her mouth and worked him gently.

'Have mercy, Alice, or I will not last any longer.' His whisper trembled.

She let him slide free. 'With you there can be nothing of mercy.' Words they had so often used in their play. 'I must be cruel to be kind, Razeby,' she said with the strangest expression on her face, but she did not take him in her mouth again. Instead, she kissed the other parts of him that made him a man. Stroked her hands slowly up the dark smattering of hair that dusted his belly, over his stomach, over his ribs and the length of his arms, from the tips of his fingers all the way up to his shoulders, as if she were trying to memorise every part of his body.

She kissed the hollow of his throat. Each shoulder. His Adam's apple. And then she looked into his eyes and watched him as she moved her legs to straddle him and lowered herself to take him into her body.

They sighed together in the relief and ecstasy of their reunion, their breaths mingling to become as one. Their gazes stayed locked as they moved together, as they found the place that only they could reach. And afterwards he gathered her in his arms and he held her and felt their hearts race together. She stroked his face, traced the line of his eyebrow, kissed his eyelids, the tip of his nose, the cleft of his chin.

There was such tenderness and love in her touch, in the way she looked at him, in her whisper of his name.

'You are mine, Alice. And I am yours.'

She smiled, but there was a sadness in her eyes.

He kissed the sadness away and held her as if he would never let her go. Come tomorrow he would save her heart, and his own, and lose his honour in doing so.

Alice lay in the bed long after Razeby had gone. Her body was contented from his loving, and when she slid her hand against the sheet that lined his side of the bed it was still warm from where he had lain. She loved him with every beat of her heart, with every breath in her lungs, with all that she was. But love wasn't all sweetness and softness and pretty things. Sometimes for love you had to make the hardest decision and do the most difficult thing in the world.

Alice had never loved before. She did not think she would ever love again. For her there was only, and would only ever be, Razeby. But he was the most determined man she knew. He had made up his mind and no amount of persuasion would turn him from it. To marry him was all she could ever have dreamed of. To be with him as his wife. To love him. And be loved by him. What more could there be in life? It was joy. It was happiness. If there could be heaven on earth, then to live like that with Razeby would be it.

But it would destroy him—and what happiness could there be in that?

So she would do the hardest thing in the world. To save the man that she loved she would sacrifice her own heart. And make him hate her for ever. It was as she had said, sometimes you really did have to be cruel to be kind.

There was only one way Razeby was going to let her go. One tack she knew would work for certain. And her heart shivered to take it, and her skin grew cold and clammy at the thought and she was so afraid, more afraid than she had ever been in her life, but she knew it was what she was going to have to do.

She closed her eyes and remembered the way he had loved her, the tenderness in his eyes. He would never look at her like that again. Never. She pushed the thought away and rose from the bed. She had to be strong enough for the both of them.

* * *

Razeby arrived at Alice's rented rooms at four o'clock the next afternoon, exactly when he had said he would—twenty-four hours after he had asked her to be his wife. She was dressed in the same yellow walking dress she had worn that day in Hyde Park and had wrapped a fawn cashmere shawl around her shoulders. There was a small fire burning on the hearth and the sun shone in through the windows, adding to the warmth of the room. But it did not matter how much coal she burned or how many layers of clothing she wore, she was frozen to the marrow and did not think she would ever feel warm again.

He was smartly dressed, wearing a black Weston riding coat and a pair of fitted buckskin breeches. The leather on his riding boots gleamed in the sunlight, as did the mahogany of his hair. He bore himself well, a slight arrogance in his walk, a confidence in the way he held himself that stemmed from being raised to lead. Everything about him spoke so loudly that he was born to be a marquis that she knew she was doing the right thing.

'So, Alice,' he said softly. 'I have come for your answer.'

Her stomach was balled so tightly she felt sick and her throat was sticking together so badly that she could not swallow.

'Will you marry me?'

Her heart was thudding hard and fast in the base of her throat. She forced her chin up, clutched the shawl so tight that her hands went numb. 'I'm afraid not. My answer is no.'

He gave a small surprised laugh, as if he did not really believe her. 'Do you think to save me from myself, Alice? Because if that is your game, I will brook no refusal.' He stepped closer.

Her heart missed a beat. 'This is no game.' She swallowed and took a step in retreat. 'I'll not marry you, Razeby.'

'Why not?' He cocked an eyebrow and his gaze bored into hers. 'I know that you love me.'

'No. You're mistaken. I don't love you. I've never loved you.' She looked away to tell the lie.

'I do not believe you. You cannot even look me in the eye to say it.'

She curled her hands so that her nails dug into her palms, forced herself to meet his gaze. 'I don't love you, Razeby.'

'And what happened between us yesterday?'

'Was sex.'

'It was a damn sight more than sex.'

'I made you think that. It's what whores are paid to do and I'm good at my job.'

He grabbed hold of her arm, hauled her to him, staring mercilessly down into her face. 'Never call yourself that word again. Do you understand?'

She nodded, afraid of the power and strength of what she saw in his face.

Something of the tension in his grip relaxed. 'Besides,' he said softly, 'I did not pay for yesterday, or the time in the theatre.'

'Consider it a couple of goodbye liaisons, for the sake of our previous arrangement.'

'I am prepared to give it all up for you and you tell me you will not have me?' He gave a laugh of incredulity and stared at her as if he did not believe her.

'Well, you see, that's the problem, Razeby.' She had thought so carefully all through the night of the words she must say—the words that would convince him. Rehearsed them in her head again and again. But now that it came to saying them they stuck sharp as fish bones in her throat. 'I'm…' She took a breath and forced them to her tongue. 'I'm not interested in a man without money or title. A man who cannot keep me in the manner to which I've become accustomed. I don't want to be a poor man's wife. I don't want to flee to another country. Or spend the rest of my life in a hovel, cooking and cleaning, with laundrymaid hands and scrabbling to make do and mend and put food on the table. I've been there. I've done that. I came to London to escape poverty and I'll not go back to it to be your wife.'

He stared at her in silence as if it took some time for the words to sink in. 'So it is not me you want at all,' he said slowly, 'but my wealth, my title, my power?'

She nodded, making sure she did not look away. Delivering every last piece of the lie while meeting his eyes.

'If it was not about love, but only gain, why did you not take the dresses, the bracelet, the money?'

'To pique your interest. It was all just a game to get you back.'

'You made me believe that you loved me.'

She swallowed and the air in her nostrils seemed chilled as ice and that in her lungs sharp as the prickle of pins. What was it he had said that day in the Exhibition Room? *Clean and quick is the best way of severing something that one has no wish to let go.* 'I never said those words, Razeby.' Her voice was quiet as she delivered the blow that would sever them for ever. 'Not once.'

She saw the words hit home. Saw the realisation in his eyes. It had worked, just as she had known it would.

'Neither you did,' he said softly. 'How remiss of me not to notice.'

The tension was stretched tight between them. She had not known that she could be so strong or so callous. To stand there second by second, minute by minute, and coldly, deliberately break his heart...and her own.

She forced her lips to curve in the echo of a smile. 'You're a nice man, Razeby—kind-hearted, generous. Great in bed.' She swallowed and the smile wavered before she forced it harder. It felt like there was something wrapped tight around her throat. 'But you see, the reason I was attracted to you was because you were a marquis and rich and high up, and good-looking, too. I know what that makes me, but then I've never pretended to be anything else.'

Razeby said nothing. He stared into her eyes, his face a mask of anger and darkness and disgust that she did not recognise. But better his contempt and loathing a hundred times over than let him destroy himself. If he thought her a selfish whore over whom he had made a mistake and had a lucky escape, then he would be glad to walk away and leave her. His wounds would heal in time. She did not think of her own. He would marry some rich, suitable woman. Breed his heirs upon her. Care for his people and his lands. Be the great man he had always been destined to be.

She could feel the intensity of his anger, the barely leashed rage, the darkness of emotion. And against her face was the warmth of his breath—but not from passion, not from loving. The intensity in his eyes was searing. She did not know how much longer she could endure it. Part of her was so close to falling to her knees, to blurting all of the truth, to wrapping her arms around him and cradling him to her, and telling him that she loved him. And another part, the strong part that knew she would move heaven and earth to save him, stood there quiet and resolute.

He did not say a word, not one word. Just took some coins from his purse. He put the purse away again and held out his hand, palm flat, offering her the two gold sovereigns that lay glinting upon it.

She knew what they were. She understood what he was paying for—their loving of yesterday and in the theatre. She stared at the coins and could not move.

'Take them,' he said in a deadly quiet voice.

The final test. The final sacrifice that must be made.

She reached out her hand and took both sovereigns from where they lay.

He curled his lip with disgust and gave a tiny disbelieving shake of his head. Then he turned, and without a glance back strode out of the bedchamber. She could hear the hurried, purposeful tread of his boots on the stairs, and across the hallway, the almighty slam of the front door that reverberated throughout and made the whole house tremble. And she did not move, just stood there, frozen in horror and shock and pain at what she had just done. Stood there, and stood there, while time ceased to be and somewhere around her was a whole world moving on.

She did not know how much time had passed before she heard the girl's voice. 'Are you all right, ma'am?' The youngest maid, Rosie, stood wide-eyed and timid outside the open bedchamber door.

She nodded. 'Go,' she managed to whisper.

But the maid just stared at her with horrified fascination and concern.

'I said, leave me.' Stronger this time.

The girl bobbed a curtsy, shut the bedchamber door and the light footsteps hurried away.

And still Alice stood there. Unmoving. Frozen. Staring at the floor, blind to the pale Turkish rug and the dark polished floor boards. Blind and deaf and dumb. Slowly she turned and walked to the bed, sat down on the edge of it. It felt like there was a great band of iron wrapped around her chest, crushing her, making it hard to breathe. She felt hollow where she had placed her hand within her chest and ripped out her own heart.

Razeby was safe. But the cost had been herself. All of herself. All of her heart. Everything she was. Every one of those words of deceit had been a cut to her own soul. In hurting him she hurt herself a hundred times over. In freeing him she sentenced herself to a living death. She felt numb, shattered, disconnected. There was nothing she could do or say or think.

She sat there, and the seconds stretched to minutes and the minutes to hours. She sat there and the sun moved away to set in the west and the daylight faded and the darkness came. And all the while her right hand was curled tight and hard.

A knocking sounded. The older maid, Meg, opened the door a crack and peeped in. 'Shall I bring you up a tray of dinner, ma'am?'

'Go away,' she said and her voice sounded like someone else's.

The door closed again.

She leaned to the side. Lay down on the bed, her feet and legs still dangling over the edge. She lay there, eyes open, staring into the darkness. Until the sounds of the carriages and the passers-by faded to nothing and there was only silence. Until, eventually, the silver of the moon crept in through the window and moved its way, inch by inch, across the room to light the curled tight fist of her right hand lying on the counterpane, white and bloodless as a dead thing. She looked at it as if it were not a part of herself. Slowly, she loosened the fist, uncurling her fingers inch by tiny inch until they lay flat and stretched, her palm exposed in full. She stared at the two large coins that lay upon it. Gold painted Judas silver by the light of the moon.

The pain hit her then, savage and merciless, and black beyond all despair. And all of the barriers crumbled, and the breaking was so sudden and swift and complete that there was nothing she could do to stop them. She wept, as she had not wept in all these weeks. She wept for the loss of the man that she loved and the loss of the woman she had been. She wept and she did not think that she would ever be able to stop.

Three days later Alice packed her travelling bag, and left her rooms in Mercer Street. She caught the mail to Southampton, boarded the first boat she could find and went home to Dublin.

Chapter Seventeen

There was silence in the drawing room of the Darrington town house in fashionable Upper Grosvenor Street.

Miss Darrington took a tiny sip of her tea. Her golden hair was perfectly coiffured, her body robed in an expensive pink silk.

'So what is your preference for the colours of flowers for the wedding breakfast table?' Mrs Darrington enquired of him.

'I am content to leave the decisions on such matters to yourself and Miss Darrington.' Razeby said. 'I am sure you will make an admirable selection.'

Mrs Darrington smiled and nodded.

'Such a pleasure that you have decided to ally yourself with our family. And with such eagerness for the nuptials.'

'There is no point in delaying when the decision has been made,' he said.

'A man after my own heart, Lord Razeby,' agreed Mr Darrington. 'Seven weeks should be more than long enough. Although Mrs Darrington is already getting herself in quite the flutter over arranging so speedy a wedding.'

Razeby forced a smile that could not touch his eyes. 'Such is the prerogative of ladies.'

Mrs Darrington gave a nervous giggle. 'La, there is so much to be done!'

'So much indeed,' said Miss Darrington. 'Perhaps seven weeks is not long enough. There is lace for my dress, the silk… Perhaps it would be better to defer the wedding until—'

'Seven weeks will be more than enough time,' Mr Darrington interrupted, fixing his daughter with a warning eye.

'If Miss Darrington is in agreement?' Razeby looked at her.

Miss Darrington gave a nod.

Seven weeks and he would stand before an altar and make Miss Darrington his wife. It would be done.

'More tea, Lord Razeby?' Mrs Darrington asked.

'Thank you,' he murmured and allowed her to fill his cup.

The clock on the mantel ticked its slow steady rhythm in the background. The large bouquet of flowers that Razeby had brought sat beside it in a cream-and-blue glazed vase.

'To marriage, Lord Razeby.' Mr Darrington raised his teacup as if making a toast.

Razeby raised his teacup in return. 'And duty,' he returned and smiled a cold hard smile that did not touch his eyes.

Alice climbed down from the cart's seat and walked up the garden path of the small cottage that lay on the

outskirts of Dublin. The surrounding trees were all
in bud, the first signs of green touching their winter-
stripped branches. In the garden the heads of the daf-
fodils had withered, but their leaves still grew thick and
lush amongst the long untended grass through which
a carpet of early bluebells was woven in vibrant splen-
dour.

She felt a sense of relief and of home coming to be
here. The air was cleaner than in London, and sweeter.
Just a breath of it felt like it cleansed all of London's
filth from her lungs.

Mr MacCormack lifted her travelling bag down from
the back of the cart and set it down by the doorstep.
'Your mammy will be glad to have you back home for
the visit, Miss Flannigan.'

The doxy, Miss Rouge, and the actress, Miss Sweetly,
had been left behind in London. Here, she was plain
Alice Flannigan, the same as she had been born, on the
outside. But inside…that was a different story all together. She smiled at the old man and gave him a few
extra coins as a tip and he ambled away, tugging the
peak of his soft cloth cap as he did.

The front door still had not opened. And from the
cool grey sky overhead came the first smir of rain. From
inside the cottage she could hear squabbling voices and
the running patter of small feet.

She raised a gloved hand and banged all the harder
on the door. 'Mammy, are you going to open this door,
or leave me standing here on the doorstep for the rest
of the day? Anyone would think you're not wanting to
see me.'

The door opened. Her mother stood there, staring in

disbelief. 'It's yourself, Alice. All the saints in heaven be blessed. I didn't know you were coming for a visit.'

Visit. Alice smiled again and did not correct her mother's misconception, just as she had not corrected that of the old carter.

Her mother took her face between her work-worn hands, her eyes raking her face, filled with welcome and with the sheer joy of reunion. 'Oh, but it's good to see you again, Alice, truly it is.' And something inside her suddenly welled up so that she felt like weeping and she could only be glad when her mother pulled her against the familiar old pinny and hugged her. Alice embraced her mother just as if she were a small girl again, squeezing her eyes shut, struggling to stopper the tears.

'It's good to be back, Mammy!'

'Look at us out here on the doorstep. Come in. Come in.' Her mother took hold of her arm and drew her inside.

The cottage interior was darker than Alice remembered and much of the furniture was missing.

Six-year-old Annie sat on her older sister Jessie's knee, having her hair combed. Molly was sitting in the only armchair in the room, weaving strips of rags to make a rug. They all looked at her, smiling but shy as if she were some stranger come to visit. She went to each one in turn, chucking their chins and teasing their hair just as she had done when they were small, and kissed their cheeks. From outside came the sound of wood being chopped and shrieks of laughter of girls playing in the background.

'Christie! Maggie, Cathy! Our Alice is back!' Her mother wrenched open the window and shouted out at them to come in. Alice's eyes moved to the small three-legged stool which was the only place that her mother could be sitting. There were two iron buckets set before it. One held dirty water, the other glistening newly washed potatoes. By her feet sat a small scrubbing brush and an old cloth potato sack.

'You'll be wanting a drink of water, Alice. Or I've nettle tea in the pot.'

'Water would be grand, Mammy. But you sit yourself down. I'll fetch it myself.'

'Indeed, you will not.' Her mother was already bustling through to the kitchen to fetch the water.

Thirteen-year-old Christie came in, the sleeves of his shirt rolled up, looking more grown up than she remembered.

Alice dropped a kiss on his cheek. 'Look at you, Christie! You've taken a stretch and no mistake. You're taller than me now.' And thin as a bean pole.

He blushed a vivid red, grumbled a protest and pulled away, but he was smiling all the same.

'He's the man of the house now,' her mother said as she came back through from the kitchen carrying a cup of water and a slice of bread.

'Where's our David away to?'

'Took the King's shilling at the beginning of last year and has been away fighting in King George's army ever since,' her mother explained. 'He sends money when he can.'

Maggie and Cathy were red-cheeked from the fresh air, their clothes ragged and worn from being passed down through so many older sisters before becoming their own.

'You look like a grand lady, Alice.' Cathy smiled

and touched a hand to the dark-blue skirt of Alice's travelling dress.

Alice smiled and hugged each of her little sisters, glad in heart to see them, but shocked at the level of poverty she saw around her.

'Christie, bring your sister's bag in from the front step. The rain's coming on.'

Her brother went to do as he was bid.

'And where's all the rest of them?' Alice asked looking round for the rest of her sisters.

'Our Martha's away married to a fella in Kilteel.'

'Married?' Alice's eyes widened.

'He's a shepherd and got his own cottage. They got married last summer just in time for the arrival of the baby, thank the Lord.'

'That's good news.' Alice smiled and felt something shift inside her.

'And our Mary and Bernadette both managed to find positions in the same big house in Dublin.'

'That's grand.'

'It is,' her mother said, but Alice looked in her mother's face and saw the lines of worry that had not been there two years ago when last she had seen her.

What are you not telling me? she wanted to ask. Where had all the money she had sent gone? Her eyes moved over the bare poverty-stricken room and those she loved. But there would be time enough for such questions later. For now she was just glad to be away from London and the terribleness of what she had left behind there. Glad to be home with the secrets of which she tried so hard not to think.

* * *

It was the afternoon of the next day before Alice learned the truth of what she had come home to.

The cottage was empty save for Alice and her mother. Molly and Jessie were out in the back garden, pegging clean washing on a line.

'So this Mr Feeney that you married—' Alice said carefully.

'It turns out we never were married after all. The dirty lying scoundrel already had a wife and six wee ones in Dublin!' Her mother interrupted. 'They say there's no fool like an old fool, and he had me reeled in all right, hook, line and sinker.'

'You weren't to know.'

'Maybe not,' her mother muttered. 'He was a charmer right up to the moment on Christmas Eve when he told me he was going back to his wife. I only discovered once he'd gone that he'd run up debts all over the place and relieved me of my savings before leaving. The bastard!'

'And you've been struggling to get by ever since.' She knew now where the new clothes and furniture had gone, bit by bit.

'We've managed up to now.'

'Thank God the cottage is bought and paid for.' *With the money that Razeby had given her.* 'At least he couldn't touch that.'

Her mother looked away, an uncomfortable expression on her face. 'It's not quite so simple, Alice.'

'I had the lawyer put the deeds in your name.'

'Everyone thought we were married. Even I thought we were man and wife. My property became his.'

There was a sense of dread in Alice's stomach. 'What did he do?'

'He mortgaged it behind my back. Gambled away the money on the horses. The first I knew of it was some gentleman at the door telling me he's the new owner and that he's putting the rent up. He's charging a fortune.'

'But I've been sending money.'

'Not enough. He's asking such a lot. And we can't go without food or coal. And he's putting the rent up again. Where on earth can I find more money? He says we owe months in arrears and that he'll turn us out in the street if I don't pay.'

'Don't worry, Mammy. I'll sort it out.' She thought of her savings at the bottom of her travelling bag.

'And that's not the worst of it.' Her mother looked at her.

How much worse could it get?

'It's our Molly.'

Alice hid the worry from her face and waited.

'Some lad from the village has got her pregnant. She's four months gone and he won't marry her. What am I going to do, Alice?'

Alice thought of Razeby and all the pain of that last scene between them, all because she refused to yield to her heart and marry him. Irony could be very cruel. Taking her mother's hand in her own, she patted the work-roughened skin. 'I've some money put by. There's enough for the cottage and for the baby when it comes. And to see you all right for a while.'

'You've still got your fine acting job at the proper theatre?'

Alice nodded. 'I've still got my fine acting job.' But

she'd walked out on Kemble and the theatre season was coming to an end.

'Oh, thank God!' Her mother's face crumpled with relief and she squeezed her eyes shut. 'What on earth would we do without you, Alice?'

Within the ballroom of the Earl of Misbourne's town house situated only a few houses along the street in Leicester Square from Razeby's own, the first ball that Venetia and Linwood were hosting was in full swing. Most of the *ton* were present, with only a few small exceptions who refused to accept Venetia into polite society. Not that their absence would have any effect on the ball's outcome. Linwood and his father, Misbourne, had used their contacts to land the Prince of Wales himself as a guest. And as the Prince was now on the floor dancing with Venetia, her acceptance by the *ton* was guaranteed. Miss Darrington had excused herself to go to the ladies' withdrawing room and showed no sign of hurrying back, much to Razeby's relief. He stood alone with Linwood in a corner of the room, both of them sipping champagne as if they were enjoying themselves, when in truth neither of them were; Razeby knew that Linwood felt the evening as much a strain as himself.

'I have seen the change in you, Razeby.'

Razeby ignored the comment. He kept his mind focused on his marriage ahead, of his duty, steering his mind coldly, ruthlessly from dwelling on anything else.

'I am telling you this as your friend because it has not gone unnoticed by the rest of London. Indeed, I wonder that Miss Darrington has agreed to marry you.'

Razeby thought of the woman who had not. The one

woman to whom he had offered everything that he was, only to have it thrown back in his face as not enough.

'It is hardly surprising that she has spent so much time in the withdrawing room thus far this evening,' added Linwood.

'It is a marriage of convenience for us both. She understands how these things work.'

'Maybe,' said Linwood. 'But are you going to tell me what is going on, Razeby?'

'I am marrying Miss Darrington is what is going on.'

'And Miss Sweetly?'

'Alice and I are no longer together.'

'I had worked that one out,' Linwood said. 'She is gone from London. Walked out on Kemble and the theatre. Venetia went looking for her. She thinks Alice might have gone home to Ireland.'

'I do not give a damn where she is.' He felt the simmer of red rage at the edges of his mind and in his chest was that familiar lance of pain that cut deep whenever he thought of her.

Linwood's dark eyes seemed to see too much. 'The last I saw you, you were harbouring feelings of a more tender nature towards Miss Sweetly.'

'I have changed my mind.'

'So easily?'

He gave a nonchalant shrug of his shoulders, but Linwood was not dissuaded.

'Damn it, Razeby. You were talking of marrying her!'

Razeby glared at his friend.

Linwood held his gaze with those calm black eyes. 'If you are truly done with her, then all well and good. But I do not think that to be the case.'

'You are mistaken.'

'Am I? Is that why you punched Devlin the other night?'

'He suggested going to the Green Room of the Covent Garden theatre.'

'He was trying to cheer your ill humour!'

Alice's name whispered unspoken between them.

'I have no wish to visit the Green Room of any theatre.' Razeby stared straight ahead, his jaw stiff and stubborn. Both of them knew the significance of the Green Room in Razeby and Alice's relationship, but neither man made mention of it.

He had loved her. And believed she loved him. He had almost dishonoured all that he was as a man, turned his back on the one thing he had to do in his life, given it all up for her—a woman who had taken his heart and trampled it into the ground. What an actress she was. She had fooled him completely and utterly.

The bitterness of the illusion she had spun seemed to gnaw in the pit of his stomach. He did not even think of telling Linwood the truth. That she had rejected his offer of marriage—that she had ripped out his heart and ground it to a pulp before his very eyes. That he was such a fool that he had been prepared to put his honour aside. It was too raw, too intense, too private. Too damn shameful! He had not come to terms with it himself, let alone start revealing such vulnerabilities, even to Linwood.

Linwood said nothing, but Razeby could feel his friend's discerning gaze upon him.

He glanced across and saw Miss Darrington re-enter the ballroom.

There was still time enough before his thirtieth birthday. He had to stay focused. And do what had to be done.

Alice sat in the lawyer's office in Dublin beside the man she was paying to represent her. Over on the wall were square-shaped box shelves, each one filled with scrolls piled high, every scroll tied with a red ribbon. The light from the office window lit the faded brown leather of the seats a warm chestnut and glanced off the glass of the pictures on the wall. A grandfather clock in the corner of the room ticked slow and steady, punctuating the silence. Tiny specks of dust floated in sunlight, softening the drab interior of the room. Alice, dressed in her best blue day dress and pelisse, sat across the desk from the lawyer and tried to keep calm.

'A thousand pounds? You cannot be serious, Mr Timmons.'

'If you wish to buy the cottage, Miss Flannigan, that is the price Mr Lamerton is asking.'

'For a cottage in the country, with its roof in need of a new thatch?'

'He has offered to re-thatch the roof as part of the selling price.'

'Then you can tell him he may keep it. There are other cottages to be had in the village.'

'Mr Lamerton owns all of the properties in the village.'

'There are other villages nearby.'

'There are, Miss Flannigan. But you seem not to be aware that Mr Lamerton inherited some considerable acreage in the area from his late uncle. He is a landowner of wealth and influence. Perhaps your mother might consider moving out of the parish.'

'No.' Alice knew that her mother had been happy in the village. She had friends there. And besides, the house represented much more than four walls and a roof over their heads. After the years of living on the street, of shifting from a shared room in one relative's house to another, it had been the one point of stability in their lives. Her mother had always sworn she would never move again. Never go back to that life of constant shift and insecurity. 'I would not ask that of her.'

'The price is unreasonable, I agree, Miss Flannigan, but there is little else I can do.'

A thousand pounds. Alice's savings. From her time with Razeby. And her earnings from the theatre.

'Maybe I could speak to Mr Lamerton about reaching some arrangement over the payments for the rent that is outstanding.'

And Lamerton would have her mother over a barrel for the rest of her days. 'A thousand pounds and my mother would own the cottage outright?'

The lawyer nodded. 'That is the case, Miss Flannigan.'

'Tell him I will give him nine hundred and arrange myself for the roof to be thatched.'

'I will make the offer, as per your instruction, Miss Flannigan.'

In the crowded bedchamber of the little cottage Alice stole from the bed she shared with her sisters and crept through to the living room. The moon was high in the sky, its quiet silver light spilling in through the small lead-latticed window. She stood by the window and looked up at the moon, the same moon that shone down on Razeby in London. She wondered how he was and what he was doing. Every time she closed her eyes she could see his face.

The night was the cruellest time, for he came to her in her dreams, always in tenderness. He made love to her and gathered her in his arms and told her that he loved her. And always, always, it ended with those words that she had spoken, those lies and deceptions. And him staring down into her face with such anger and disgust. And always in the darkness it seemed that she could feel the press of two golden sovereigns against the palm of her hand. And every night she wept silently in the darkness.

She stood there and watched the full moon. Once upon a time she would have wished on it. But she did not do that now. A month had passed since she had come to Dublin. The cottage was paid for. A new fresh thick thatch upon the roof. Furniture and new clothes bought. The larder stocked full and ten bags of coal emptied into the coal cellar. And all save five pounds given into her mother's hands. But the money would not last for ever. She could not shirk her duty. It was time to go back to London. Besides, there was another reason she could not stay here. But she did not want to think of that right now. Not until she was sure.

Chapter Eighteen

It was two weeks until Razeby's wedding.

He sat in White's Gentlemen's Club with a group of his friends and pretended to laugh at some crude joke that Fallingham had just cracked. Devlin was guffawing by his side, the drink flowing freely.

'Another three bottles of champagne,' Razeby said.

'Steady on, old man, someone might think you are celebrating getting yourself enmeshed in parson's trap,' Bullford teased.

'Happens to the best of us, as Linwood will tell you.' Razeby grinned as if his heart were not shattered and aching.

Linwood gave the tiniest incline of his head, but said nothing else.

'So how do you wish to celebrate your last night of bachelorhood when it comes, Razeby?' Devlin's words were already slightly slurred. 'The boys and I have been discussing it. And we were thinking a night out at a certain colourful establishment—Mrs Silver's House of Rainbow Pleasures, to be precise. You could sample one of every colour. Maybe we all could. And afterwards swap notes.'

The words touched a raw nerve. None of them knew the truth, save for Linwood. The identities of Mrs Silver's girls were a closely guarded secret. He thought of Alice working in that place as Miss Rouge and his stomach twisted tight into a small hard knot. The thought of even entering the brothel made him feel sick. Yet he showed not one sign of his discomfort.

Across the table Linwood's gaze met his and held for the smallest moment before moving away to the rest of the group.

'Hardly original,' Linwood drawled. 'Besides, he's tasted them all already.'

He had tasted one and one alone and she had snared him and bound him to her in ways he had never imagined possible.

'I concede there is something of the truth in that,' agreed Razeby, although he did not say which half of Linwood's sentence was the truth, and which the lie.

'Linwood's right,' said Bullford. 'You will have to come up with something better than that, Devlin.'

'If you are so smart, you come up with a better idea,' said Devlin.

'Maybe I shall, old man. There's time enough yet to think about it.'

Razeby lifted one of the bottles of champagne from the silver bucket of ice that the footman had just brought. He gave the bottle a shake then, laughing as if he had not a care in the world, popped the cork and necked some of the erupting froth to the cheers of his friends. He wiped a hand across his mouth as if were enjoying every dissolute moment and passed the bottle to Devlin, who did the same. 'And in the meantime why do we not take our champagne through to the gaming room and play a few hands on the tables?'

'Now, that is a damnably splendid idea,' said Fallingham and, taking out his snuff box, offered it round.

Razeby's gaze met Linwood's across the table, and there was nothing of laughter or mock merriment in either man's eyes. Razeby drew his friend a tiny nod of gratitude of what he had just saved him from. Linwood reciprocated in the same way. In the carousing and drunkenness of the others, no one else noticed.

It was almost dusk when Alice knocked on the front door of Venetia and Linwood's apartments in St James's. The hackney carriage waited out on the road, with her travelling bag still stowed inside. She pulled again at the voluminous dark hood, checking that it shrouded her identity from any of Venetia's neighbours who might be chancing to look from their windows and see the lone woman standing there. A breeze stirred the dark shroud of the cloak around her.

The footman let her in. But when he would have taken her cloak she declined, only followed him through nervously to the drawing room.

Venetia was on her feet to greet her. 'Alice!' She came to her and took her hands in her own. 'Thank the Lord! I have been so worried over you. Come in, sit down and take some tea. Your cloak…' She gestured to the butler who hovered, ready to take it from her.

But again Alice shook her head, waiting until the manservant left before she sat spoke. 'I know the hour is late and I've no wish to embarrass you amongst your neighbours.'

Venetia sat down on the sofa beside her. 'That is foolish talk, Alice, and you know it.'

'I didn't come to stay, only to…' she hesitated for the smallest of moments '…to ask a favour of you.'

'Anything,' said Venetia.

'You own a charity house out in Whitechapel. One that provides shelter for certain women and their children…'

'I do,' said Venetia and Alice could see the curiosity and concern in her eyes.

'May I stay there? It would just be for a short while, until I get myself sorted out.'

Venetia met her gaze and held it. Alice glanced away, afraid of what her friend would see in her eyes.

'You may not,' said Venetia quietly.

Alice stared round in shock. She had not thought Venetia would refuse her. 'I wouldn't ask it of you, Venetia, but I've nowhere else to go,' she admitted out of desperation. 'And you needn't worry that I'd speak anything of your connection with it. I know you hold it as a secret. I would say nothing.'

'Alice.' Venetia took her hand in her own. 'I know you would say nothing. But you cannot stay there. It is in Whitechapel, for heaven's sake. No. You will stay here with me. I insist upon it.'

'I can't stay here. Only think what it would do to your reputation. The *ton* would have a field day if they knew I was living under your roof.'

'The *ton* do not need to know. We can be discreet.'

'But what of Linwood? He won't like my being here one little bit.'

'My husband will understand my wish to help my best friend. Please stay, Alice.'

'I…' The temptation pulled at her. She knew she would be safe here with Venetia. Besides, she knew that having the celebrated Miss Sweetly in their midst would do neither herself or the refuge any good.

'I take it that is your hackney carriage waiting outside?'

Alice gave a nod.

Venetia instructed her butler to see to Alice's luggage and send the carriage away.

'I'll stay only for a few days. Then I'll find somewhere else.'

'Are you forgetting that you sheltered me, Alice, when my home was lost? I do not. You are welcome to stay here as long as you wish. I will be sincerely glad of your company.'

Alice smiled a smile of relief. Venetia was good to her; she always had been.

'Have you eaten?'

Alice shook her head. 'I'm just off the stagecoach from Southampton. I was back in Ireland visiting—' She stopped mid-sentence. 'Is Linwood at home?'

'He has business round at his father's.'

Alice felt herself relax a little, afraid that where Linwood was, Razeby might appear.

Venetia looked down into her face. 'Was everything all right with your family, Alice?'

'No.' She smiled. 'Not really. But it is now.'

'Then you had better tell me about it.'

Alice sat at the breakfast table the next morning in Venetia's apartments. Venetia sat opposite her, not yet dressed, still wearing her dressing gown wrapped around her. Alice had put on her pale-green afternoon dress and pinned up her hair.

'Won't you eat something else?' Venetia asked.

Alice shook her head. 'I'm not hungry.'

Venetia topped up both their cups of coffee and spread some honey across her fresh bread roll. 'It is Razeby, is it not?'

Alice said nothing, just forced herself to nibble on the dry roll on the plate in front of her.

'What happened between the two of you?'

'Nothing happened.' She could not meet her friend's eyes.

'You will have to hone your acting skills better than that before you go back on stage,' Venetia said quietly, but she did not press her for the answer.

Alice glanced away and massaged the tight spot of tension that ached between her brows. 'How is he?'

'Like a different man.'

She closed her eyes at that.

'He is engaged to be married to Miss Darrington.'

'I am glad of it,' she said. And she was, truly she was. It was the best she could do for him.

'The wedding is set for two weeks' time in Westminster Abbey.'

'So soon?' she whispered and swallowed.

She glanced up to see Linwood in the door frame and felt her face pale.

'Miss Sweetly.' He gave a small bow of his head. Unlike Venetia, he was fully dressed in a smart dark-green tailcoat and buckskin riding breeches.

'Lord Linwood,' she murmured as she rose and gave a small curtsy. She resumed her seat too quickly.

Linwood helped himself to a selection of breakfast

items from the heated silver trays on the sideboard.
As he lifted the lids the food smells wafted strongly
in Alice's direction. Bacon and eggs and kippers. Her
stomach tightened.

He sat down by Venetia's side, opposite Alice.

She bit her lip, averted her gaze from his heavily
laden plate and tried not to breathe through her nose.

'I hope your trip home to visit your family went
well,' he said.

She nodded and knew she could not keep staring
in the opposite direction. 'Very well, thank you.' She
forced herself to look at him, and those black eyes were
so perceptive that she wondered what Razeby had told
him of her. Her gaze dropped and she found herself
looking directly at his plate of food.

He cut into the fat fillet of kipper and the smell hit
her all the stronger.

Alice gagged and, clutching a hand to her mouth,
fled from the room.

Venetia found her in the little bedchamber up in the
attic, kneeling over the chamber pot, retching up the
remains of the half bread roll she had eaten. She came
into the room, shut the door behind her and opened up
the window.

Alice sat on the bed, leaned back against the wall
and breathed in the cool, fresh morning air as Venetia
sat beside her.

'Sorry,' Alice said. 'It must have been something I
ate at the coaching inn yesterday.'

'But you did not eat anything in the coaching inn
yesterday, did you, Alice?'

Alice swallowed and took a deep breath. 'No.'

'How many months gone are you?'

Alice did not even try to deny it. Venetia would know the truth of it sooner or later, and in a way it was a relief to be able to tell someone else. 'I've missed two lots of my monthly courses.'

'Does Razeby know?'

'No!' She sat bolt upright and the dizziness swam in her head, so she eased herself back against the wall again. 'And don't you dare tell him, Venetia. Please, I beg of you!'

'I will tell him nothing that you do not wish him to know.'

'Thank you. I don't want him to know anything of it.'

'Why not? He is not an unreasonable man, Alice. You will need a means of living for you and the baby when it comes. Razeby would hate to default on his duty.'

Alice smiled at that—a bittersweet smile at the re-membrance of how much Razeby had been prepared to give up for her.

'It is his child, too, Alice. And whatever has hap-pened between the two of you, I am sure he would take care, at least financially, of both you and the child you have made between you. You should tell him at the very least.'

'I cannot.' *The child you have made between you.* She felt the tears prickle in her eyes and pressed her hands to her face to hide them. 'You have no idea, Venetia. What I did to him…the terrible things I said.' She swallowed and swallowed, but the tightness in her throat would not alleviate. The scar of that terrible day in that bedchamber in Mercer Street was still vivid and throbbing in her memory. 'I lied to him. I made him despise me. I made him think the very worst of me.'

'Why would you do that?'

She looked up at her friend, knowing she was going to have to tell her the truth. 'He asked me to marry him. He wanted us to go away, to the Continent, to live. He was going to give it all up for me. His birthright, his heritage, his title, his people. Everything that is so important to him. Everything that he has been raised the whole of his life for. I couldn't let him do that, could I? No matter how much I want to be with him.'

'So you turned him down.'

Alice nodded. 'In the worst way possible. There was no other way he would have believed me otherwise. He's a very determined man, is Razeby.' She clutched her bottom lip hard with her teeth to stop herself from crying, but it was useless, the tears spilled over her eyes just the same. 'He thinks me the most callous and worst of whores. God only knows what he'd do if he knew I had his babe in my belly. I doubt he'd leave his child to be raised by the woman he believes me to be. And I couldn't let that happen. I won't risk that happening. Not when it's all I've left of him.' She looked at her friend. 'Oh, Venetia, what am I going to do?'

'We'll find a way, Alice.' Venetia put her arm around her. 'I'll help you.'

'I can't stay here, unmarried and with a belly that will swell to notice soon enough. I wouldn't do that to you, Venetia.'

'I will find rooms for you in the country. I will take care of the money and—'

'No.' She shook her head. 'I can't let you do that,' she said, knowing what would happen to the fragile reputation that Venetia had worked so hard to build. Besides, there was also her family back in Ireland to think of. 'I will find another way. I have to.'

'Alice, the theatres are closed for the summer. And when they open again you will not be in a position to hide your condition.'

'I know. But my mind is made up, Venetia. You're my friend. And you've already done so much for me. Getting me out of Mrs Silver's and all. But enough is enough. I won't ruin your chances of happiness in your new life. I'll leave this very minute otherwise.'

'You can be a most stubborn termagant when you choose to be, do you know that, Alice Flannigan?'

Alice smiled even though the tears were still rolling down her cheeks and she could not seem to stop them. And then she thought of Razeby again. 'You won't tell him, will you, Venetia?'

'I will not tell him.'

Alice gave a sigh of relief. 'Thank you, Venetia. For that and for letting me stay. Linwood's not too angry, is he?'

'He is not angry at all. He, too, remembers how you took me in after my house burned down, before we were wed. He is not what you think him, Alice.'

'He's Razeby's friend.'

Venetia gave a little wry smile that did not touch her eyes. 'I cannot deny that.'

'How is your head this morning?' Linwood asked as he and Razeby trotted their horses through a deserted Hyde Park early the next morning.

'Absolutely fine.'

'Then you did not accompany Devlin to that tavern in the docklands?'

'I did. It proved to be an interesting distraction.' Anything to take his mind off mulling over what a fool he had been over Alice.

'Do you know Miss Sweetly has returned to London?' Linwood asked.

Razeby's heart skipped a beat and for that small moment he could say nothing. Then the anger and determination kicked in and he recovered himself. 'I did not. Nor is it any of my concern.' His voice was cool. His eyes belying nothing of the small curve of his lips.

'Should you choose to call upon me at home, it will therefore not discompose you to know that Alice is a house guest of Venetia's for some short while.'

Razeby said nothing, but he gave a small acknowledging nod of the head to his friend. 'I will bear it in mind.'

They rode on in silence, Razeby determined not to ask one question about her and Linwood revealing nothing.

He should be glad of that, Razeby thought. There was nothing about Alice Sweetly that mattered to him anymore. That was what his head was saying. What he felt in his heart was something else all together. But Razeby had done with listening to his heart. So he did not ask. And Linwood...he did not tell.

Chapter Nineteen

Alice walked along Oxford Street the next morning. She had thought long and hard through all of the days past over her options. It was as Venetia had said. The proper theatres had closed for the holidays. And even if they had not, she was not entirely sure Kemble would have her back after the way she had walked out on him. There was no point in approaching any of the other so-called theatres. She could not dance, or hold a tune. She could not twist her body into gymnastic shapes or ride bareback on a horse. She had never been on a horse in her life, if it came to that. And she could not play a single musical instrument. She liked to draw and colour, but again, she thought the standard was insufficient to find employment through that avenue. She could launder and wash and scrub and polish as good as any maid. But the agency had turned her away, saying that without a single character to her name, or any experience, she would not find work in service. She had an excellent memory, but no employer had need of that. Even Mrs Silver would not want her with a babe in her belly, though in truth she could not stand the thought of any man other than Razeby touching her.

So she spent the day trawling the streets of London looking for work in any shop that she thought might hold the slightest chance of employment. Although in her heart she knew even if they did take her on, she was just deferring the problem for the future. Once the baby began to show, they would not have her, and the money was unlikely to be good enough to last her through. But in the end, there was nothing to be considered. Some respectable shop owners recognised her as the famous Miss Alice Sweetly and sent her packing immediately. Others would not interview her without previous experience of working in a shop. And the one establishment that showed a measure of interest needed her to record all sales in a ledger and write the customer a receipt and, given that there were only two words that Alice could write, she made her excuses and left again.

She knew that Linwood's sister was visiting Venetia this afternoon, so she did not return to the rooms, but instead headed for nearby St James's Park. There was a nip in the air, but other than that the day was fine and bright. She stayed clear of the more fashionable routes, walking along a quieter line of trees until she found a wooden park bench. Her feet and back ached from all the walking and she was tired. It seemed she was always tired these days. So she sat down in the sun and rested. She could hear the chime of St James's clock and did not intend on returning to Venetia's apartment until after six, to ensure that any visitors would have long departed.

A few people passed. Two ladies walking. An old man. A boy who looked like he was running an errand. And a gentleman on horseback. She kept her face averted from the latter, although she knew he was not Razeby. Half an hour elapsed. She felt better for the rest, and for the fresh air. And then she heard the jangle of a horse harness.

'I thought it was you, Miss Sweetly.' She glanced up to find the Duke of Hawick standing there on the grass, leading a large chestnut horse by the reins. He removed his hat and held it in his hand beside his riding crop.

'Your Grace,' she said and, getting to her feet, gave a small curtsy.

He bowed. 'Have you been away? I have not seen you in a while.'

'Visiting my family in Ireland.'

'How pleasant for you.'

'It was.'

'I trust you had a good trip.'

'Very good, thank you, Your Grace.'

He smiled and his teeth looked remarkably white against the pale golden tan of his skin. 'What brings you out here to the park?'

'It's a pleasant day. I thought to take some air.'

'The day is fine indeed. I have been taking something of the air myself. Brought Legion out for a bit of a canter.' He gave the chestnut horse's neck an affectionate half-rub, half-pat. 'Do you ride, Miss Sweetly?'

'Unfortunately not.'

'You prefer to enjoy the view on your own two legs, or perhaps in the safety of a carriage.'

'It's a less dangerous pursuit.'

He smiled again and his dark blonde hair fluttered in the breeze. 'I suppose that depends on whose hands are upon the ribbons.'

'I suppose you've the right of it.' She smiled and wished he would go away.

'We never did get to have that evening alone.'

'We didn't.' She glanced away, feeling awkward and a little vulnerable. 'I really should be getting on... If you'd excuse me, Your Grace.' She got to her feet.

'May I be as bold as to escort you home? I do not like to think of any woman walking home alone at this time in the day.'

'I thank you for your kind offer, but it's not late and I'll be quite safe.' She gave him a small curtsy and made to walk away, but Hawick came, still leading his horse, to walk by her side.

'I would be remiss in my duty as a gentleman if I were to agree. Where are you staying these days, Miss Sweetly?'

She realised her mistake. She could not tell him without drawing scandal upon Venetia. 'With a friend,' she said and did not elaborate. 'But I wasn't intending heading home immediately. I've a few chores to attend to first.'

'Anything that I may be of assistance with?'

'I appreciate the kindness of your offer, and I thank you for it, but there's nothing with which you can assist me.'

He gave a nod of his head, but he did not take his leave of her, just continued to walk slowly by her side.

There was a small time in which they walked in silence.

'Perhaps you will think me too bold and too hurried in my approach. But I am a man who has learned from past experience...' he paused for the tiniest moment and she knew he was referring to events of last year when all of London had known how long and hard he angled to make Venetia his mistress without success '…that it is best not to dally in negotiations or protracted games when it comes to such matters. I see what I want and I will have it…or not.'

She felt her stomach tighten and her heart beat harder with a sudden nervousness.

'I have made no secret of my admiration for you, Miss Sweetly.'

She kept on walking, very slowly, by his side and did not look round at him.

'And indeed your absence seemed only to cement my feelings on the matter…'

Her heart began to thump in earnest. She knew what he was going to ask her.

'You are a lady without a protector. I am a gentleman who would be happy to offer that protection.'

'Your Grace…' She stopped then and turned to him.

'I am not prepared to undergo prolonged negotiations by letter and note. I have found a more direct approach preferable, and therefore I hope you do not find my open discussion of terms to be offensive. To come to the point, Miss Sweetly, a hundred pounds a month, four new wardrobes of clothes a year, all outings to entertainments included, a furnished house in Sackville Street with a complete staff and all running costs met, and the use of a carriage and four. The agreement in full detail to be drawn up in writing between us, naturally.' He smiled charmingly, but there was a slight hard edge to his clear blue eyes.

A hundred pounds a month. Even if she were only with him for three months that would be three hundred pounds. It was enough to find somewhere safe to stay,

enough to survive on for a good while if she was careful. And yet she knew too well what being any man's
mistress entailed and the thought of that reality with
another man... What she really wanted to do was to tell
him to go away and never come near her again, that she
had no desire to sell herself to him or any other man.
She wanted to shout at him that she was not some cheap
whore to be sold to the highest bidder without any consideration for her heart or desire. But Alice knew she
could not do that. She bit her lower lip and looked away.
Because the reality was that she *was* a whore and the
only thing she had left to sell was herself.

That strange hungry sickness was gnawing in her
belly and that same slight faint feeling was in her head.
She thought of the baby that was growing inside her,
her baby and Razeby's, and the knowledge instilled a
fierce protectiveness in her, a searing determination
that she would do anything and everything to protect
their child. She could see the green of the grass beside
the pale-fawn material of her slipper and the polished
gleam of the toes of Hawick's black-leather riding boots
standing not so very far away.

'You surely can't expect me to give you an answer
right now, Your Grace.' She raised her gaze to meet his.

'That would be unreasonable. And I am not an unreasonable man. I would have your answer by the end
of the week. I can be found here exercising Legion most
days at this time. Or you may send a note to me at my
town house.' He slipped a card from his pocket and offered it to her.

She said nothing, but she took the card from him.

'Such a pleasure to have met you here this afternoon, Miss Sweetly.' He took hold of her gloved hand

and pressed a kiss to it. After a bow he placed his hat on his head, slipped one foot into his stirrup and mounted his horse. He looked down at her from where he sat for a moment, then he gave a small smile, and with a nod of his head, rode off in the direction from which he had come.

She watched him ride away and the thought of what he was proposing made the queasiness rise in her stomach. She took a deep breath, stowed the card inside her reticule and kept on walking.

Alice sat on the edge of the bed in the tiny bedchamber in Venetia's attic in her long plain-white nightdress. The house was in darkness and silence. From somewhere outside she heard the cry of the watch.

'Two o'clock and all is well.'

The soft patter of rain sounded against the window and the darkness of the night sky was complete, the moon and stars shrouded by thick charcoal-streaked clouds. The candle, which sat on the cabinet by the side of the single bed, burned lower and she pulled the wool shawl more tightly around her shoulders to ward off the night's chill. In her hand she held the card that Hawick had given her that afternoon in the park. A smooth, thick white card, printed with expensive black ink, but the words that were there could have said anything. It did not matter how many months she had studied letters and words, they were always just a strange jumble of symbols and patterns that made no sense.

Hawick had had famous mistresses in the past. Indeed, his negotiations to make Venetia his mistress when she was still an actress and before she had married Linwood were renowned. He was reputed to have offered her ten thousand pounds and still Venetia had turned him down. Twelve hundred pounds was a far cry from ten thousand, but it was still a fortune in money, even if she was not able to stay the course to collect all twelve hundred. Once he discovered she was pregnant, he would not want her in his bed.

She wondered how many months it would take before it became obvious. It would be difficult to hide from him given what it was he wanted from her. She closed her eyes at that thought, unable to bear it. But she knew that beggars could not be choosers. She had made her bed and now she must lie in it, quite literally.

She clutched a hand to her stomach and tried to stopper the tears. Tears and sensibilities and regrets would not provide for the baby, she told herself angrily. And it was not as if she had not slept with men in order to survive before. Men that she was not attracted to. Men that she had not loved. But the little voice at the back of her mind whispered that that had been before Razeby. And Razeby had changed everything.

But she could not stay here. She would not ruin Venetia's chance of happiness and acceptance. And she could not go to Ireland and put her own problems on to her mother, not when her mother had aged ten years in the last one and was already worried sick over their Molly. Alice was the one who solved her family's problems, not added to them. And come a week Tuesday, Razeby would be married to Miss Darrington.

When she thought it all through like that there was not really any decision to be made. All this weeping could not be good for the baby. She forced herself to breathe, to wipe away the tears from her cheeks. Then she climbed beneath the covers of the bed, blew out her candle and lay there in the darkness.

'Miss Sweetly.' Hawick smiled and drew the horse to a halt some little distance from the bench on which she sat waiting for him the next day. 'I am delighted to see you again, and so swiftly following our previous meeting.'

There was no sunshine today. The sky was a light dove grey and the grass beneath her feet was still wet from the earlier shower.

'Your Grace.' She stood and drew him a small curtsy. And did not resume her seat.

He removed his hat and came to stand before her.

She could not smile, could not speak anything of the niceties and prevarications that she should. The rehearsed words came to her lips. 'With regard to your offer of yesterday…'

His blue eyes were trained on hers.

'For two hundred pounds a month, I will accept.'

'One hundred and fifty,' he said with a smile.

'Two hundred,' she repeated and loathed herself for what she was doing.

He looked at her a moment, let his gaze move down over her body, blatantly appraising what he would be getting for his money. Her breasts felt larger than normal and more tender. Hawick's eyes lingered upon them. There was no other visible evidence of the baby's presence…yet.

When his gaze came back to her eyes he smiled again. 'You drive a hard bargain, Miss Sweetly. But two hundred it is.'

The relief flowed through her.

'I will have my lawyer draw up the contract. To take effect from…shall we say tomorrow?'

'Tomorrow? So soon?' The words were out before she could prevent them.

'Unless you have a reason to delay?' The hard look was back in his eyes. He raised his eyebrows ever so slightly and waited for her reply.

Delay would only make it worse. So she shook her head.

'Where shall I send the carriage for your move to Sackville Street?'

'There's no need for a carriage. I'll make my own way.'

'If that is your preference.'

'It is.'

'The house is Number 44.'

'You have leased it already?'

'I own the street,' he said.

'Oh, I did not realise,' she replied.

They looked at one another.

'Until tomorrow, Miss Sweetly.' Hawick took hold of her hand and it was all she could do not to snatch it from his grasp. He took it to his lips and kissed her gloved fingers, holding her gaze with his own as he did so, so that she saw the lust there and the arrogance and sense of ownership. A ripple of panic shivered through her. She lowered her eyes that he would not see it and curtsied.

'Your Grace,' she murmured.

'I would offer to walk you home, but I have a feeling that you will refuse me that pleasure.'

'Your feeling is right, Your Grace.'

'But you will not refuse me tomorrow, will you, Alice?'

'No. I'll not refuse you tomorrow,' she said quietly.

He smiled at that and, mounting his horse, rode away.

Chapter Twenty

Alice finished the last of her explanation and turned away from the expression in Venetia's eyes.

'You do not have to do this, Alice. You can stay here.'

'I can't stay here, Venetia. We both know that. You're risking much in just having me here for a few days. If it gets out, it could undo all the good work that your ball accomplished.'

'Alice…' Venetia's brow furrowed with concern as she came to take her hand, but she could not deny the truth; they both knew Alice's presence here was a liability. 'You can stay at the house in Whitechapel, it is a rough part of town, but there would always be food and shelter. They would not turn you away.'

'I know.' But it was too late for that. Besides, Alice needed to earn money for the baby and for her family back home in Ireland. She smiled to soften the refusal. 'I didn't unpack my travelling bag. I'll leave for Sackville Street first thing in the morning.'

'What are you going to do when Hawick discovers you are pregnant?'

'I'll deal with that when it happens.'

'If you change your mind about Hawick, or if there is trouble with him or anything else, you must come to me. Promise me that, at least.'

'There won't be any trouble.' Alice said it with a confidence she did not feel.

She felt Venetia's hand squeeze around her own. 'Promise me, Alice.'

She looked into her friend's eyes and saw the compassion and concern in them. She remembered all that they had shared and how very much Venetia had done for her.

'I promise,' she vowed but she knew she would not risk ruining Venetia's reputation unless it was a matter of utter desperation.

Venetia hugged her and they both wiped the tears from their eyes.

The next afternoon Alice faced Hawick across the finely furnished drawing room of the town house he kept for his mistress in Sackville Street. Upstairs in the master bedchamber her travelling bag was already unpacked, her dresses hanging in the wardrobe, her underclothes folded neatly in the drawers.

'So let me get this straight—you are telling me that you have your monthly courses and cannot sleep with me this night?'

'It is most unfortunate in its timing.' She looked him boldly in the eye to tell the lie.

'Unfortunate indeed,' he drawled and did not look pleased. 'You made no mention of it yesterday…when you were abroad in the park. Does not such a malady usually keep women housebound?'

'It only came on this morning,' she said and saw his

gaze drop to where her fingers were worrying at the crocheted strap of her reticule. A little spurt of fear rippled through her at the direction of his interest and she threw it down on to the corner of the sofa behind her, casually, as if the reticule and its contents meant nothing to her. She wondered what he would do if he were to open it and discover the letter and the engraved silver pen from Razeby.

'You are not having doubts over our arrangement, are you?'

'Of course I'm not.' Another lie to compound all the others. 'I can't defy nature, now can I? No matter that I would wish it otherwise.' She smiled teasingly and forced herself to touch her lips to his cheek.

'How long do your courses last, Alice?' he asked, and for all the intimacy of the question the strange thing was that she was thinking that at no point had he asked her permission to call her by her given name.

'Only a week.' It was the longest she could ask for without arousing his suspicion. And until she had at least his first payment in her hand she could not afford to do that.

'Next Saturday?' He raised a brow to ask the question.

She nodded.

'Then I will wait a week,' he said and traced along the edge of her bodice, his fingers skimming the skin of her breasts that were constrained within it. 'And hope our union is all the sweeter for it.'

She nodded again, but her flesh was crawling where he touched her and the sickness in her stomach was not from the baby.

She had a week's graciousness. One week. And then

there could be no more deferring. She would have to give Hawick what he was paying for. She heard the retreat of Hawick's footsteps. Heard the close of the front door. She sagged back against the wall and prayed that the days would pass slowly.

Razeby had prayed the same thing. But the week during which he spent too few of the days with Miss Darrington and too many of the nights carousing in White's or some gaming hell, trying hard to prove to the world that he was having a great time in his life, passed in a blur of speed. That he was just making the most of his remaining bachelor days, rather than hiding a man whose life felt like it was falling apart. He did not want time to think, to brood, to ponder. He spent every night in company and then, when it was late and he was alone in his town house, he drank himself into oblivion.

Saturday came. Saturday. He lay in his bed and winced against the lance of sunshine that crept between the curtains to impale his eyes. His stag night. Three more nights and he would be standing before an altar with Miss Darrington and, once the deed was done, this torment would be over. Once she was his wife and he had begotten his heir upon her, he would welcome his thirtieth birthday and the end it would bring. He had spent a lifetime dreading it, doing every damn thing to deny it. Now he longed for it and the relief it would bring. For only that final end would wipe the spectre of Alice from his mind. God help him, nothing else did.

The clock downstairs in the hallway struck midday. He pushed back the covers, sat up and swung his legs over the edge of the bed. He sat there, naked, unshaven, feeling dreadful; too many late nights, too much brandy and wine and champagne. Too many cigars. And not a one of them salved the anger that raged in his blood or the bitter taste in his mouth…or the damnable ache he would not admit to another living soul that throbbed in his chest.

He leaned forwards, elbows on knees, hands cradling his head, wondering how the hell he was going to get through marrying Miss Darrington on Tuesday when he did not even know if he could maintain this façade through the night that was to come. He raised his head and peered across the room at the black domino that hung on the outside of the changing screen and the black face mask that hung by its side. No matter that he did not feel one bit like celebrating, a stag night at a masquerade ball was preferable to one spent in Mrs Silver's high-class brothel. With a snarl he crushed the thought of Alice that had crept into his head and rang the bell for his valet.

At four o'clock that afternoon Hawick arrived at the house in Sackville Street in which Alice had spent the week alone in the bedchamber, feigning a woman's condition that was the very opposite of the condition which beset her body.

'Alice,' he said, capturing her hand in his and touching it to his lips.

She ignored the string of maids and footmen that hurried past them carrying parcels and packages and long covered garments on hangers and managed to resist the urge to snatch her hand from his grasp.

'Won't you come through to the drawing room?' she offered. 'I'll have some tea brought up for us, or something stronger, if you prefer.' Anything to keep him occupied so that he would not kiss her or get other even worse ideas.

He gave a nod of agreement and followed her as she led them through to the drawing room. 'I trust you have recovered from your affliction.'

She was so tempted to beg just one more night, but she knew she could not do that. 'Indeed.' She nodded. 'I'm my usual self, Your Grace.'

'I am relieved to hear it.'

She said nothing.

'And I think, given the intimacy of our…friendship, that you may dispense with "Your Grace". My given name is Anthony.'

'Anthony,' she said, and the smile she forced to her face felt more like a grimace. 'But "Your Grace" comes so readily to my lips.'

'Well, we'll have to see what we can do about changing that tonight, will we not?'

Her stomach clenched tight at the thought. She smiled all the harder to hide her dread.

'In view of your recovery and to celebrate our new arrangement, I have a little surprise planned for tonight.'

'A surprise?' She tried to sound pleased rather than worried.

'A ball,' he said, 'with a little twist to make it a bit more exciting. I thought we could attend.'

'That would be a grand way to spend our first night together,' she said. All the while she was out with him in public there was a limit to the intimacy of what he could do. And then she remembered Razeby and the Covent Garden theatre and what they had done there in that public place.

'I love to dance.' The dance floor would be safe.

'Good,' he said. 'I'll look forward to our dancing together.'

The smile was starting to hurt her mouth. 'I'll ring for the tea, shall I?'

'I did not come here for tea, Alice.'

'No?' It came out a little too high pitched.

'Let's go upstairs.'

'Upstairs? Isn't it a little early in the day for—'

He laughed and, taking her hand in his, led her up the stairs to her bedchamber.

Her knees were knocking by the time she got there. The sweat prickled beneath her arms and her hands felt both clammy and chilled.

He stopped her outside the door. 'Close your eyes,' he instructed.

'Why?' she asked suspiciously.

'Because if you do not it will spoil the second half of the surprise I have waiting for you inside.'

'To be honest, I'm not great on surprises, Anthony.'

'Trust me, you'll like this one.'

Alice was not so sure, yet she could do nothing other than close her eyes.

She heard him open the door, then he took hold of her arm and guided her inside.

'You can look now.'

She opened her eyes and there laid out on the bed before them was a dress of brilliant scarlet silk, the bodice sewn with a thousand glass beads that glittered like rubies in the sunshine. The neckline plunged indecently low. The silk of the skirt was so sheer as to be almost transparent. Beside the dress was spread a scarlet domino with a deep-cowled hood. And positioned between them on the bed sat a Venetian mask to match their colour precisely. It was adorned with tiny glittering glass beads and vibrant red feathers, and from either side there was a length of thin scarlet ribbon that would bind it to her upper face.

Whatever horror Alice had been anticipating, all of her expectations paled into insignificance beside the reality of what lay upon that bed. The dress and the mask were similar to those she had worn as Miss Rouge during her time in Mrs Silver's brothel.

'For every woman needs a new dress to attend a ball. And none more so than for a masquerade ball.'

She felt a dizziness swim through her head at the shock of seeing the outfit and clutched a hand to the thick mahogany poster of the bed to support her. Her heart was hammering in her throat and it felt like her stomach had dropped clear of her body, through the floor beneath her feet into the drawing room below.

'It's red,' she said in a stilted voice that sounded nothing like her own. She turned her head to look at him, wondering if somehow he knew the secret of her background—that she had been the woman forced to play Miss Rouge behind the mask. Wondering if this was some cruel torture he was inflicting upon her.

But Hawick's gaze held only lust and appreciation. 'I have always found red to be a most stimulating colour.'

'I've never thought of red as a colour that suited me,' she said carefully through stiff, cold lips.

'On the contrary, I think it will suit you very well indeed.' He paused and stepped closer, brushing his fingers against her *décolletage*.

She could feel the heat and moisture of his breath against her forehead. She could smell the cologne scent of him too strong in her nose.

'Wear it for me tonight, Alice,' he commanded, and she knew she could not refuse without raising his suspicions as to her aversion to the colour, or their arrangement, or both.

'Of course.' She nodded.

She saw his gaze was focused on her breasts, watched it drop lower to sweep over the rest of her. He skimmed a hand against her buttocks, making her jump.

'You seem a little nervous, Alice.' His gaze met hers.

'You're a duke, for goodness' sake, Anthony. That's enough to make any woman nervous,' she said by way of excuse and prayed with all her might that he did not mean to take her right here and now.

'I wish I had time to show you that you have nothing to be nervous about right now, but, unfortunately, I have another commitment elsewhere. So we will just have to wait until after the masquerade.'

She could barely contain her relief. Her smile was all genuine this time.

'I will pick you up at nine,' he said.

She nodded and did not think to ask what colour of domino he would be wearing.

The bell of St James's Church sounded ten o'clock. The sky overhead was as dark as the long dominoes and moulded black face masks that Razeby and Linwood were wearing within the dimmed interior of Razeby's town coach.

The coach slowed as it approached the Argyle Rooms on the north side of Little Argyle Street at the corner of King Street. The entire building lit up the darkness of the night with the candlelight from the huge crystal-dropped chandeliers glittering through the windows that lined the west ballroom and the flambeaux that flamed in their holders high on the wall outside the magnificent front door.

'Go in without me. I will join you later. There's something I have to do,' Razeby said.

'You do intend on coming later?' Linwood asked.

'It is my stag night. I can do nothing other. The *ton* will expect a dissolute celebration of the end of my bachelorhood—and we shall not disappoint them.' He glanced across at his friend, glad of the shadowed gloom of the interior. 'I am glad it is not Mrs Silver's House to which we go this night.'

Linwood gave a nod of acknowledgement. 'This thing you have to do...'

'It is closure, Linwood. Something I should have done weeks ago.'

Linwood gave a nod, but he made no move to leave. 'Razeby...' Linwood leaned forwards '...there is something that I think you should know, concerning Miss—'

But at that very moment the coach door was opened by the footman.

'I will tell you later,' said Linwood and climbed from the coach, leaving Razeby inside alone. The door closed again and he was off and travelling through the night towards Hart Street.

Inside the house everything was just as he had left it. The candles had been lit in the hallway and the main rooms as he had instructed. A low fire burned on each hearth, so that the house was warm in contrast to the chill that clung to the night air outside. He had not slept here in weeks, but everything was prepared just as if he was due to arrive, just as Alice had run it.

He set the black Venetian mask he was holding down on the opened surface of the bureau as he surveyed the room around him. A small fire burned on the hearth just as it had done when he and Alice had spent their evenings in here. Darkness already shadowed the skies outside and although the candles of the chandelier had not been lit, those of the wall sconces and on the branch upon the occasional table blazed. The room had a comfortable atmosphere to it as if Alice and he still lived here. The faint scent of lavender and beeswax polish still hung in the air.

Tomorrow he would terminate the lease. And there would be no trace left of his life with Alice. He did not even know why he had kept the place on. Why even now he felt reluctant to let it go. It was nothing but torture to realise what a fool he had been and how close he had come to throwing everything away for a cold-hearted harlot. His jaw tightened. His father would have turned in his grave. His mother would never have forgiven him. He wondered if he ever would have forgiven himself. Looking back at those days, he could barely believe he had even considered such a ridiculous course of action. Some kind of madness had fixed himself upon his brain...upon his heart. And Razeby swore that in the short time he had left that nothing would ever affect him like that again.

He let his gaze wander around the room, from the two armchairs on either side of the card table where Alice and he had played *vingt-et-un,* to the sofa on which they had played games of a more intimate nature and the rug before the hearth on which they had made love. There was a bitter taste in his mouth. He hardened his heart and his expression and made to pick up the face mask from the bureau, remembering all the times he had come in and caught her hiding secret letters, her fingers stained with ink, her cheeks flushed with embarrassment. His eyes narrowed at the memory. He felt the suspicion stir through him as he wondered just who the hell she had been writing to so often.

He left the face mask where it was and searched the bureau.

In the pen holder lay an old cheap pen, its nib blunted from excessive use. Of the expensive silver pen he had bought for her and had engraved there was no sign. She had probably hawked it, he thought sourly. Most of the compartments and drawers were empty. There were a few stubby pencils, some eraser putty and a stick of sealing wax in one. And in another, a pile of his old letters, letters that his footman had brought following their daily delivery to his town house each morning. Letters that he had dealt with here and left with Alice to be burned. He frowned and pulled the pile out, wondering what she had been up to.

The letters appeared just as he had left them, until he turned them over. Across every sheet of paper were lines and lines of letters of the alphabet. A row of a's followed by a row of b's and so on, pages of them, like pages from a copy book, crudely formed as if from the hand of a young child. Some had been written back to front or upside down. He leafed through the pages and then he stopped dead, for there was a page on which two words had been copied again and again and again. The pages underneath were the same. The same two words painstakingly practised until she had written them perfectly—*Alice* and *Razeby* and between the two words a heart. Razeby felt his chest tighten and his own heart shift. At the bottom of the pile was a sheet on which she had sketched a pencil portrait of him. It was roughly drawn, but it had captured his likeness, and in it he was smiling at the artist, smiling in a way he no longer smiled any more.

Oh, God! He understood what she had been doing all of the hours of all of those days and why she had not wanted him to see them. And he understood, too, why he had never seen her read a newspaper, or receive a single letter, or ever even sign her name. Alice 'heart' Razeby—she did not know how to write the word 'loves'. Alice loves Razeby. Not Razeby 'heart' Alice, as he had had engraved upon the silver barrel of the pen.

In his head he heard again those words that had haunted his nightmares and made him turn his hurt into bitterness and anger. *I never said I loved you. I never used those words.* Both carefully and callously uttered. She had not said them, but she had written them again and again when the cost of doing so was very great. And as he stood there his blood trickled cold against his neck, there was a sinking realisation in his stomach and he had the horrible sensation that he had got this all wrong.

Alice loves Razeby.

He folded the pile of letters, placed them in his inside pocket and grabbed the black face mask from where it sat on the bureau. The length of his domino swept out like a great black wing behind him as he left the room.

Chapter Twenty-One

The masquerade ballroom was crowded.

Up on the balcony a small orchestra was playing. The high stone ceiling curved around the haunting baroque-inspired melodies so that the music seemed to come from the surrounding walls. The crowd was colourful as the courts of fifty years ago. Men and women wore dominoes of peacock colours, their upper faces hidden by intricate white or black masks similar to the ones that both Alice and Hawick wore. It seemed the masking lent an air of liberation and sensuality and barely suppressed recklessness to the night. Alice was very conscious of the scarlet that she wore. Beside her Hawick had chosen black, like many of the other gentleman that packed the floor.

She thought she had escaped Miss Rouge and all that time in her life had held but, garbed in the bold sensual scarlet silk and with Hawick's hand possessive against her arm, she knew she was that woman once more. Miss Rouge, a harlot, a whore who must sell herself to the highest bidder. The one mercy that would make the night bearable was the mask that covered her face, so that all of London would not know her shame.

She closed down that part of her mind. Did not let herself think. Refused to feel. So the woman by Hawick's side moved and danced and replied when she was spoken to, but she was not Alice, she was an empty façade. She was Miss Rouge. And Miss Rouge could get through this night, when Alice could not.

Everyone was drinking, laughing, dancing. It felt like some Bacchanalian orgy from days of old. Hawick's hand slid beneath her domino, stroking against the small of her back, encircling her waist.

'Let us dance, Alice.' His breath was hot against her cheek. She could smell the tang of red wine on his breath. She let him guide them out onto the dance floor and take her hand in his as the music began again.

The hammering of the brass knocker against its strikeplate resonated through the street all around. The front door opened to admit him. Razeby did not wait for an invitation, just stepped past the gaping butler into Linwood's hallway.

'Lord Razeby to see Miss Sweetly,' he said.

The door closed behind him. The butler's cheeks flushed as he tried to speak firmly, but politely. 'There is no Miss Sweetly here, my lord.'

'I know damn well she is here, so fetch her and be—'

Venetia appeared in the doorway that led into the drawing room, dressed in a dress of pale fawn. She was as calm and confident as ever she was, with that air of assertion. 'Razeby,' she said in her smooth low voice.

'I know she is here, Lady Linwood, and I am not leaving until I have seen her.'

Venetia nodded her assurance to the butler and dismissed him before she addressed Razeby. 'You are supposed to be at the masquerade ball for your stag night.'

'I am going nowhere until I have spoken to Alice.'

Venetia's brow furrowed ever so slightly, the one small sign of discomposure. 'Has Linwood spoken to you?'

'Of what matter, ma'am?'

She shook the expression away with a small half smile. 'No matter,' she replied smoothly and paused before adding, 'Alice is not here.'

'Do not seek to deceive me. Linwood told me you have been sheltering her since her return to London.'

'She was here. And now she is gone.'

'Gone where?'

'What do you want with her?'

'I have discovered that she has not been entirely honest with me.'

He thought he saw something shift in Venetia's eyes, but when she looked at him again her expression revealed nothing.

'Where is she, Venetia?'

'You will find out soon enough.'

He arched an eyebrow and felt his nostrils flare. 'Which means?'

Venetia's gaze was steady and composed as it held his.

'Please, Venetia…' he begged. 'I love her.'

Venetia glanced away. 'Oh, Alice,' she whispered softly beneath her breath and closed her eyes. She took a deep breath before she looked at him once more. 'She does love you, Razeby, no matter that it may appear otherwise. All that she has done, all that she does…she has her reasons. She would not stay here or let me help her because she was convinced it would turn the *ton* against me. Her family has troubles of its own. And there are other complicating factors at play of which I can say nothing. Had you come last week…' He saw the concern and worry on her face and the tiny furrow that wrinkled her brow. 'You are too late, Razeby.' She hesitated and he saw the pain in her eyes. 'She is gone to Hawick a week since, to his house at 44 Sackville Street.'

'Hawick,' he said and even to his own ears his voice sounded too quiet and loaded with danger.

'I am sorry.'

But Razeby was already halfway down the stone stairs that led from the front door down on to the street.

Alice felt the surreptitious caress of Hawick's hand against her hip as he turned her on the dance floor.

'Red becomes you well, Alice, but I am in anticipation of divesting you of it tonight,' he whispered close by her ear. Her stomach tightened with trepidation, but she was saved from having to answer by the steps of the dance which drew them apart.

She stared through the crowd towards the exit, wishing with all her might that she might turn away from what lay ahead, thread her way through the bodies on the dance floor to walk out of the hallway, out of the main door and keep on walking away from Hawick, away from this nightmare. As she looked she saw at the edge of the dance floor was a group of men cloaked in black dominoes like so many others, but who had not yet fixed in place their masks. Alice stared in horror as her eyes moved over the faces that she recognised too well: Devlin, Fallingham, Bullford, Monteith and Linwood.

Her heart stumbled and gasped. Her stomach plummeted in fear and dread. Her blood ran cold as ice as her eyes scanned frantically for the sixth member of that male party, dreading to find him. Her heart was hammering so hard and fast that she felt herself tremble, her blood roaring in her ears. Of all that she had thought she must endure this night… Please, God, she begged, do not let him be here, for she could not bear Razeby to see her with Hawick, to see her dressed like this. God must have heard her pleading. Razeby was not there with his friends. And for that she could only be grateful.

Across the dance floor Linwood's dark gaze shifted to meet hers. And she felt her blood run cold and her face burn with shame for she knew that the viscount recognised her. Then the bodies on the dance floor moved to block her view and she saw him no more.

She glanced longingly at the exit. But Alice could not run away from her responsibilities. She turned her gaze away and followed the steps of the dance that led her back to Hawick.

'Miss Sweetly is not at home.' The footman standing at the door of 44 Sackville Street was young, still wet behind the ears, but he knew who was paying his wages. 'Nor is His Grace the Duke of Hawick.'

'Where have they gone?' Razeby asked in a deceptively soft voice.

'I'm not at liberty to say, sir.'

'Of course not.' Razeby smiled. 'One must have

trustworthy staff. It would be more than your job's worth to tell me, I suppose.'

The young man gave a nod.

'How much *is* your job worth?' Razeby leaned against the door jamb in a relaxed fashion.

The footman looked uncomfortable.

Razeby smiled again and, slipping a wad of white banknotes from his pocket, began to flick through them. 'This much?' he asked after a few pound notes had passed and saw how the footman's eyes were transfixed by the sight. 'Or perhaps this much?' He fanned through half the pile. 'Or, maybe even a little more?' He opened out the whole wad of notes and smiled at the footman. 'Two hundred pounds, such a lot of money for such a little answer. London is a busy place, in which I could have heard the same answer from any number of sources.'

'His Grace took Miss Sweetly to the grand masquerade ball at the Argyle Rooms.'

Razeby smiled and handed the money to the footman, who slipped it straight into his pocket before glancing around suspiciously.

Razeby climbed into his waiting coach and tied the black mask in place across the upper half of his face.

In the heaving masquerade ballroom of the Argyle Rooms, Razeby wondered how the hell he was going to find Alice and Hawick. The crowd was a rainbow of coloured dominoes and masks. Most of the men had opted for black, while the women were in gold and silver, white and yellow, blue and green. The music swayed and lilted, reverberating throughout the stone walls of the hall.

Razeby wove his way through the revellers, past footmen who waited with silver salvers laden with glasses of champagne. The light glittered on the jewels on the women's masks and around their bare throats and *décolletages*. It was one of those rare events in which *ton* and *demi-monde* mingled side by side and all of scandal and intrigue and whispered debauchery was acceptable behind hidden identities.

He saw Linwood and the rest of his friends, their smart white-tie evening wear hidden beneath the shrouds of their black dominoes, but their faces unmasked. He gave a grim smile, knowing that they had deliberately removed their masks that he might find them.

The music played on, the sets moved upon the floor. Razeby made his way to Linwood. 'Linwood.'

'Razeby,' said Linwood and tied his mask back in place as did the others once they saw him.

'Alice is here with Hawick. I need to find her.'

Linwood's eyes glittered black as the devil's behind his mask. 'This is your stag night. You are marrying Miss Darrington on Tuesday.'

'Am I?' he muttered. His jaw clenched tight. 'I will have the truth from Alice regardless of what happens on Tuesday.'

'Razeby…' Linwood lowered his voice and leaned closer '…there is something you should know before you see her. I am sworn to silence, but you are my friend, and you did ask me to tell you if I were ever to know that all was not well with Alice.'

Razeby stilled, seeing the intensity in Linwood's eyes, and waited with a fear beating in his chest.

Linwood hesitated for a second before saying, 'She is carrying your child.'

'God in heaven,' Razeby whispered, then gritted his teeth with determination. 'How the hell am I going to find her in here?'

Linwood's eyes gestured to the figures moving in unison upon the dance floor. 'Perhaps with a deal less difficulty than you anticipate.'

And there, in the middle of the floor, dancing with a black-cloaked man was a woman in a scarlet-silk domino that swirled around her legs when she moved to reveal the figure-hugging scarlet dress beneath. Her fair hair hung long and straight and wanton over her shoulders in such contrast to the current fashion. And across her eyes and nose was tied a scarlet Venetian mask with holes cut for the eyes. Miss Rouge for all the world to see. His heart skipped a beat. He knew what being Miss Rouge had done to Alice, knew how very much she loathed even to see the colour. He pushed emotion aside, sharpened his focus.

'Be careful how you do this, Razeby,' cautioned Linwood.

'I am done with care.' Razeby gave a hard smile. 'I need to find myself a dance partner. And so do the rest of you. It is my stag night, after all.'

The dance came to a halt and Hawick kissed Alice's mouth, hard and brief, right there on the dance floor. No one seemed to mind. Other men were kissing their masked ladies, too.

'Shall we have a little rest for a while, over in the corner?' he breathed so close to her ear that her skin crawled.

The next dance was called.

'Can we not stay upon the floor a little longer? Please, Anthony?'

'It is a progressive dance. Are you so eager to find yourself a new partner, Alice?' He smiled as if joking, but there was no joke in his eyes.

'The dance will deliver me back to you. One turn round the circle.'

'I do not know if I wish to wait that long.' Hawick's gaze drifted lower to linger upon her exposed *décolletage* where the scarlet domino gaped. 'I want you, Alice.'

'What an impatient man you are,' she managed.

'Only when it comes to you.' He smiled.

And so did she, but the horrible sensation in her stomach churned all the more.

Upon the dance floor, the ladies formed one large circle, the gentlemen a slightly smaller inner one, like dark masked ravens in their black dominoes. Each faced their own partner. The music started up once more. The ladies curtsied. The gentlemen bowed.

The melody played and Hawick took her in his hold. They moved with and around each other, dancing the steps before Hawick handed Alice on to the next gentlemen and received his new lady in her stead. And so she gradually passed on from one gentleman to another.

Every gentleman that Alice partnered was garbed in the same long black-silk domino, overlying the same black-and-white formal evening wear. Every face was obscured with the same dark domino mask. She did not speak to them, barely even looked at them, feeling only relief that they were not Hawick. The music with its slight macabre undertone seemed to resonate through her. She moved through the dance, its every step taking her further away from him, through one man and then the next, dancing with each one in turn until they handed her on. Five men, all tall, all dark, all masked, all in black dominoes. And on to the sixth. She stepped in towards him and something made her glance up into his face. And masked though it was, what she saw there made the breath catch in her lungs.

The eyes behind the mask glittered too dark, too familiar. Even masked she would have known him anywhere. Her heart leapt into her throat. Her blood rushed too hard, pounding loud in her ears. She swallowed hard, forced herself through one step and then the next. He reached out, caught her hand in his and, even had she not recognised him through the mask, her skin thrilled to his touch and her whole body reacted to his proximity, making it impossible not to realise his identity.

He pulled her close to turn her beneath his arm, and the scent of him, so familiar, sent a shiver of longing all the way down her spine. It was only halfway through the turn that she realised he had shifted them both out of the circle. The space closed invisibly behind them, and when she looked more closely she realised that the men with whom she had danced before Razeby were all of Razeby's friends. But she was already being hustled away.

'Alice, you did not really think to escape me so easily, did you?' Razeby whispered into her ear as he steered them both to be swallowed up by the surrounding crowd. She tried to turn, but his grip was unyielding. She could do nothing other than go where he directed her, away from the dance floor, threading a path through the close-packed bodies out into the crowded hallway where he pushed her against the recess of a wall and, shielding her with his body, unfastened the ties of her domino. The expensive red silk slipped to land on the floor by her feet.

'What are doing? You can't just—'

'I thought you did not like red, Alice.'

'You know I don't, but—'

He unfastened his own domino and swept it around her shoulders, enveloping every inch of the indecent scarlet dress in which Hawick had dressed her with the black silk. For a moment she yielded to her instinct, snuggling into his domino, breathing in the scent of him, before common sense reasserted itself. Razeby stepped closer still, until his body was hard against hers and her face touched against the lapels of his black evening tailcoat.

'What are you—?'

But his fingers were untying the red mask that hid her face. Throwing it to the floor as if it were a piece of worthless tat.

She gasped and had to crick her neck to stare up into his face. 'Would you reveal me to all of London that is here? Have mercy on me, for pity's sake, Razeby, I beg of you.'

'I have told you before, Alice, that when it comes to you, I have no mercy.' His voice was hard, but from his pocket he produced a plain black Venetian mask and tied it where the red mask had been.

'Razeby...' She hated to say the words, but knew that she must tell him, now, before any more harm was done. 'I'm with Hawick now.'

'Are you? I do not see Hawick out here.' He smiled, but it was a chilling smile, a dangerous smile. 'Besides,

I want to talk to you, Alice.' And the quiet, determined, angry way he said it stroked a shiver all the way down her spine. 'Shall we go somewhere a little quieter?'

He took hold of her arm, in a grip that was firm but unbreakable, and led her up the staircase towards the upper floor. Behind them the crowd closed and the scarlet domino and mask were trampled underfoot.

Upstairs he drew her into one of the dark shadowy private rooms that led off the main floor. Beside the brightness of all the candles and crystal of the ballroom and hallway the room seemed to be in blackness. It took a moment for her eyes to adjust enough to see the soft flood of moonlight that glowed through the window.

'You're marrying Miss Darrington on Tuesday. I'm Hawick's mistress. What more is there to say between us?' She tried to make her voice sound as if she did not care, but it was impossible. It hurt to look him in the eyes, knowing the truth of what she had done to him and the truth of their child within her belly. But she could not look away.

'What more indeed?' he said quietly and behind the mask his eyes looked blacker than Linwood's. 'How about the truth, Alice?'

Her heart gave a stutter. 'I don't know what you mean.'

'Shall we start with this?' From inside his tailcoat he produced some sheets of paper folded over.

Oh, God! She knew what they were before he opened them up and showed her. She dropped her gaze, biting at her lip and feeling the shame scald her cheeks.

'You said that you did not love me. But…' He had found the sheets on which she had written both their names together a hundred times or more.

'Idle scribbles,' she murmured and could not look at him.

'I do not think so, Alice.'

'I have to go. Hawick will have noticed I'm missing.'

'You are not going anywhere.' He stepped closer, backing her against the wall, catching hold of both her wrists and securing them behind her back. 'There is another matter of which you have been remiss in telling me.' He held both her wrists in one hand, leaving the other free to brush gently against her lips.

Her breathing grew heavy. She was too conscious of his touch, of his body so near to hers, of the dangerous quiet control that barely leashed the force of his anger.

He trailed his fingers slowly over her chin, traced them down over the column of her throat.

'Please, Razeby,' she whispered. 'Don't do this.'

But the dark eyes just glittered dangerously behind the mask. 'Why not?'

'You know why not!' she cried, her voice hoarse with emotion.

His fingers trailed against her collar bones, then lower over her *décolletage,* tantalisingly close to her breasts, so pale and barely concealed by the blood red of the dress. 'Because of what is in here?'

She gasped and arched as he slid his fingers beneath the bodice to cover her heart. Beneath the dress she wore no shift, no underclothes of any description. He stroked gently against the aroused peak of her nipple, before capturing the fullness of her breast, making her heart thrill and thud to his touch.

In one smooth movement he had ripped the bodice of the dress open, the tear of silk a hiss in the silence between them. Her breath grew ragged as his hand explored lower, over her rib cage, over her stomach, sliding tortuously, slowly, to her abdomen where it rested flat against her skin and what lay beneath. He could not know, she told herself.

But Razeby lowered his voice and looked directly into her eyes. 'Or what is in here?' he said.

Chapter Twenty-Two

Alice closed her eyes against the accusation she saw on Razeby's face.

'Venetia told you,' she whispered.

'Not Venetia,' he corrected. 'Her lips were sealed, on that secret at least.'

'Then how…?' She opened her eyes and looked at him.

'It does not matter,' he said harshly. 'What does matter is why the hell you did not come to me? You are carrying our child, Alice. Did you honestly think I would have turned you away?'

'You don't understand…'

'Damn right, I do not understand!' he snapped. 'Were you even going to tell me? Or perhaps you were planning on cuckolding Hawick?' He stared down into her eyes with a ruthless and tightly coiled rage she had never seen there before.

'No!' she cried, horrified at the suggestion. 'How could you think I'd do such a thing?'

'I wonder,' he said.

She caught her breath as the words cut her, but she

knew she deserved his wrath. After what she had made him believe of her, she could not blame him for thinking so badly of her.

'Hawick would have to be a complete fool to believe the babe his, when I'm two months gone and haven't even slept with him.'

'You have not slept with him? How have you managed to avoid it when you have been with him for a week?'

She sagged back against the wall. 'The oldest excuse in the book.'

'How ironic.'

She said nothing, just averted her gaze to a distance beyond him.

He removed his hand from where it lay warm and flat and possessive against her belly. The chill of the night air against her naked skin made her feel its loss all the more. Capturing her chin between his fingers, he brought her face round, forcing her to meet the full raze of his gaze.

'What did you think he would do, Alice, when he discovered you were carrying my baby? Keep you on as his mistress? Claim my child as his own?'

'Stop it!' she cried. 'He would have turned me off without a farthing more.'

'And yet you went to Hawick knowing that, rather than come to me,' he said in a hard voice.

'I never went to Hawick. He came to me. I've nothing else I can do to earn a living.'

'You are an actress.'

'The theatres are closed for the holidays, Razeby. I've not a penny to my name. Do you think I'd be selling myself to Hawick were there any other way? I can't read and write. I can't write entries in a cash book or receipts for customers. I can't sew or sing or dance. Without a character they'll not take me in a shop or a workshop or in service. And I won't ruin Venetia's chances of happiness in her new life. What else could I do?'

'You could have come to me,' he said harshly.

'When I had worked so hard to make you believe me a cold heartless whore who had used you for your money and was moving on to the next man who could offer her more?' She stared at him incredulously. 'I couldn't come to you. What sort of man would leave his child to be raised by a woman like that?'

'You thought I would take the child from you to raise myself.' His voice sounded suddenly weary. He rubbed a hand against his forehead as if it ached there and glanced away.

She nodded. 'Wouldn't you have?'

'It would never have come to that.'

'Why not? Don't you want the child?'

'Oh, I want the child, all right. But you see, I want you, too, Alice.'

'Even after I made you believe…' She let the words peter out, realising just how much she had admitted.

He smiled a hard smile. 'You admit that you lied to me.'

She swallowed and tried to look away, but he held her chin and would not let her.

'You love me.'

She pressed her lips together to stop them from trembling. It had gone too far for lies. He knew too much. He knew the truth of her. He knew of the baby. She closed her eyes to stop the tears, but they leaked out just the same.

His breath was a caress against her cheek. She felt his lips brush against her mouth, her cheek, her ear. 'Answer me, Alice,' he demanded.

She opened her eyes and looked into his, 'Of course I love you, Razeby. I've always loved you. Why else did I refuse to marry you?'

'You were trying to save me from myself. It was my initial gut instinct to your refusal. I should have listened to it.'

'I couldn't let you give up the Razeby estate and title, all that you had worked so hard for, your birthright, your heritage. It's your duty, your destiny. Razeby needs you. You would have regretted it for the rest of your life.'

'What is left of it,' he murmured beneath his breath. Then more loudly, his voice still harsh, 'You were right, Alice. It would have been a mistake to turn my back on Razeby and my duty. If a man does not retain his integrity, he ceases to be much of a man. I will not dishonour either Razeby or myself.'

She nodded and her heart ached even as she smiled her approval and understanding.

'So I suppose I should thank you for breaking my heart and putting me through sheer hell.'

'If it's any consolation, I broke my own in doing so.'

'I do not doubt it.'

They looked at one another through the moonlight.

'We have much to discuss, Alice. But not here. I am taking you home to Hart Street.'

'We can't!'

He arched an eyebrow and the dark dangerous look in his eyes made her shiver. 'I will brook no refusal.'

'What about Hawick?'

'Do you want me to kill him?' he asked softly.

'No!' The word shot from her mouth because she did not know whether he was serious or in jest. 'He could sue, and the last thing you need is a scandal.'

'Do not worry, I will sort matters with Hawick.' He brushed his lips against hers, as if sealing a promise, and only then released her bound wrists.

Wrapping his domino more tightly around her to cover her semi-nakedness, he scooped her up into his arms and carried her down the stairs, through the crowded hallway and out into the night.

The house in Hart Street was exactly as she had left it. In every detail. All the servants were still in place. There were flowers in the hallway vase. Lamps were aglow.

It felt cosy and warm and safe. As if she had never left.

He took her straight upstairs and into the bedchamber, kicking the door shut behind him, before setting her down on her feet.

A small fire burned on the hearth, casting their shadows to dance upon the walls.

What had happened between them the last time they were in this room seemed a lifetime ago.

'Take off that dress.' She saw the way his expression hardened when he looked at the remains of the dress that still hung on her body.

She stripped it off, letting it fall on the floor around her ankles like the blood of her shame.

'I couldn't tell him of Miss Rouge. He didn't understand when I said I didn't like red.' She stared at the dress, remembering the horror of everything that it represented for her and wondering if she would have been able to go through with it tonight with Hawick, had Razeby not saved her.

She let the silk fall away and stood there naked. Razeby's glance held hers, then he lifted the dress from where it lay and, taking her hand in his, led her to the fireplace.

He passed her the crumple of red silk and she threw it into the flames. Hand in hand they stood there and watched it burn, watched in silence until it curled and blackened and crumbled away to ash.

Turning to him, she looked up into his face. The tears were spilling from her eyes to roll down her cheeks, but they were tears of love and relief, tears of what just being with him at this moment meant. 'I don't know why I'm crying. I hardly cried all my life. And now I just can't seem to stop. I've turned into a watering can.'

He smiled and gently kissed away her tears.

He did not say a word. Just stripped off all of his clothes until he stood naked before her. Her man. Her lover. The father of the child that grew within her. A child made of their love. He was so tall and strong and handsome...so beloved.

She reached out her hand and laid it against his heart, feeling the rhythm of its strong steady beat. He captured her fingers, placed a kiss in the very centre of her palm that had lain against his heart. There was no need for words.

He carried her to the bed. And he made love to her. And she made love to him. And it was the gentlest, most moving moment of her whole life. A merging of hearts and souls. An acknowledgement of a love that defied all. And afterwards he held her in his arms and looked deep into her eyes. He said nothing in all those minutes. Just studied her.

His own eyes looked dark and serious in the amber glow of the firelight.

'You do know that I am not going to let you go, Alice?'

She smiled at that, but there was a sadness in her heart. 'You are marrying Miss Darrington on Tuesday.'

'How can I marry Miss Darrington when I love you and you love me, and…' his gaze dropped to her belly '…you are carrying our child?'

She swallowed. 'Are you asking me to be your mistress?'

'Not my mistress. And not asking.'

Her eyes widened as his meaning hit home. 'We can't marry, Razeby!'

'We can't not, Alice.'

She stared at him.

'What would you not give to protect the babe in your belly from hardship and censure and danger? What would you not give to ease his way in a difficult world?'

'Nothing,' she said. 'I would give my all.'

'And so, too, would I, Alice.'

She could feel their hearts beat in unison, hear the soft sound of their breath as they lay there.

'Would you have our child bear the label of bastard? Would you deny him the protection of my name, my wealth, my rank? Or our son his birthright, to accede to Razeby and inherit all that he is due?'

Her heart swelled with the enormity of what he was saying, what he was offering. She stared into his eyes, knowing he was right. 'No,' she said softly. 'I would not.'

'The child changes everything, Alice,' he said.

'Yes,' she whispered. 'Yes, he does.'

Their eyes held, locked in such tenderness.

He smiled. 'You do know you are going to have to marry me?'

She smiled, too. 'I suppose that I do.' But the tears began to spill again, tears of happiness and of joy.

He reached out and wiped each precious one away. 'Console yourself, my love.' A teasing light shone in his eyes. 'I am a marquis, wealthy, good looking and great in bed—or so I once was told.' He smiled with that wicked gleam that made her heart bloom.

'Stop it, you wicked man!'

They smiled together.

But as he looked into her eyes the teasing faded away. His gaze was soft but serious. Very gently he brushed a tender kiss against her lips. 'You are my love. You will be my wife and the mother of my child. And as such, there is something that you need to know, Alice. Something I probably should have told you a long time ago.'

A shadow moved in the depths of his eyes, and her heart tightened and she knew that something bad was coming, before he stoked her cheek one final time, before he moved away to sit naked on the edge of the bed.

How did a man tell the woman he loved such a thing? He did not know the words to say. They had been hidden for a lifetime, never spoken to another soul. Every single one that came to his tongue seemed clumsy and inadequate. He raked a hand through his hair and felt the dread seep through his blood. He took a deep breath.

Alice seemed to understand, for she rose and came to sit on the edge of the bed by his side and took his hand within her own.

'Start at the beginning, Razeby,' she said. She was so calm.

He nodded and did as she instructed. 'I was seven years old when my father's final illness claimed his life. He knew he was dying. On that last day he sent my mother away and bade me sit with him. The doctors had dosed him with so much laudanum, but he was still in pain.'

Alice did not rush him. She did not question. She was just there beside him, with him, and it was enough.

'He told me that my grandfather had died at thirty years of age. That he, too, was dying at thirty. That a weakness of the lungs runs in the men of our family. That it was some sort of curse from which we could not escape.'

Razeby closed his eyes at the memory. He saw his father frail and wasted in that dim-lit room and heard again that laboured and breathless voice. 'Marry and breed before you are thirty. Marry and breed an heir before it is too late.' Razeby spoke those same words aloud.

For Razeby and its future. Do you understand, James?

In his mind he saw the boy who had stood there and answered, *I understand, Father.*

'I held his hand and watched him die.'

'Razeby,' she whispered and her fingers warmed the chill from his own. 'That is much for a boy of seven to bear.'

He swallowed and turned his gaze to meet hers. 'I will be thirty in four months, Alice.'

It took a moment before the realisation crossed her face. 'You have lived your whole life believing that you will die at thirty,' she said slowly.

'It sounds ridiculous now I come to say it out loud.'

'You were seven years old, Razeby. It's only natural for a boy to believe his father's words and take them to his heart. Even a father who was dosed high on laudanum.'

Her words made him see it in a different way. When he looked back he saw how disturbed his father must have been by the drug and the prospect of his imminent death. 'They never left my heart. Beneath their shadow I sought hedonism and thrills and pleasure. I had a plan, you see, of exactly when to undertake that last task of duty.' He paused. 'And then I met you.' He threaded his fingers through hers. 'And I did not want to give you up. You changed everything. You changed me. I fell in love.'

She smiled and brought his fingers to her mouth and kissed them.

'It is why I did not ask you to marry me. I would have done it in a heartbeat, but we both know that the same people who love you as Miss Sweetly will despise you as the Marchioness of Razeby. I could not subject you to that cruelty, knowing I would not be here to protect you. But the baby changes everything.'

'Oh, Razeby,' she said with a sad smile.

They sat in silence and her eyes studied his. 'Your father was a sickly man.'

'Weak lungs, the doctor said. The same as my grandfather before him.'

'But not you.'

'We cannot know that.'

'You're forgetting, Razeby, I know exactly what you can do with that breath of yours. And there's nothing weak about it.' She arched her eyebrow, teasing him, but her eyes were soft.

He smiled.

'Atholl's father, your father's brother—did he pass away at thirty?'

'He died last year, aged fifty-seven, having drunk a bottle of port every day of the last twenty years.'

'No weak lungs there, then.'

'No.'

They smiled.

'My granddaddy used to say that the length of a man's life was as uncertain as the wind.' She smiled, but it had a poignancy to it. 'Thirty years, or three score and more, who knows? Why worry, Razeby? Just to live is the miracle. To love, even more so.'

'Maybe you have the right of it. You are my miracle, Alice.' She shone a light in the darkness and made it fade away.

'And you're mine. Come here, you foolish man.' She rose and moved to stand before him. sliding her hand to rest against the nape of his neck and pulled his mouth to hers. 'You should have spoken to me of your worry long ago.'

'I should have,' he admitted.

'What am I going to do with you, Razeby?'

'Do you wish me to give you a few suggestions?' He smiled.

'Maybe later,' she teased and then the teasing dropped

away and she kissed him in earnest, with tenderness and with love.

He wrapped his arms around her and they lay back on the bed and loved. And Razeby knew that she was right. Everything was going to be all right. Because of Alice and their love.

Razeby left Hart Street and had his coach take him directly to St James's and Linwood's apartments. It was midnight when he knocked on the door.

Linwood had not long returned from the masquerade. His black domino still lay over the back of the sofa where he had thrown it. The black Venetian mask sat on the occasional table alongside a half-full glass of brandy. Of Venetia there was no sign, but the door that led into Linwood's bedchamber was closed.

'Forgive the late hour of my call.' Razeby moved to take the wing chair opposite Linwood's and accepted the glass of brandy that his friend pressed into his hand. 'I am come from Hart Street.'

'You spoke to Alice?'

'I did. Thank you for telling me, Linwood, and for all that you did this night. But there is one more favour I must ask of you. And it is not an insignificant one.' He paused.

'I am listening,' said Linwood.

'When your father pulled strings with the Archbishop of Canterbury to arrange your marriage to Venetia…'

Linwood smiled.

On Monday morning Alice woke alone in a beam of sunshine shining through the window. She felt a feeling of warmth that she was here and safe with Razeby, even if he had not yet arrived.

Over on the little hearth the maid had already been in and lit the fire. The bedchamber was warm and cosy. All it lacked was Razeby.

She was about to get up when there was a knock at the door and the maid appeared carrying a tray of light breakfast—bread rolls and toast, butter and jam and honey, a pot of chocolate and one of coffee.

'Master's orders,' said the maid and sat the tray on the bedside table. 'I'll be back in half an hour to help you with your *toilette*.'

Alice glanced across at the emerald-green silk dress that hung ready and waiting for her, over the dressing screen, the dress that had so much significance for her and for Razeby. So much had happened to her wearing that dress. And today she would be wearing it when she married him.

She dressed carefully, hearing the front door open and the soft murmur of voices in the hallway downstairs as she did so, and knew that Razeby had arrived. He came to her, dropped a kiss on one exposed shoulder before leaning back against the bed post to watch while she pinned her hair up in the same simple style that he loved.

'How did Miss Darrington take the news?' She addressed his reflection in the looking glass.

'She wept,' he said.

Alice spun round to look at his face. 'Oh, I feel terrible!'

'Do not! They were tears of most adamant relief.'

'I thought she wished to marry you.' Alice looked at him quizzically.

'So did I, but it transpires that wish belonged only to her parents. I suspect that Miss Darrington's heart, like my own, is engaged elsewhere.'

'Oh!' Alice said.

'Oh, indeed.' Razeby smiled, his eyes moving over her in appreciative perusal. 'You look beautiful, Alice. But there is something missing.'

'What have I forgotten?'

'This,' he said and from his pocket he took a small black-leather box and handed it to her.

Within the box was the most beautiful emerald-and-diamond ring she had ever seen.

'To match the dress,' he explained as he slipped it onto her betrothal finger.

She touched the ring lovingly then slipped her arms around his neck and kissed him. 'Oh, Razeby,' she whispered. 'My love.'

When Alice walked into the drawing room half an hour later, on the arm of Linwood's father, the Earl of Misbourne, it was to find the room decked in the prettiest of summer flowers. The sunlight streamed through the window to light the room golden and bright as the love in her heart.

In the rows of chairs their friends sat dressed in their smartest: Monteith, Devlin, Bullford, Fallingham and Sara. Arlesford and Hunter and their wives. Ellen and Tilly. And Venetia.

Razeby, with Linwood as his best man, stood at the front of the room before a dark-robed priest.

Razeby glanced round when he heard her step,

watching her with love in those liquid brown eyes of his and smiling that smile that was all for her as Misbourne led her to him.

She placed her right hand in his and, before God, the priest and their friends, Alice married the man she loved.

Epilogue

Razeby House, Yorkshire—two years later

Alice, Lady Razeby, stood on the small wooden bridge and stared down into the river. The water was shallow here and so clear that the sun peeked through the overhanging green canopy of leaves to glint golden shimmers upon the brown gravel of the river bed and the speckled trout that rested upon it. They were large fish, well fleshed, ripe for Razeby's fishing net if he saw them, but, much as she enjoyed the taste of fresh trout, she preferred that they remained free.

A soft breeze stirred through the surrounding woodland, bringing with it the sweet scent of wild summer flowers and the quiet drone of bees. From the branches overhead she could hear the cheery chirp of sparrows and from further afield the rhythmic cooing of a woodpigeon. All of it sounded against the gentle sound of the river's flow.

In that beautiful, idyllic, peaceful setting she slipped a piece of paper from her pocket. The paper was tattered at the edges, with creases that were well worn where it had been opened and folded closed again so many times. She let her eyes wander over the words that were penned upon it. The ink had faded a little with time and sunlight, but she knew each of those words by heart.

She traced her finger along each line, saying the words of the love letter that Razeby had written to her all those years before quietly to herself. She could read and write now, of a fashion, since Razeby had patiently taught her, but it was still a struggle for her and always would be. But Razeby had also taught her that it was nothing to be ashamed of and that it was no reflection upon her intellect. She smiled at the thought of the man she had loved almost from the first moment she had met him.

The sound of distant voices broke the still calm of the moment—a woman's voice, louder and more forceful than the rest, singing an old-fashioned nursery rhyme. Alice smiled all the more as the tramp of feet came closer along the woodland path and, folding the letter, she slid it safely into her pocket just as the littlest voice giggled and called out with excitement, 'Mama!'

She turned to the tiny child sitting on Razeby's shoulder, a boy whose light brown hair was a mix of her own blonde and Razeby's dark locks, and whose eyes were a rich warm brown all from the tall, handsome man who was his father.

'James junior caught his first trout,' announced the Dowager Lady Razeby, holding up a fine fat trout fixed to a string looped around her hand. She had hated Alice with a vengeance, but all of that had changed with the birth of James junior when the dragon dowager had transformed into a doting grandmother. 'My grandson is advanced for his years.'

Alice laughed.

Razeby lowered his head and lifted the little boy off his shoulders, passing him to her. James junior wound his little hands, all dirty from where he had been playing in the mud, around her neck and she kissed his soft baby cheek. 'He's a clever boy all right.'

'Just like his mama,' said Razeby and, sliding an arm around her waist, pulled her back to snuggle against him that he might drop a kiss on the top of her head.

The dowager began to sing again, the same old nursery song that Alice's own mother, who now lived with Alice's youngest brother and her sisters in a large house on the outskirts of the local village, had been teaching James junior.

Razeby joined in and so did Alice, and James junior clapped his hands together and smiled and smiled with his little chubby cheeks.

And Alice's heart glowed with happiness.

* * * * *

REQUEST YOUR FREE BOOKS!

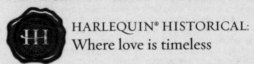

HARLEQUIN® HISTORICAL:
Where love is timeless

2 FREE NOVELS PLUS 2 **FREE GIFTS!**

YES! Please send me 2 FREE Harlequin® Historical novels and my 2 FREE gifts (gifts are worth about $10). After receiving them, if I don't wish to receive any more books, I can return the shipping statement marked "cancel." If I don't cancel, I will receive 6 brand-new novels every month and be billed just $5.44 per book in the U.S. or $5.74 per book in Canada. That's a savings of at least 16% off the cover price! It's quite a bargain! Shipping and handling is just 50¢ per book in the U.S. and 75¢ per book in Canada.* I understand that accepting the 2 free books and gifts places me under no obligation to buy anything. I can always return a shipment and cancel at any time. Even if I never buy another book, the two free books and gifts are mine to keep forever.

246/349 HDN F4ZY

Name   (PLEASE PRINT)

Address   Apt. #

City   State/Prov.   Zip/Postal Code

Signature (if under 18, a parent or guardian must sign)

Mail to the **Harlequin® Reader Service:**
IN U.S.A.: P.O. Box 1867, Buffalo, NY 14240-1867
IN CANADA: P.O. Box 609, Fort Erie, Ontario L2A 5X3
Want to try two free books from another line?
Call 1-800-873-8635 or visit www.ReaderService.com.

* Terms and prices subject to change without notice. Prices do not include applicable taxes. Sales tax applicable in N.Y. Canadian residents will be charged applicable taxes. Offer not valid in Quebec. This offer is limited to one order per household. Not valid for current subscribers to Harlequin Historical books. All orders subject to credit approval. Credit or debit balances in a customer's account(s) may be offset by any other outstanding balance owed by or to the customer. Please allow 4 to 6 weeks for delivery. Offer available while quantities last.

Your Privacy—The Harlequin® Reader Service is committed to protecting your privacy. Our Privacy Policy is available online at www.ReaderService.com or upon request from the Harlequin Reader Service.

We make a portion of our mailing list available to reputable third parties that offer products we believe may interest you. If you prefer that we not exchange your name with third parties, or if you wish to clarify or modify your communication preferences, please visit us at www.ReaderService.com/consumerschoice or write to us at Harlequin Reader Service Preference Service, P.O. Box 9062, Buffalo, NY 14269. Include your complete name and address.

HH13R

*Let Michelle Willingham take you on a journey to
ninth-century Ireland where you can fall in love with the
most gorgeous Viking hero ever to grace its shores!*

Slowly, he stood, eager to escape the confines of this place.
He struggled to open the door, but when he stepped outside,
he breathed in the scent of freedom. All was quiet, the night
cloaking the sky with darkened clouds. In the distance, he
spied the flare of a single torch.

Caragh.

He gripped the chains to hold his silence as he tiptoed
into the night. Soundlessly, he made his way toward the
beach where he saw her staring intently at the sand. Alone,
with no one to help her.

In her face, he saw the dogged determination to survive.
It was breaking her down, but she kept searching. He'd
known men who were quicker to give up than her.

She walked alongside the water, the torch casting shadows upon the sand. In the faint light, her face held a steady
patience. Her skin was golden in the light, her brown hair
falling over her shoulders in untamed waves.

She was far too gentle for her own good. What kind of
a woman would capture a Norseman and then give up her
own food? Why would she bother treating his wounds,
when he'd threatened her?

And why was there no man to take care of her? No husband or a lover….

Styr remained in the shadows, even knowing that he
shouldn't be here. He ought to be studying the perimeter of

the ring fort, searching for hidden supplies or information about these people.

Instead, he couldn't take his eyes off Caragh, as if she were the vision of Freya, sent to tempt him. Like the women of his homeland, she possessed an inner strength he admired. Though Fate had cast her a bitter lot, she'd faced the grimness of her future.

Taking him prisoner was the action of a desperate woman, not a cruel one. He knew within his blood, that if he left her now, she would starve to death.

He shouldn't care. He owed her nothing.

And yet, he couldn't bring himself to walk away.

Styr Hardrata sailed to Ireland intending to trade, never expecting to find himself held captive in chains by a beautiful Irish maiden, Caragh Ó Brannon. They are enemies, and yet there is something between them neither can ignore....

Look for Michelle Willingham's
TO SIN WITH A VIKING
Coming August 2013
from Harlequin® Historical

SADDLE UP AND READ 'EM!

This summer, get your fix of Western reads and pick up a cowboy from some of your favorite authors!

In August look for:

CANYON by Brenda Jackson
The Westmorelands
Harlequin Desire

THE HEART WON'T LIE by Vicki Lewis Thompson
Sons of Chance
Harlequin Blaze

TAKING AIM by Elle James
Covert Cowboys Inc.
Harlequin Intrigue

THE LONG, HOT TEXAS SUMMER by Cathy Gillen Thacker
McCabe Homecoming
Harlequin American Romance

Look for these great Western reads AND MORE available wherever books are sold or visit
www.Harlequin.com/Westerns

HARLEQUIN® HISTORICAL:
Where love is timeless

FROM THE FABULOUS
BRONWYN SCOTT
COMES BOOK TWO IN THE WICKEDLY NAUGHTY AND SENSATIONAL DUET

Ladies of Impropriety
Breaking Society's Rules

According to Society, I, Elise Sutton, haven't been a lady for quite some time—a lady couldn't possibly run the family company and spend her days on London's crowded, tar-stained docks. And she most certainly wouldn't associate herself with the infamous Dorian Rowland—privateer, smuggler and The Scourge of Gibraltar himself!

But I need Rowland and his specialized expertise—especially with the wolves circling, waiting for me to fail. I yearn to feel alive and Rowland, who can kiss like the devil, inflames my senses and makes me dare to break free....

A Lady Dares
August 2013
Available wherever books and ebooks are sold.